No Comfort

Hurricane María
Murder On The Beach

Pedro Miranda

Printed in the United States of America

First Printing, 2018

ISBN 978-0692186053

www.PMirandaBooks.com

"A writer who is afraid to overreach himself is as useless as a general who is afraid to be wrong."

Raymond Chandler

Chapter One

November 2017

"What is that on the sand over by that fishing boat," remarked Linda.

"Where?" asked Fred.

"Over there, by that boat. It's a woman," said Linda. " Could she be sleeping? What time is it?"

"Nine. Let's go see," replied Fred.

They hurried over, and as they got closer, Linda saw who it was. "It's Pat," she said.

"Who?" asked Fred.

"Pat, from last night. You remember the Navy nurse that was with your two friends."

"I do," he replied.

"She's covered with sand," said Linda. "Oh, Fred, is that blood on her face and her hair?"

"Wait here. Let me take a look," he replied.

Fred walked ahead, and Linda followed close behind, disregarding his admonition. Pat was lying on her stomach. She had on the same clothes from the previous evening, blue jeans and an un-tucked, collared white shirt with long sleeves rolled up to her elbows. Her head was turned to one side, and her eyes were open. Fred was about to touch her when Linda stopped him.

"Don't, Fred. She's dead. We need to call the police."

"Yes," he said. "I'll call."

It took nearly an hour for the police to arrive. By then people were starting to come down to the beach. Many walked toward Linda and Fred, who tried to keep them away from the body. Linda placed a beach towel over Pat, covering her as best she could. Two policemen walked up to what was by now a small crowd. One of the two, Sergeant John Lopez, asked Linda whether she had found the body. He was a big man and was sweating profusely in his blue uniform.

"Fred and I found her," said Linda.

The sergeant said that they would have to wait for the duty district attorney who, under local law, was the only person who could authorize the removal of the body.

"She lives in Aguadilla and is not going to be happy about having to work on a Sunday morning. It will be a while before she gets here," said the sergeant.

"There's not much point standing under the hot sun waiting for her," he said. "Let's go over to that restaurant. It's closed at this hour, but they have tables on the terrace, out of the sun, where we can sit and talk. If you two stay under this sun much longer, you will regret it."

Linda knew what he meant. When she first arrived in Puerto Rico, she had lain on the beach at her hotel for two hours trying to get a tan, and had paid for it with a severe sunburn. She woke up in pain the following morning, and it took her days and liberal applications of humidifying skin cream to recover.

Fred was a surfer and was used to being outdoors under the intense sun. He was deeply tanned and would have no problem waiting on the beach.

"That's The Islander, where we met the lieutenant and her friends last night," said Linda.

6

Lopez ordered the other policeman to stand guard by the body, while he, Linda, and Fred walked to the restaurant.

It had a terrace with several tables overlooking the beach. Linda and Fred sat across from the sergeant at one of the tables, and he asked them for their names, addresses, and occupations.

Fred went first: "I'm in Puerto Rico doing relief work for the Red Cross. I stay at the Condado Vanderbilt Hotel in San Juan, and you can reach me through the front desk," he said.

"I also work for the Red Cross," said Linda, "I'm staying at the La Concha."

"Do either of you know who she was, the deceased?" asked the sergeant.

"Her first name was Pat," said Linda. "We were with her and her two friends last night, had a few drinks together and then Fred and I left. We wanted to turn in so we could get up early the next day for a final stroll before leaving for San Juan. Pat and the other two were going to a party on the beach."

"What was her last name?"

"Pat? I don't remember her last name. Do you, Fred?" asked Linda.

"Do you know, Mr. Rogers?" asked Lopez.

"I'm not sure, but I think it's Colberg," said Fred. "I mean we only met her last night. I think that's it, Colberg. I believe she was a lieutenant in the Navy, a nurse."

"If that is so, we will have to notify the FBI," said the sergeant. "Please write down the information you gave me, including your names, who you work for, and where you're staying."

They looked towards the beach, their attention drawn by a woman was approaching at a fast clip, and the other policeman who was waving them over.

"That would be the district attorney. We should go," said Sergeant Lopez.

The sergeant walked to the woman, while Linda and Fred stayed a few feet away. She spoke with the sergeant, took some notes, and then walked over to Fred and Linda.

"My name is Sandra Ocasio," she said, "and I am the duty district attorney. I know Sergeant Lopez has asked you a few questions and has pretty much covered everything. I have only one more question—well, maybe a couple. Linda, again, what is your last name?"

"Perkins."

"Yours, Fred?"

"Rogers."

"How old are you, Linda?"

"I am twenty-nine years old, will be thirty next month."

"You, Fred?"

"Thirty-two."

"Thank you. Fred, the sergeant tells me that you and Ms. Perkins met the victim last night. What are the names of the two colleagues who introduced you to her?"

"Ann Miller and Sandra Martinez."

"You told the sergeant that the deceased was a nurse and a naval officer. Are you certain?

"As far as we know. It's what we heard. Right, Linda?"

"Yes, that's what she told us," answered Linda.

"What are you doing in Puerto Rico, Fred? Where are you from?"

"As I already told Sergeant Lopez, I'm here as a relief worker with the Red Cross. I come from Phoenix, Arizona, and I've visited Puerto Rico before to surf Rincón."

"You're a surfer from Arizona?" asked Ocasio. "Why do you bring it up, that you are a surfer?

"I guess to explain why I'm in Rincón. As to being a surfer, I took up the sport in California, where I went to school."

"I see. How about you Linda? Where are you from and why are you here?"

"I came with the Red Cross, same as Fred, to work on relief after the two recent hurricanes. This is my first time in Puerto Rico, and I'm not a surfer, although Fred is teaching me. We were spending the weekend here, taking a break from our jobs. I'm from Tennessee and I volunteered for the Red Cross looking for a change after I broke up with my fiancé. But please forgive me, that's personal information and has nothing to do with all this. I don't know why I brought it up."

"Anyway," she continued, "Pat Colberg was in Puerto Rico for the same reason we are, to help after the chaos created by two major storms in the space of two weeks. What happened to her is just tragic. But why do I go on, she is dead and why any of us are here is irrelevant."

"Not at all," said the district attorney. "Everything that you tell us, including why you are here and what you found, is important."

"I don't have anything else at this time, so I'll let you go unless you have any questions or anything that you want to say. Thank you. Someone will be in touch."

Chapter Two

Liz and Jack had been married for almost three years and were partners in the law firm of Diaz and Hardy. A trim brunette in her late thirties, Liz Diaz was a former FBI agent with expertise in martial arts, weapons, and self-defense. She left the Bureau to practice law in Puerto Rico. Jack Hardy was a seasoned trial attorney in his mid-forties who, after marrying Liz, closed his practice in Philadelphia, moved to Puerto Rico, and joined his wife in the re-named firm.

"Liz," he said, looking down from his window at the city below, "there are two cruise ships berthed in the tourism terminals."

"I see them," she said. "And the financial district seems fine, but look at all those blue tarps on the houses."

"Yes, there's still a lot of damage," he said.

"Jack, that's our building, isn't it?" She asked.

"It is," he said. "By the way, I spoke to Andy yesterday and he told me that we have power most of the time."

"Jack, I think he and Joyce may be having second thoughts about moving to Puerto Rico to work with us," said Liz.

"Why, because of the hurricanes? I'm sure they are," said Jack. "But they've been with me a long time and were glad to come when I offered. It'll pass."

"You can't blame them," said Liz. "Two major hurricanes in the space of two weeks is enough to scare anyone."

"I understand," said Jack, "but they made their choice when I closed my office in Philly and moved down here. They could have stayed there. I'm glad they came, don't get me wrong, both he and Joyce have been with me a long time. Andy is an invaluable and trusted assistant, and Joyce a top-notch paralegal, and I do appreciate having them. Of course they are stressed, but don't worry; they'll get over it."

"I never get tired of the view whenever we fly back," said Liz. "Morro Castle guarding the entrance to the bay, the old walls that protected the old city, and the city beyond. The port, the beaches, the hotels, I find them all so beautiful. It breaks my heart to think of the destruction caused by those hurricanes, the deaths and the desolation, the suffering."

As soon as they landed, Jack called Andy.

"Hi, Jack, welcome back," said Andy, "How was your trip?"

"Hectic. Al has a number of business-related issues that need work. We'll discuss them tomorrow."

"But tell me, what's happening down here?" asked Jack.

"Several motions have been filed in court. Rita is handling them. You have appointments with current clients, and I have penciled one in for both of you with a gentleman who wants to see you regarding his son who is a suspect in the murder of a woman in Rincón. By the way, boss, you know you can check your appointments on your tablet, right?"

"I know, Andy, but you know that I'm old-fashioned and like to check in with you. Anything I should tell Liz?"

"Nothing aside from that appointment."

"See you tomorrow," said Jack.

They collected their bags and walked outside, where Bill Heinrich was waiting for them. Bill was a big, affable, and polite man; a native of Nebraska. He and a few others had been hired to provide security for Jack, Liz, their team, and their witnesses during the Miller case, after a number of violent incidents. Two men had died, one of them murdered, and the other one probably so, and one key witness had been kidnapped, tortured, and abandoned in the El Yunque forest, presumably to die. After the case was over, Liz and Jack hired Bill to work with the firm on a permanent basis as an investigator and security advisor.

"Welcome back," Bill greeted them.

"Thank you, Bill. How are things?" asked Liz.

"Not very different from when you left. Recovery is still slow, and the port is choked with supplies that aren't making it out to the communities and the people that need them," said Bill.

"Why that's happening, or who's to blame, is anybody's guess. Everybody is pointing their finger at someone else, some at the governor, some at the mayor of San Juan, and many at the federal government. Federal help has been slow in coming. I'm sure you remember the president's visit in October, and the video that shows him throwing rolls of paper towels into the crowd."

"Aside from that," he continued, "the usual stuff. Politicians still playing their games, handing out lucrative contracts to cronies, and the people continue to suffer, waiting at the end of the line."

As they entered the highway, heading from the airport to San Juan, they ran into heavy traffic.

"Traffic lights are still out?" asked Jack.

"Yes, most of them."

"Unbelievable," said Liz.

"Watch it, Bill, that guy is going to cut you off," said Jack.

"I know, and I'm going to let him. Everybody is under stress, and it's best to be patient. You never know who's going to pull a gun on you during a simple traffic incident. Everybody around here seems to have one; a gun, I mean. I guess we're part of the United States after all."

They made it to their apartment in the Condado, an affluent neighborhood in San Juan, and were happy to find that the power was on, at least in the lobby.

"Thank you, Bill. See you in the office tomorrow morning."

"Yes, see you both there."

Liz and Jack picked up their bags and headed for the building's big glass doors. Jaime, the security guard, an efficient young man, let them in and helped with their luggage.

Their apartment was on a high floor in an older building on Ashford Avenue, close to the sea; a corner unit with a balcony that wraps around two of its sides, north, and west, and offers impressive views of the city and the Atlantic Ocean. From their high perch, everything looked almost normal. Up here they were comfortable, except when they lost power or water, which, since the hurricanes, happened often enough. The apartment was ample for two people. They both loved it, however, and reasoned that they had adult children who might visit. Liz's daughter Cris, who attended NYU, came home often for the holidays and at other times.

"Liz I'll see you later. I need to go to a meeting," Jack said a few minutes after they entered their unit, where they found that the power was also on.

Jack drove a couple of miles to an old building across from the Puerto Rico Supreme Court and climbed up the stairs to a room on the second floor. He always felt apprehensive about coming; asked himself why he needed to be there in the first place, thereby proving that he did. Others had already arrived and were waiting for the meeting to get started. Once it did, and after they addressed some preliminary matters, the participants had the opportunity to share. Jack got up and walked to the podium.

"Hi, my name is Jack, and I'm an alcoholic."

"Hello, Jack," said the others.

"I've been sober for twelve years, and by now alcohol doesn't tempt me—or, I thought it didn't. You know, I don't think that I'm about to rush out to get a drink. Maybe I'm fooling myself, that's what we alcoholics do, isn't it? Anyway, what I wanted to say is that it scared me the other day when I saw a picture on a magazine advertising a well-known brand of Scotch whiskey, the brand I used to drink. Out of the blue, I could smell and taste the damn thing as it passed over my tongue and down my throat. So that's why I'm here today, to remind myself that I am still an alcoholic despite many years of sobriety. Thank you."

Chapter Three

"Mr. Montes, how can we help you?" Liz asked the middle-aged man sitting across from her and Jack. He looked tired and haggard, with a three-day beard that Liz knew wasn't a fashion statement. His name was David Montes, and federal and local authorities were looking for his son.

"I am worried for my son. He is the one who needs you. You can help me by protecting him. Everyone is after him."

"Who is your son?" asked Jack.

"Robert Montes. The police want to find him. They say that he killed a woman soldier in Rincón."

"He hasn't been picked up? Does he know the police are after him?" asked Jack.

"Yes, he knows that the police, the FBI, the Navy, and others, are looking for him."

"Mr. Montes we know you're upset and worried. Still, you and your son need to understand that it is not good to avoid the police," said Liz.

"Robert doesn't want the police to get him before he talks to you."

"Where is your son?" asked Jack.

"I don't know where he is."

"Let him know, wherever he is, that he needs to turn himself in as soon as possible."

"I told you he won't do that. He's scared."

"Of the police?" asked Liz.

"And of others."

"Why?" asked Liz.

"I don't know. He won't tell me."

"So you've talked to him?" asked Jack.

"Yes, he called me."

"And what do you want us to do?" asked Jack.

"I want you to talk to him, and to help him."

"How?" asked Jack.

"What do you mean how? By defending him, by making sure that he's treated fairly, and by finding out what happened to that woman that was killed."

"Finding out what happened is what the police are doing," said Liz.

Montes stood up.

"I thought you would understand that they sometimes don't. As far as they're concerned they have solved the case. They already have their man; they have my son."

"Are you saying that your son is innocent?" asked Jack.

David Montes glared at Jack with contempt. He was a rough man who had grown up poor and had no illusions about how society, the police, and the legal system treated the poor. He was beginning to wonder whether he was in the right place.

"He assures me that he's innocent, and I believe him. But in any case, he's entitled to have an attorney, right? That's why I'm here."

"For us to be able to help he must turn himself in. We can talk to him before he does and we will be with him, but there isn't much time. The longer he waits, the worse it will be," said Liz.

"So that's your advice, that my son turns himself in? What is it, you don't think I have money to pay for you to defend him?"

"No, that's not it. We can defend him, but your son doesn't want to hide from the authorities. It would make things much worse for him and difficult for us," said Jack.

"Will you talk to him?"

"If you can arrange it, yes," said Liz.

"I'll get a message to him right now. Can I have some privacy?"

Liz and Jack got up and let David Montes have the conference room. When they returned, he said that his son wanted to meet with them.

"You'll have to go to him. He's too scared to come here."

"Look," said Jack. "We're willing to talk to him if he comes here, or we can talk to him over the phone, but we're not going anywhere."

"Please, he's not far, but he doesn't want to be caught before he can discuss his case with you."

"You told us that you didn't know where he is," said Jack.

"I wasn't sure. Besides, I wouldn't have told you unless you agreed to talk to him," replied David.

"I have a question," said Liz. "Why did you come to us?"

"Everybody knows what you did in the case of the murdered students. I figured that if you were able to find out who killed them, you could help my son."

"Mr. Montes, I know that you are aware that your son is in serious trouble. Lieutenant Colberg's death will be investigated by several agencies that, for different reasons, have jurisdiction. Puerto Rico Police will investigate for the obvious reason that she was killed here, while the Navy and the FBI will investigate because she was a naval officer. Other federal agencies such as the DEA could also be involved, depending on preliminary findings," said Jack.

"The person suspected of killing the lieutenant could find himself, or herself, facing charges in both local and federal courts," said Liz.

"We will talk to him with the understanding that he will turn himself in. If he agrees, we will make the arrangements for him to do so and will make sure he is safe. Where is he?" asked Jack.

"With friends in one of the public housing projects in San Juan, Llorens Torres. But whatever happens, he won't turn himself into the Puerto Rico Police."

"Llorens is one of the most dangerous places in Puerto Rico," said Liz. "It has been raided many times by police, sometimes with the support of National Guard troops, like in the mid-nineties, when hundreds of National Guard soldiers and police conducted what was, essentially, a military operation."

"I remember," said David. "They had helicopters and it was like a war, with many soldiers and police going in with rifles and other weapons. They were searching for drugs and guns, and they arrested a lot of people."

"Wasn't it a few weeks ago that the drug lords prevented the Philharmonic Orchestra from entering to give a free performance?" asked Liz.

"Yes. But there is no need for you to worry. We will drive you to where he is. You won't have a problem."

"If we agree," said Liz, "when could we see him?"

"Now. My son's friend is downstairs in his car, and I'm coming with you."

"Liz, this could be dangerous," said Jack.

"If we go we would need to bring another person with us, Bill, our security person," said Liz.

"No problem. Is he here?"

They called Bill, and all four went downstairs to the street, where David Montes led them to a car parked nearby. The driver was a young man in his early twenties, dark-skinned, with close-cropped hair and several tattoos adorning his arms and his neck. He remained impassive as they got in his car. As soon as they were settled he drove off without saying a word, leaving Old San Juan and heading east on the road that leads to the airport. Marcos turned out to be an excellent and careful driver, never exceeding the speed limit and always observing the rules of the road, which was no mean feat with so many traffic signals not working, and drivers more aggressive than ever.

It didn't take them long to reach the housing project, where they parked next to one of the many buildings. All of them looked alike except for the murals painted by talented residents, and the graffiti. Many young women and men were milling about, and they did not look friendly. Liz was sure that if they hadn't come with Marcos, they would be in serious trouble.

"Jack, do you see the mural over there, the one with two flags and three faces?" asked Liz.

"Yes."

"The flag on the left was used by pro-independence revolutionaries in an uprising against Spain in 1868 known as El Grito de Lares. The three men depicted are Ramon Emeterio Betances, Eugenio María de Hostos, and Pedro Albizu Campos, three heroes of the pro-independence movement. You already know that in Puerto Rico politics and the issue of sovereignty are ever-present and all-consuming."

Chapter Four

Marcos led them to the third floor of one of the buildings. He knocked twice on the door of one of the apartments. Once inside, David Montes embraced a young man and introduced him as his son, Robert.

Robert was a tall man, almost six feet, thin and olive-skinned. He had a shaved head, a well-groomed beard, and was in his early thirties. He spoke rapidly, moving his arms and his hands in emphasis.

Everybody sat in the tiny living room of the stifling hot apartment, and Jack was miserable. He couldn't get used to the heat and the humidity when there was no air conditioning. To make matters worse, he was the only one wearing a coat and tie. The rest knew better.

Jack's Spanish was rudimentary, so it was up to Liz to question Robert, even though she was confident that everyone in the room spoke at least some English.

"Robert," she began, "you need to surrender yourself. You don't want to be labeled a fugitive ever, but more so in a case like this, where an American military officer has been murdered. They will hunt you down and it won't end well for you."

"I know that. I know this is serious. That's why I want to go to the police with my attorneys," said Robert.

"There's no time to lose," continued Liz. "I have a good friend in the FBI, and we can make arrangements to bring you in to her. We would accompany you."

"Now, if you want to tell us anything you should first hire us as your attorneys," said Jack. "That way whatever you tell us will remain confidential. It's called Attorney-Client Privilege and means that anything that you discuss with your attorneys is secret, and subject to certain exceptions, we cannot reveal it unless you allow us to do so."

"I understand," said Robert. "Yes, I want you to be my attorneys."

"Let's write something down, and we will both sign it," said Liz.

Once they did, Liz asked him to tell her what had happened.

"The last time I saw Pat was when I ran into her in Rincón. I had met her a few days before in Old San Juan, so I went up to her to say hello," said Robert. "She told me that she loved Puerto Rico, especially Rincón and its beaches. We spent some time together that evening, and the next day someone found her body on the beach."

"How do you know when and where her body was found?" asked Jack speaking English. By now he had loosened his tie and removed his coat.

"Everybody was talking about it. Rincón is a small town," said Robert.

"But you had spent the evening with her?" asked Liz.

"I spent some time with her," Robert replied. "That night there was a party on the beach. They had built a bonfire and people were drinking and doing other things. I was with Pat, and we had a few drinks. After a while, we went for a walk. Sometime later I left, and I assumed that she would return to where the others were," he continued.

"Do you know if she did?" asked Liz.

"No, I don't know, and I never saw her again."

"How did you find out that people were looking for you?" asked Jack.

"I have many friends. One of them told me that the police knew that I was with Pat that night, and that they were asking where to find me."

"So what did you do?" asked Liz.

"I knew that Pat was a Navy officer. I got scared, and I left Rincón."

"You said that you had gotten together with Pat a couple of times. Does that mean twice or a few?" asked Jack.

"A few."

"Robert, we need details. How many times is a few?" asked Jack.

"Four."

"How did you and she meet?" asked Liz.

"We met one night at a bar called El Batey in Old San Juan. I was sitting at the bar, she came, sat next to me, and introduced herself. She told me that she was in the Navy and that she liked Puerto Rico. We had a few drinks and then played some pool. She was an expert player. She beat me twice, and I beat her once."

"What else?" sked Liz.

"Nothing else. She gave me her phone number, and I left"

"You left by yourself?" Liz continued.

"Yes, alone."

"Did Pat also leave?"

"No, she stayed."

"So that's one time and the last time in Rincón makes two. You said that you saw her four times. When were the other two?" asked Jack.

"I'm sorry. It was three times, not four. The other time was at El Patio de Sam, you know, the restaurant on San Sebastian Street across from San Jose Church. I walked in to get something to eat, and she was there sitting at the bar eating a hamburger. I joined her and had one myself. We sat and talked for a while until she told me that she had to meet someone. She didn't tell me who or where."

"Where do you live? Is it San Juan, Rincón, or somewhere else?" asked Jack.

"I live in a small house that I rent in Rincón."

"What do you do for a living in Rincón?"

"I am a handyman and do odd jobs here and there for businesses and private individuals. I know everyone in town, and everyone knows me."

"How did you end up here in the Llorens Torres housing project?" Continued Jack.

"We used to live in Santa Teresita, near Llorens. Robert grew up there," said David, answering for his son. "He came home with a black eye or worse many times from fighting with the Llorens boys in a nearby park, but he kept going back, and before long befriended Marcos and a few others. My son has always been a gregarious person. He makes friends easily and has never been picky about who his friends are, not when he was a boy and not now."

"Pop, that's how I met the people who are helping me now. Anyway, I thought Llorens was the safest place for me, so I came."

"Robert here's what we suggest you do. Take this notebook and write down the names and contact information of everyone that you know in Rincón, everyone you interact with. Then indicate which of them were there that night at The Islander and which of them are close friends. In the meantime, I'm going to call my friend and arrange to bring you in. Do you agree?" asked Liz.

"We promise that we will get to the bottom of this," said Jack. "Another thing, who else are you afraid of? Your father said that there might be others."

"Look, I don't know who killed Pat, and I don't know why they killed her. She was mixed up in something, she must have been. Otherwise, why would anyone want to hurt her?"

"Even so," said Liz, "why would you be at risk?"

"I don't know. I suppose by association."

Liz called her friend in the FBI, Special Agent Frances Day, and told her that she wanted to bring Robert in.

"Liz, the police are looking to arrest him not the FBI," said Frances Day. "We're still investigating. We don't know that he's our guy. We want to question him, yes, but we're not ready to arrest him. The investigations have moved quickly, and although the agencies involved are not in agreement on the details of the crime, the Navy is pushing for a quick resolution. That's why arrest warrants have been issued for your client, who was the last person seen with the lieutenant.

"So, as far as you people are concerned he's not a suspect?" asked Liz.

"I didn't say that Liz. He may be. We're still investigating but are not yet ready to make an arrest, that's all."

"We don't want the police arresting him. We would rather turn him in to the FBI. I just met Robert. We're not hiding him. On the contrary, we convinced him to turn himself in. We want to accompany our client and have him turn himself in for questioning."

"When can you bring him in?"

"Not to the federal building. We could run into the police who would arrest him, which would defeat the purpose," said Liz. "Why don't we meet in my office? He can turn himself in to you there. You can hold him as a suspect, correct? He doesn't want to be out on the street, where he feels he's in danger. He thinks that there may be other bad actors out to get him."

Chapter Five

After Liz finished talking to Frances, they left the apartment to return to the firm's office. When they reached the ground floor and walked out of the building, a group of two dozen young men and women confronted them and blocked their way.

Bill knew that things could get ugly. Even though the people barring their way were young, they were tough and full of hostility, hardened by a life on the streets. Most of them had participated in many turf battles. They ruled Llorens, where they ran the drug points and protected their turf armed to the teeth. They controlled the neighborhood by instilling fear on the other residents, and intimidating them into silence.

"What are you doing here, gringos?" shouted a young woman. "Who the hell do you think you are, coming here without permission? We will show you what happens when you disrespect us."

David Montes was a hard, no-nonsense man who was protecting his son. He stepped in front of the aggressive youths and challenged them, told them that Liz, Jack, and Bill were friends who were there to help his son. Robert stood next to him as did Bill, Jack, and Marcos, who was a resident of Llorens. Marcos had done time in prison and was respected by the other youths.

"Why are you with these gringos?" shouted the same young woman, apparently the ring-leader.

"Because my brother Robert is in trouble and they are helping him," Marcos shouted in reply. "I don't care who they are. I don't like them, but Robert and his father do and asked for their help. They trust them, so I trust them. Nothing happens to them in Llorens, understood?"

A few other friends had joined Marcos, and the situation had the potential of erupting into violence. Many of the people on both sides were armed, so if things got out of hand the consequences wouldn't be pretty. People would get hurt, and the police would come and make arrests. Robert would be found out and arrested.

"If you don't let us pass, there's going to be blood," said David. "Many will get hurt, and the police will come, along with the ambulances. There will be arrests, and some will leave in those ambulances. They will take some of you, and some of us, including my son Robert, who they are looking for."

"Very well, this is your lucky day. Get the fuck out and don't bring gringos here ever again," said the same young woman.

"My father is no pushover," said Robert on the way back. "He won't talk about it, but he saw action with the 82nd Airborne Division during the invasion of Grenada in 1983."

"I wasn't aware that he was a veteran much less that he saw action. I'm not surprised. Most soldiers aren't comfortable talking to others about their experiences," said Bill.

"Did you see action Bill? I know that you're a veteran," said Jack.

"No, Jack I didn't. Perhaps contrary to what people think most soldiers don't. So I salute you, David Montes."

"That's enough. Stop it," said David.

They returned to the office and waited for Agent Day. Robert, his father, and Jack stayed in the conference room. Liz would receive Frances in her private office; she wanted to talk with her before Robert was taken into custody.

"Frances, Robert Montes wants to be sure that his son is treated fairly, that's all. He says his son didn't do it," said Liz.

"Maybe, maybe not. It wouldn't be the first time that a parent is the last person to find out what his son is capable of doing. You know that. But we're still investigating. He is an obvious suspect. NCIS and the police think he did it. Now, as I said, we're not ready to file charges. We feel that we don't have sufficient evidence to establish probable cause before a judge. I don't know what evidence the police have, but right now the FBI has nothing solid. We can hold him a while for questioning, that's it."

"I know," said Liz. "Whether you will, at some point, arrest him remains to be seen, hopefully not."

"So where is he?"

"Next door, I'll bring him."

When Liz went to get Robert, the scene in the movie Papillon where the character played by Dustin Hoffman arrives on Devil's Island came to mind. Like the character that Hoffman played in that movie, Louis Dega, Robert looked like a man defeated.

"It's time Robert. Special Agent Day is waiting for you in my office. Are you ready?"

"No, I'm not ready. Are you sure this is the right thing to do?"

"We discussed this. It may not be comfortable for you; we understand that. It is, however, the only thing to do if you don't want to be arrested by the police, or risk the street as a fugitive," said Liz.

Robert walked with his father, Liz, and Jack to turn himself in.

"Are you Robert Montes?" asked Frances Day.

"Yes, I am."

"Mr. Montes, I am Special Agent Frances Day with the FBI. I want to ask you some questions regarding the death of Lieutenant Pat Colberg. Are you willing to come with me to my office?"

"Yes, I suppose I am," answered Robert.

"Thank you. This way please."

With that Robert Montes left the office with Special Agent Day and her two companions.

"So what happens now?" asked David.

"What happens now is that the different agencies will continue to conduct their investigations, the police, the NCIS, and the FBI," said Jack.

"And what do we do?"

"Well, we either wait for them to do their thing, and then decide what to do when they arrest your son, or we do our own thing. We try to find out ourselves what happened," said Liz.

"Can we do that?"

"Yes we can, Mr. Montes, as long as we're careful not to obstruct or interfere with the official investigations," said Jack. "It's your call, sir. What do you want us to do?"

"They already think my son did it. If we don't do anything, he doesn't stand a chance."

"I sure as hell don't believe that justice is blind," he continued. "I am a skeptical man. I've seen too much, and I know how things work. I know that money, or the lack of it, position, and connections too often determine how a person is treated by society and by the law. I may not have position or connections, but I do have a modest capital, and I am not content with leaving my son's future in the hands of the authorities."

"Of course, in our system of justice there is a presumption of innocence when a person is charged with having committed a crime," said Jack, "but the reality is that once law enforcement fastens their attention on a particular person, that presumption may fly out the window and they will be looking for evidence to confirm their suspicion."

"That's what I'm saying," said David. "As far as they're concerned, my son did it."

"Right," said Liz. "But we would be looking at it from the opposite side, assuming that Robert is innocent. Although the burden of proof is on the prosecution to prove guilt beyond a reasonable doubt, we would prefer not to rest on that. We would be looking for evidence to prove your son's innocence, or at least to raise that reasonable doubt."

"I think we should not sit around and wait for justice to take its course," said David.

Chapter Six

The next morning, Liz, Jack, and Bill met to discuss how to proceed. They decided that three things needed to be done right away. They had to go to Rincón to look at the crime scene and gather information, they had to find out who Lieutenant Colberg was, and they had to talk to Fred Rogers and Linda Perkins. They called Rita, the other attorney in their office, as well as Andy and Joyce, the administrative assistant and the paralegal, and asked them to join them in the conference room.

"Guys, we're representing Robert Montes who you saw leaving the office yesterday with Frances Day," started Liz.

"He is the main and only suspect in the murder of Lieutenant Pat Colberg in Rincón. I'm sure that you're all familiar with that crime because it is all over the news."

"Robert says he didn't do it," said Jack. "Not surprising, you're thinking."

"Well, surprising or not we're going to try to make sure that they have the right person," added Liz. "There's work to do, and we need to do it now."

"Rita you need to contact Fred Rogers and Linda Perkins," said Jack. "They were the two persons who found the body, and we need to interview them. According to the newspapers they're staying at the La

Concha and Vanderbilt hotels in the Condado so you can start there."

"Joyce and Andy, you can start looking for information on Pat Colberg," said Liz. "We know that she was a nurse aboard the USNS Comfort, which is still docked in San Juan. They won't let you on board without some authorization, but they must have an information officer who you can contact."

"In the meantime, I'll be going to Rincón with Bill," said Liz, "and I'm going to ask David Montes to come along. Jack will be staying in San Juan taking care of other business; this isn't our only case. He will also be our point of contact."

After the meeting broke up, Liz went to her office and called David Montes.

"David, we're going to Rincón tomorrow morning. I assume that since your son lived there you have some familiarity with the town. Is that so?"

"I do. I never lived in Rincón, but my wife and I would take Robert and his sister to the beaches there when they were young. We lived in San Sebastián which is not very far inland. I used to work in the sugar mill a few miles outside of that town, Central Plata. When the mill closed in 1996, I lost my job, and we moved out."

"So you know the area. That's why we think it would be helpful if you would come with us," said Liz.

David asked whether his son's friend Marcos could come with them. He explained that he was street smart and was a good driver.

"I think it would be good for us to bring him along," he said.

Liz hesitated. She remembered the many tattoos on Marcos's arms and neck. She had seen others like them when she was with the FBI and knew that some indicated membership in some very dangerous gangs, while others marked events that had taken place in prison. She told David that she didn't think it was a good idea.

"I assure you that he won't be a problem, assuming he agrees to help us," said David. "We wouldn't have gotten out of Llorens without his help, and he will do anything to help Robert."

Liz talked it over with Jack and Bill. They didn't know what trouble they could run into in Rincón, and although Bill was their security person, he was not a local. Setting aside their misgivings, they decided that since David vouched for him, and since Marcos had stood by them during the recent confrontation at Llorens, they would consider taking him with them to Rincón.

Liz called David again. "Can you be here this afternoon with Marcos? We will talk with both of you and then decide whether to bring him along to Rincón with us."

Marcos came, which was something, but true to himself remained quiet, glaring at David Montes. He had told David that he didn't want anything to do with this woman and her two gringos, that he didn't trust them. They were from a different world. They were not his people. He had grown up mistrusting them, convinced that most of them had no use for those like him.

"Mr. Montes," said Marcos. "You know that I have broken into their homes and their cars, not these people, but others like them. That I have stolen from them, and that I have done time in jail for doing so."

David told him that he knew that, and understood how he felt, but that he trusted them and they were helping his son. He said that he needed his help, and so did his friend Robert, so he agreed to go.

Marcos accepted with the same reluctance with which he had been asked. It would be an uneasy alliance on all sides.

The next morning they left early for Rincón, tucked away on the northwestern side of Puerto Rico, it was an apt location for a town whose name translates to corner.

"I can't believe this traffic," said Liz.

"I know," said Bill. "After María, getting out of San Juan is a nightmare. Once we get on the expressway, though, it will get better." Marcos was silent all the way, and any attempt to engage him in conversation got nowhere.

They bypassed Arecibo, a town that had been severely affected by the hurricane. When it hit, the river that borders the city had jumped its banks, flooding nearby neighborhoods. David said that he had heard that many houses bore watermarks eight feet high on their inside walls.

Liz suggested that they stop at Ramey Runway, a restaurant in the town of Aguadilla. Liz and Jack knew the owner, Gloria Perez, who had opened the restaurant with her husband, George Lindemuth, when he retired from the Air Force. It was located close to Ramey, the vast Strategic Air Command base, and served the large population of active duty and retired military personnel in the area. Ramey had since closed, and George had passed away. The restaurant, however, remained open and thrived.

Chapter Seven

"Good to see you again," Gloria said to Liz when they arrived. "It's been a long time."

Gloria greeted Bill whom she knew, and Liz introduced David and Marcos. David graciously responded. Marcos, as ever, did not.

"Son," said Gloria, "you seem to be pissed off at the world and everyone in it. I think I know where you're coming from. I, too, had it tough when I was growing up. I was raised in the projects here in Aguadilla and ran with a rough crowd. We can compare notes someday."

"Listen," she continued, un-acknowledged by Marcos. "Life may not have started out great for you and me, or fair, but being mad at everyone won't get you anywhere. You make your own way. These people aren't your enemies. I hope you'll come to see that if you haven't already. Stop sulking. Sit down and eat."

Instead, Marcos turned around and left the restaurant.

"Let him go," said Gloria. "I know what's going through his head. Leave him alone. Someday I'll sit down and talk to him. Anyway, it's good to see you, but why are you here?"

"First things first, Gloria," asked Liz, "how did you manage with the storm? How are you coping?"

34

"Well, I have a pretty large generator here in the restaurant, and a few of my employees and I weathered the storm and slept here for at least a couple of weeks. We get by like everyone else, heading out every day to hunt for necessities—water, food, toilet paper, to name a few. Diesel fuel for the generator. It hasn't been easy, that's a fact. We were able to open the restaurant with a minimal menu. We've given away free food to needy neighbors and paying clients are returning."

"Volunteers have helped," she continued, "and we've had some assistance from the government, but not that much. Too many people are still without power or clean water. The official response has been, at best, disorganized, and at worst misleading. Hell, the initial official death count was sixty-four, what a sick joke. If you ask people associated with hospitals, funeral homes, the morgue, or people who have lost someone, the number of deaths is in the thousands. Sixty-four was a ridiculous number."

"We appreciate the help and the generosity of many," she went on, "but we also hear the voices of idiots who say that we either brought this on ourselves or that we expect things to be done for us and are plain lazy. You tell that to people who are stringing ropes across rivers to ford them where bridges were washed away."

"You know what I say?" Gloria exclaimed. "Fuck'em! They aren't here and if this happened to them—living without adequate shelter, power, water, medicine, food, for weeks, as we have, and God knows for how much longer—they wouldn't stand for it. Some say they treat us like second-class citizens. It sure looks that way."

"I'm sorry for the sermon," she said. "It's so frustrating to deal with all of the incompetence and the misinformation. But enough about me, Liz. Again now, why are you here?"

"Our client is a suspect in the murder of a woman whose body was found on the beach in Rincón," replied Liz. "This is his father, David. His son's name is Robert. We're on our way to Rincón to see what we can find out."

"We already have an appointment to meet with the police officer, Sergeant Lopez, who was first on the scene and who interviewed the two people who discovered the body," said Bill.

"I've heard about it," said Gloria. "She was a naval officer, right?"

"Yes, she was with the USNS Comfort, the hospital ship that's docked in San Juan," said Liz.

"Robert Montes was with her the night before she was found dead, and he was, supposedly, the last person to see her alive. He admits to being with her but assures us that he left her on the beach alive and well," said Liz.

"You know," said Gloria, "Rincón is a popular destination for surfers and other young people. But the entire western coast of Puerto Rico can sometimes be a dangerous place, popular with smugglers who bring in illegal aliens, drugs, and weapons, particularly drugs and illegal aliens. We're just so close to the Dominican Republic that these criminals use that country as a springboard. It's about eighty miles across the Mona Passage. A short distance, for sure, but the sea is rough, deep, and quite dangerous. The people that come across are desperate, and desperate people do desperate things."

"I know the area well," said Bill. "I lived in Ramey when my father, Bill senior, was stationed in the SAC base. Dad retired from the Air Force before the base closed in the mid-70s, but we continued to live in Aguadilla. Both of my parents died here and are buried in the National Cemetery near San Juan."

"Many of Puerto Rico's best surfing beaches, Little Malibu, Domes, María's, Tres Palmas, Sandy Beach, Pools Beach and Antonio's, are in this area, including in Rincón," Bill told them, adding that the 1968 World Surfing Championship was held in Domes Beach and that in 2007 Rincón hosted the ISA World Masters surfing competition where local surfer Juan Ashton won first place.

"Surfers from around the world often visit Rincón," said Bill, "and the town now has a thriving tourism economy with entrepreneurs offering scuba diving, snorkeling, and other water-borne activities. Interestingly," he added, "the town has also become popular with internet-based companies that have come to set up shop."

"Domes Beach takes its name from the nuclear reactor that was built nearby in the early 60s. It shut down a few years later, but the dome is still there. It was Puerto Rico's only-ever nuclear reactor." Continued Bill.

"What a stupid idea, building a nuclear reactor here," said Jack. "Can you imagine? An accident would have wiped out the entire island."

"Thank God it was never brought online," said Bill.

"I was born in Nebraska and love my home state," he said. "I still have family there and visit often, but Puerto Rico is where I grew up, and this is my home. I love these beaches, and I hate all the crap that's happening around them."

"I'm glad you came back," said Liz. "You are invaluable to us at Diaz & Hardy, and a dear friend."

"Gloria, we have a couple of rooms at the Rincón Beach Resort, which I understand is a short drive from Rincón," said Liz.

"Yes, the hotel is near the town of Añasco, not Rincón. Close enough though," said Gloria.

"Have you heard anything about the murder?" asked Liz.

"No, I haven't, other than what's been reported by the press. I do have a friend in Rincón who you may want to look up," said Gloria.

"Her name is Peggy Ramos. No relation, that I know of, to your Lieutenant Ramos," she said, referring to a police officer involved in the Miller case. "She owns a bar in Rincón, and if anybody has heard anything, it would be her. If you want, I can give you her number, and can call to let her know who you are and that you're coming."

"That would be great Gloria, thank you," said Liz.

It was still early, so they decided to drive to Rincón and visit Peggy. Gloria called, as promised, and they were off. On the way, Liz also called Peggy, and she gave her directions to her place, called La Ola, which was right in the center of town, facing the main square. The drive was mostly uneventful, although slow because of ongoing Hurricane María debris cleanup and road repair.

They got to Rincón, in many respects a typical Puerto Rican town in its layout and its culture, but different because of the influence of its surfer population. They drove to the square, in the center of the city as it was in every other town laid out per Spanish colonial specifications, and went by the Catholic Church, Saint Rose of Lima, looking for La Ola. They went around the square, passing by the town hall and the Presbyterian Church of Rincón, as well as by many traditional buildings and institutions sitting side-by-side modern businesses that cater to the ubiquitous surfer population.

The town was recovering well from the hurricane, although there were pockets still without power, and things were not yet entirely back to normal. For example, many businesses, gas stations, as well as others, were still not accepting payment with credit cards, a minor inconvenience to be sure, but one additional thing which, along with many others, made daily life more challenging.

They found La Ola easily enough. Finding a spot to park was a different story. They had to drive around to find one, a common problem in small towns not built for the onslaught of vehicle ownership and traffic. Marcos parked on a side street some distance away, and they walked to the bar where they hoped to find Peggy. When they stepped into the bar, they were forced to stand for a few seconds waiting for their eyes to adjust from the brightness outside. It was not hot or stuffy, as the many open doors and four ceiling fans provided excellent ventilation.

"That wouldn't be Peggy, of course," said Liz, referring to the attractive young woman behind the bar who looked to be in her twenties.

Bill walked up to her and asked for Ms. Ramos. The young bartender told him that she had left to run an errand and would return soon. She then directed them to a nearby table and asked whether they wanted anything to drink. Marcos declined and excused himself. The rest of them ordered beer.

"Where are you going?" David asked Marcos.

"I have some friends here that I want to visit," replied Marcos.

"Please don't be long," said Bill.

Chapter Eight

"That should be Peggy," said Bill as a tall woman in her fifties, with short gray hair and a deep tan, walked in.

She glanced at their table and came over.

"Liz?" she asked. "Pleased to meet you. I'm Peggy."

"Yes, pleased to meet you," answered Liz. "This is Bill, my associate, and this is David Montes. He and his son, Robert, are our clients."

"How can I help you, Liz?" asked Peggy. "My friend Gloria didn't say much, other than that you're looking for information. Let me check how things are going. I'll be back in a few minutes, and we can talk."

"You're not from here are you?" Liz asked her when she returned. "I mean not from Rincón and not from Puerto Rico."

"I'm not," said Peggy. "I came during spring break in 1980 with my college roommate, whose parents lived in the city of Mayaguez. I met a local surfer, Ricardo Ramos. He taught me to surf, and we got along very well. Too well as it turned out."

"I returned to Puerto Rico after graduating from Boston College and got a job teaching at the University in Mayaguez. Ricky and I got married, and we later bought this place and renamed it, La Ola. The marriage did not work out, and we divorced. We had no children, and Ricky had zero interest in the bar, which was heavily mortgaged anyway, so he signed it over to me."

Peggy said that she had decided to keep her married name because it made her feel like she belonged. The locals still saw her as a gringa, one of many in town, but by now they almost accepted her as one of their own. They did like her better than her ex, Ricky, who they all regarded as a no-good troublemaker.

"Peggy, David's son, is suspected of having killed that lieutenant, Pat Colberg, on the beach here in Rincón. As far as we know, he is the only suspect. He and his father say that he didn't do it and hired us to be his attorneys. We're here to see what we can find out that can help us show that Robert didn't do it," said Liz.

"Mr. Montes, I know your son, Robert. He has been in my bar many times, often drinking more than he should. He hangs out with a rough crowd, most of them bikers. They no longer come here because I threw them out for good. They don't mess with me, but they are capable of anything. I don't think that Robert is quite in their league. He may have gotten mixed up in things out of his depth."

"Have you heard anything regarding the incident?" asked Liz.

"No, I haven't, at least nothing that would be useful to you. I mean, I heard about the party on the beach, and I heard that some young woman had been found dead the following morning. I also heard that some of Robert's hoodlum friends had been at the party."

"Do you know the names of these friends? Are they local kids?"

"Yes, they are locals, but they're not kids. I understand that they resent what they see as too many outsiders in their town, especially the surfers. They can't stand the surfers."

"Do you know where we can find them?" asked Bill.

"As I said, they used to come here sometimes, until I kicked them out. I have seen their bikes at a place a few minutes outside of Rincón, on the road to Añasco. I think it's called Mi Sitio."

"Do you know any of those guys?" asked Bill.

"I know that one of them is the nephew of my ex-husband and is as worthless as his uncle. I haven't seen him in a while. His first name is Santos. I don't remember his last name because he is the son of my ex's sister, so he goes by his father's name, not Ramos."

When Marcos returned, Peggy, used to identifying and dealing with potential problems, looked at him with suspicion as he entered the bar. Marcos looked like trouble to her. She was surprised when he came to the table, and even more surprised when Liz introduced him to her. After a few minutes, Peggy excused herself and left.

"Where have you been, Marcos?" asked Bill.

"I was visiting a friend," he replied, looking at them with by now expected hostility.

"Did you ask your friend about the murder?" asked David.

"Yes, and he told me that he was down there with a group of friends. It wasn't their crowd, mostly surfers and people from San Juan, blanquitos. They went because of the girls, some of whom are always attracted to locals."

"Blanquitos: rich, spoiled kids. Right, Marcos?" asked Liz.

"Yes."

"He said that Santos and some of his friends were there, although not with Robert, and that he saw Robert leave with a gringa. He wasn't there when they returned."

"Anything else?"

"No, only that there was an altercation involving Santos and a couple of the people from San Juan."

"What about?"

"He didn't know."

"We should go visit that place, Mi Sitio," suggested Bill.

"Good idea," said Liz, "and we can stop by the beach where the body of the lieutenant was found. Is it on the way?"

"No, It's in the other direction, on María's Beach, close to the Punta Higueras Lighthouse. Our hotel is closer to Añasco in the direction we would head if we were going to Mi Sitio. We could go to María's Beach first and then double back to Mi Sitio and our hotel," said Bill.

After thanking Peggy for her help they left for María's Beach, traveling on one of the few roads that were in good condition. They soon made it to the beach and found The Islander, a favorite watering hole for the surfing crowd. They went in and ordered food and drinks.

Liz asked their server if he knew about the murder and where the body had been found. He replied that he had just started working at The Islander, and that although he had heard of the crime, he didn't have any firsthand knowledge. Bill asked the young man whether there was anyone there who had been at The Islander when the events had taken place. He said that there was, and waved at a young woman who was at the bar. The afternoon was slow, so she was able to come over and talk to them. Her name was Sue, and she said that she had yes, she been present on the night that everything happened.

"It was pretty busy, a mix of locals and people from San Juan who were down for the weekend," said Sue.

"Did you know the woman that was killed?" asked Liz.

"I didn't know her, but I had seen her here before. Her name was Pat Colberg."

"How about Robert Montes? I'm his father."

"Yes, I know Robert. He drinks too much."

"Was he here that day?" asked Liz.

"Yes, he was here. So where those idiot friends of his. They always make a scene. They want to show that they are bad boys. Bunch of losers is what they are. They don't mess with me, though. I've dealt with far worse. One of them grabbed me once, and I hit him over the head with a tray. Ever since then they give me my space and they respect me."

"Can you tell us anything about the lieutenant?"

"She was with two girlfriends that night. I also saw her speaking with a man and a woman, a couple, who joined them. From what I heard, the man works with the two girlfriends. Then the lieutenant and her two friends left for the beach, and the couple went somewhere else. I think they were going back to their hotel. I heard that they were the ones who found the body the next morning."

"Did you see Robert talking to the lieutenant, or anybody else other than the friends he came with?" asked Liz.

"No, I don't think I saw him talking to anybody."

"Did you go to the beach party?" Continued Liz.

"Yes, after we closed at ten that night."

"Did you see the lieutenant or Robert when you went to the beach?" asked Bill.

"No, I didn't. But I just now remembered that back at The Islander I did see Santos talking with the lieutenant when she was leaving to go to the beach. Her two friends went on ahead, and she stayed with him for about fifteen minutes."

"That's a long time," said Bill.

"I know. The conversation seemed intense."

"Did they go to the beach together?" asked Liz.

"No, she went to the beach. He went to get his motorcycle and left. He went south, maybe towards Mi Sitio, where he and his loser biker friends hang out."

"Do you know the place?" asked Bill.

"I've been there maybe twice. I don't like it. Too macho and stupid. They're all stupid. Nazi flags and decorations all over the place. Can you imagine, Puerto Rican Nazis? They think Adolph would see them as members of his master race. Shit for brains, that's them."

"By the way, do you know Santos's full name?" asked Liz.

"No. I think few people do. He goes by Santos."

Chapter Nine

"María's Beach used to be Rincón Point," said Bill. "After the 1968 World Surfing Championship was held there and at Domes, the surfers renamed Rincón Point after a local woman called María Garcia, who had a Coke machine next to her house by the beach and sold soft drinks during the event. You already know that Domes was named after the nuclear reactor dome. Point of interest, that was the first time that network television covered a surfing event, ABC's Wide World of Sports."

They walked along the beach and saw that to the north of The Islander there were no other buildings and the beach looked desolated. It was easy to see how something could have happened to Lieutenant Colberg there without anybody noticing.

"Many things happen on those beaches that go unnoticed," said Bill, "particularly at night."

"Remember what Gloria told us about the beaches attracting other, more sinister, characters, who use them to smuggle drugs, weapons, and people into the country?" he asked. "This is one of the places where it happens."

"Some of the contraband, human, drugs or weapons, stays in Puerto Rico. The rest continues to the United States mainland. There is money to be made in all three of those endeavors, and they are all interrelated," he said. "Most of the weapons are brought for the gangs and the local drug lords."

"The estimate is that 75 percent of the homicides in Puerto Rico are drug-related," said Liz, "and although the numbers have declined in recent years, they spiked after Hurricane María. Criminals take advantage of unsettled circumstances. With much of the island plunged into darkness, drug gangs look to grab territory, taking advantage of the disarray."

"We're not the worst," she continued. "Many places in the region are deadlier. Countries like Venezuela, El Salvador, Jamaica, Honduras, Brazil, Guatemala, Colombia, and Mexico. But Puerto Rico, with 20 homicides per 100,000 inhabitants, is still very high on the list, and it has gotten worse after María, with an average of 56 homicides per month. Can you believe that, 56 homicides every 30 days, that's almost two a day? No wonder people are scared to leave their homes after dark."

They walked along the beach for a few minutes. By then it was beginning to get dark, and they decided to be on their way. They drove south on Highway 115 until they reached Mi Sitio. There were several motorcycles and cars in front, but they were able to park their car. They walked inside, found a table and sat down. Nobody came to take their order—it didn't look like a place that would have table service anyway— so, after a few minutes, Bill asked everyone what they wanted and he and Marcos walked to the bar to get their drinks.

"Is Santos here?" Bill asked the bartender, a woman dressed in full outlaw biker regalia, with a mohawk haircut, tattoos, and piercings, whether Santos was there. She pointed to a man playing pool at one of two pool tables towards the back of the room.

"That's Santos back there," said Bill when he and Marcos returned to the table with the beers.

"Look over there at the wall," said Liz. "That's a poster depicting Hitler reviewing his troops, and next to it is one of him, Eva Braun, his girlfriend, and others at The Berghof, his vacation home in the Bavarian Alps."

Apart from the posters that Liz pointed out, the walls were full of Nazi, Ku Klux Klan, and white supremacist flags and banners.

"This is scary and revolting," said Liz. "I wasn't aware that we had such places in Puerto Rico or such people."

"Let me go over and talk to Santos," said David. "I think I stand a better chance of getting him to talk to us than any of you, although, who knows, with all this white supremacist crap, maybe he would like Bill better." It wasn't clear to the others whether he was joking or being serious.

When David got up and went to talk to Santos, Marcos followed him at a discreet distance. David waited until the game was over and then walked up to Santos and tapped him on the shoulder. Santos was a big man, at least six feet tall and around 240 pounds, solid, not fat. He had brown hair gathered in a ponytail that reached down to the middle of his back and was starting to thin at the top. He wore dark glasses, even inside the dark bar, and had a pockmarked complexion, probably the result of teen acne. He was wearing a leather vest adorned with Nazi and white supremacist patches, and he had tattoos on both arms and on his neck. He wore heavy jewelry—a necklace, bracelets, and an earring on his left ear—and he had a teardrop tattoo below his right eye. Typically such a symbol would mean that the person had killed someone, or had attempted to do so, or had a friend who had been killed. Of course, it could also be false advertisement.

"Are you Santos?" asked David.

"Yes, I am Santos. Who are you and why are you bothering me?"

"My name is David Montes. I am Robert Montes's father. I think you know him, and I'm sure you know that he is a suspect in the killing of a navy lieutenant, Pat Colberg, on María's Beach. My friends and I are trying to get information that would help clarify what happened. Would you be willing to talk to us?"

"Listen, old man, I think you should stop asking questions, and you and your friends should turn around and leave this place while you're still able to do so."

Santos pushed David away and immediately doubled over in pain from the hard punch that the old man landed on his stomach. With that, three of Santos's friends moved towards David brandishing pool sticks. One of them was able to strike David across the shoulders, but Marcos was right on him, followed by Liz and Bill. Santos's friends made the mistake of disregarding Liz. How were they to know that she could more than hold her own in any fight with her expert knowledge of the self-defense techniques of Krav Maga?

They probably had never even heard of Krav Maga, a martial art created by a man named Imi Lichtenfeld in the 1930s to help members of the Jewish community protect themselves from brutal Nazi forces. It had served Liz well many times and proved as useful this day against these wannabe successors of those far deadlier Nazi thugs of the 1930s.

Liz took down one of Santos's men. Marcos and Bill took care of two others in short order, and Bill saved Marcos from another stormtrooper who was getting ready to crack his head open with a pool stick.

But proficient though they might be, they were outnumbered, and things would soon start going downhill. Bill pulled them back, and they were able to get away while Santos and his friends were still confused by the unexpected response. They made it to their vehicle ahead of some of Santos's men who followed hot on their heels.

They decided that it was too dangerous to go to the nearby hotel where they had booked rooms, so they called to cancel their reservations, explaining what had happened. Liz called Gloria in Aguadilla to let her know that they were on their way to Ramey Runway.

Chapter Ten

"I don't know why they attacked us," said Liz. "Was it because we were outsiders, or because we were asking questions about the murder?"

"Well, one thing seems certain, we're not getting any information from Santos. That is a dead-end," said Bill.

"I think we should return to The Islander and see whether we can talk to Sue again. She might be able to direct us to someone else who can help us get more information," said Liz.

"I'm sure my son has other friends in Rincón. I mean, besides that trash at Mi Sitio," said David. "I'll get in touch with him and ask."

"You know that there's a Coast Guard Station here in Aguadilla, at the old base. They may not be able to give you anything specific to your case. They can, however, provide you with some helpful information about what goes on around here. It may be worth your while to talk to them," said Gloria.

"We already have a general idea of what goes on. What we need is someone who can point us in the right direction regarding the murder," said Liz.

"I understand," said Gloria, "but it can't hurt to talk to the people who have an intimate and detailed knowledge of what goes on in the beaches around here. Maybe what happened to Pat Colberg is tied to something else, and they can shed light. You have nothing to lose. Talk to them."

"You're right. We don't have much. It's worth a try," said Liz.

"I'll get you an appointment to see the Command Master Sergeant of Air Station Borinquen in Ramey. He is a friend, and I'm sure he will be happy to fill you in with anything he knows and is allowed to share. Are you staying around until tomorrow? Let me make a phone call."

Liz and Bill agreed that it wasn't efficient for the four of them to continue together. They needed to go to two places tomorrow: Air Station Borinquen and Rincón. It took them a while to figure out who should go where. Bill and Liz would have to go separate ways as they couldn't send David and Marcos out as a team by themselves, so the question was who would go with Liz and who with Bill.

In the end, they decided that Bill would be more effective with the Coast Guard and that he didn't need anyone to go with him. Liz would return to Rincón, the more dangerous assignment. David and Marcos would go with her to see Sergeant Lopez, the police officer who had first investigated the case on the morning that Pat Colberg's body had been found on the beach. Liz wasn't sure how helpful he would be. The police were always reticent about sharing information with civilians. She still hoped that he would be willing to give them something, maybe about his conversation with Fred and Linda. Later, they would try to find Sue, the bartender at the Islander. It was going to be a busy day, and they only had one car. Gloria said that she had a second one which she would let Bill use to go to the Air Station.

They stayed overnight at a bed and breakfast that the team had used in their previous case to hide a witness who was in danger. It hadn't worked out then, but this time they didn't expect trouble. The next morning they met for breakfast at a local bakery that served good croissants and excellent coffee, Levain Bakery. Afterward, Bill continued to his early appointment at the Air Station, and Liz, David, and Marcos returned to Rincón.

"The main mission of Coast Guard Station Borinquen is search and rescue," the master sergeant told Bill. Sergeant Kennedy was a man in his mid-thirties, with the deep tan of a person who makes his living outdoors, and he was impeccably dressed in his white Coast Guard uniform.

"We're also involved in law enforcement and provide support to Coast Guard vessels and aircraft, as well as to other Department of Homeland Security agencies, including the Border Patrol and Customs, that deal with drug trafficking and alien smuggling. We have about 200 military personnel and 150 civilians working for us."

"I take it that smuggling is a significant problem in this area," said Bill.

"It is, for two reasons," said Sergeant Kennedy. "First, this is a US Territory, and with so many beaches and so many islands close by, it is a convenient back door for those who want to enter the country, either to stay in Puerto Rico or to continue their trip to the mainland. Second, this place has a significant drug trafficking problem and, again, the beaches provide a convenient way for the drug lords to get their supplies."

"All kinds of weapons and related accessories are smuggled into Puerto Rico," he continued, "from handguns to assault rifles, AK-47s, AR-15s, extended magazines, scopes, lasers, and armor-penetrating, cop-killer, guns and ammunition, all destined for local drug trafficking organizations. Drugs are a big problem in Puerto Rico. For example, although places such as the seaside slum in Old San Juan known as La Perla may have become chic and fashionable to many, it is still the heroin capital of the island."

"Puerto Rico has 311 miles of coastline, all of it patrolled by Coast Guard cutters looking for smugglers. We're also on the lookout for vessels that leave Puerto Rico to link up with delivery ships, transfer the contraband, and return to the island. It is easy for the returning boats to blend in with the many legitimate recreational and fishing vessels near the coast, or to reach shore under cover of darkness."

"Sergeant, as a boy I lived in Ramey when it was a SAC base because my father was stationed here before the Air Force pulled out. I left Puerto Rico when I joined the military in the mid-80s and returned twenty-five years later when I retired. So I've lived here most of my life. This is my home, although it's a different world now than back in the 70s," said Bill. "We didn't have all that contraband activity back when I was a boy, nor many murders on the beaches, that I remember. At least as far as murder it is still a rare occurrence, isn't it?"

"Yes, it is."

"What do you think happened? What are we dealing with here? Do you have any idea?" asked Bill.

"I don't know, and I won't speculate on a matter that is under investigation."

"Of course. I understand. Thank you for your time, you've been very helpful."

As it was still early, Bill called Liz and arranged to meet with her and the others at The Islander. The call went to her voicemail, and he left her a message letting her know his plans. Liz called back almost immediately and told him that she had decided not to go to The Islander because she wanted to get back to San Juan. Bill was to wait at Ramey Runway for her to pick him up.

In Rincón, Liz and David met with Sergeant Lopez. Marcos did not go with them, given his general appearance and attitude. He said that in any case, he preferred to stay away from police officers. The meeting with Sergeant Lopez was unproductive and disappointing because he was reluctant to share any information regarding an active investigation, but it was not a total loss. Although he wouldn't discuss the case itself, he did tell them that Santos and his friends were a problem in the area and that the police had intervened several times with the gang. He said that he had no substantial evidence, but suspected that they were involved in drug trafficking and worse. Lopez also told them that he and his men had been to Mi Sitio several times following up on complaints about fights, and had arrested Santos and his friends. They had always made bail, but several of them had cases pending.

"Mi Sitio is not a place that you want to visit," said Lopez. "Although the name translates to My Place, it means their place, not yours."

Chapter Eleven

It was a perfect night to conduct their business, dark and overcast at that hour despite it having been a clear night earlier, throughout the unexpected beach party and the latter distractions that could have derailed their operation. By two o'clock in the morning they had the beach to themselves. Still, they were cautious and stayed hidden among the sea grapes and other vegetation, away from the open expanse of sand. They knew what they were doing. They had done it several times before. There was a dirt road several feet behind them where two windowless vans, painted dark, were parked, waiting. They had one sentry posted by the vehicles and one farther out, where the dirt road fed into the asphalt state road, and kept in touch by walkie-talkies, preferring them to their cell phones, which were less secure. They only used the devices if there was a problem. Otherwise, they did not speak or make a sound. Those waiting by the beach knew what they had to do. Each of them had their job, and there was no need for dangerous chatter.

They were waiting for two boats that would come ashore with their illegal cargo. The boats, too, observed strict silence. The only sound was that of their motors as they sped towards shore. They would be in and out before they could be detected unless law enforcement was waiting for them, not often the case. Once the two boats landed, the shore party sprang into action.

The boats this night would bring two types of cargo: weapons and drugs. Other nights, on different beaches, they might carry people. Whatever the contraband, security considerations demanded that they use different beaches to conduct business. This night they were in Rincón. A few days before they had been in Aguadilla and the cargo had been human, people attempting to enter the country illegally, most of them looking for a better life than the ones they were leaving behind in their impoverished lands.

Of course, the jobs, the work, the planning—every aspect of what they did—was different depending on the type of contraband. Human cargo lost its value once it landed. If the smuggled people were caught, it was unfortunate for them but did not carry immediate consequences for the smugglers as long as they weren't also apprehended. Weapons and drugs, however, posed different challenges, as they had to be delivered to the customers. The loss of that cargo could cause very unpleasant reactions from irate customers prone to violence.

"There they are," Santos whispered to the five men crouching with him in the brush. He looked at his watch. It was two fifteen in the morning. He wanted to get the boats unloaded, and the contents stashed away in their safe house before daybreak. "Let's go; we need to move fast."

"Flaco," he said to the man on his right, "you, Cholo, and Luis go to that boat," he said pointing to his right.

"Jesse, you and Jose Luis come with me. We'll take the one on the left."

"C'mon, move. Don't waste time. The sooner we get off this beach, the better."

They ran, crouching, to their assigned vessels, and started unloading the cargo. They would have to make at least three trips to bring the weapons and the drugs to the brush where they had been waiting. From there, they would carry them to the waiting vehicles. The important thing now was to unload the boats, so that they could leave, and get off the beach where they were more exposed.

It went like clockwork. They unloaded the merchandise, the two boats left, they loaded everything into the two vans, and they took off, driving to an old farmhouse twenty-five minutes away between the towns of Moca and San Sebastian.

Santos was riding shotgun in the first van, giving directions to the house once they left Highway 111 out of Aguadilla.

"Make a right," he said, directing the driver to a narrower, single-lane road. They followed it for two or three minutes before turning left and climbing up a steep incline. The driver had to downshift, or the van wouldn't have been able to climb.

Ahead and to the right stood a ramshackle wooden house, unpainted, and, as far as any casual observer could see, uninhabited. Those in the van knew better; this was the house where Santos's father, Primitivo Otero, Primo for short, lived. He had once been a mean drunk. Now he was a drunk on his last legs. Santos brought him food and liquor, and in turn used the house to store the merchandise.

They parked the two vehicles. Santos and Flaco got out and climbed up three steps to the front door, which was hard to open because the bloated wood stuck. The whole wooden structure tilted to one side, and the floorboards sank with the weight of the two men. They walked into a small living room, and the smell of decaying food, stale breath, and God knew what else was overpowering. Primo was there sprawled on a sofa, drunk.

"You know, I used to live in fear of this wreck, as did my mother and many in our neighborhood. Now look at him," he said, pointing at the bedraggled figure on the sofa.

"Tell the others to bring the boxes inside."

Santos went to a secured door, removed the padlock, and swung it open.

"Do you see all of this stuff? The old bastard's brain has been fried by rum and drugs to the point where he doesn't even notice that there is a locked room in his house. Believe me, if he did, he would pry it open and sell everything inside. Flaco, tell them to hurry, we need to get out before anyone notices we're here and gets curious or calls the police."

"Cholo, you need to call our customers tomorrow and make arrangements for delivery and payment."

Cholo was an intimidating presence, a big man with long hair starting to turn gray, untrimmed beard, and four gold upper teeth. He had an explosive temper that could erupt into violence at any provocation, real or imagined.

It often landed him in serious trouble and had gotten him a dishonorable discharge from the Army. A young sergeant had made the mistake of waking him up early on New Year's Day and ordering him to mop up his barracks, which were a mess following a drunken party the previous night. Cholo got up, half-drunk, and beat the sergeant to within an inch of his life. A court-martial had followed, and Cholo spent some time in the stockade, lost his rank, and was dishonorably discharged.

"I'll take care of it, Santos. Usual place?"

"Yes."

Chapter Twelve

In San Juan, Rita called the reception desk at the La Concha Hotel and left a message for Linda Perkins, explaining that her name was Rita Shelby, that she was an attorney, and that she wanted to speak to her about an urgent matter. She left her phone number and asked that she please give her a call. The next day Linda called and Rita told her that she would come to the hotel to meet with her. Linda asked what it was about. Rita explained to her that her office was representing a man who was a suspect in the killing of Lieutenant Pat Colberg. That his name was Robert Montes, and he claimed that he was innocent. Linda remembered that she had met Robert at The Islander and agreed to meet with Rita.

"Ms. Perkins, thank you very much for agreeing to meet with me. I also left a message for Fred Rogers at the Vanderbilt. I still haven't heard from him. I know that you two are friends. Do you think you could get him to meet with us when I come over?"

"I'll try. When do you want to come?"

"How about this evening? We could meet in the lobby around seven o'clock," said Rita.

"Seven is impossible. How about eight thirty?"

"That's fine. I'll see you, and hopefully Mr. Rogers, tonight at eight thirty."

Rita was an excellent attorney, smart, quick-witted, and resourceful. She had proved herself under challenging circumstances in their previous case and had earned the trust of Liz and Jack. Although she was sure that she wouldn't have a problem interviewing Linda and Fred, she decided to ask Jack to come with her. When she called him on the intercom and asked to go to his office, he told her that he was finishing a memo to Al Miller on a matter that they were handling for him and that if she could wait fifteen minutes, he would come to her office when he was finished.

"Hi, Jack. I could have come to you."

"No problem, Rita. How can I help?"

"Well, I'm going to see Linda Perkins, and perhaps Fred Rogers, at her hotel tonight. She is staying at the La Concha, and Fred at the Vanderbilt. Apart from having been the ones who discovered the lieutenant's body, they were among the last people to see her alive the previous night. We know that they spoke at The Islander before the lieutenant went to the beach party with her friends, Ann Miller and another one of Fred's co-workers."

"I remember who they are," said Jack. "Do you mind if I go with you?"

"Not at all. That's why I wanted to talk to you. I would appreciate it if you did."

"Fine. We can meet at the hotel. I won't be in the office the rest of the day. Al Miller and his wife, Betty, are flying in from Philadelphia and I am picking them up at the airport, and spending the day with them. They haven't been here since the hurricane. I'm sure they will be shocked. What time should I be at the La Concha?"

"I'm supposed to meet Linda at eight thirty, so how about eight fifteen?"

"Perfect, see you then."

Rita looked out from her office at the cruise ship terminals. San Juan is a major destination and hub for several cruise lines, and the hurricanes had hit the industry hard, not only because they tore Puerto Rico apart, but also because they also did a number on many of the usual ports of call in the Caribbean. But San Juan was recovering, and many of the large ships had resumed service a few weeks after Hurricane María. The port again looked busy, if not quite as busy as a few months earlier. There was a ship docked in the tourism pier with the attending activity of local entrepreneurs. Many tour buses, however, were missing, as several of the destinations outside of the city were not ready for business.

Rita recalled reading that the rainforest at El Yunque had been denuded, and that it would take decades to recover, in some areas up to fifty to one hundred years. The financial damages were also significant. The disruption to tourism caused by María would affect the big and the small, from the cruise companies to the souvenir shops and many other small entrepreneurs down the line.

Rita was a young woman, and she had never seen such devastation, nor, in truth, had anybody else in living memory. She prayed that things would soon return to normal.

Her more immediate concern, however, was to get ready for her appointment at the La Concha. She had to call her live-in girlfriend, Sam, to let her know that she would be coming home late.

"What, Rita?" asked Sam. "You're going to be late again tonight?

"The office is busy, Sam," said Rita. "There's a lot more to do, and I'm flooded with work. This new case is complicated."

"You should have talked to Liz a long time ago. This is unacceptable," said Sam.

"I know, Sam, and I will talk to Liz, but not tonight. I wish I could come home for dinner," said Rita, "but you know that with the horrible traffic, the blackouts, and the malfunctioning traffic lights it would be impossible, and the roads aren't safe anyway."

"You'd better talk to Liz soon and get this resolved, Rita," said Sam before hanging up on her.

At six in the afternoon, Rita thought about going downstairs and getting something to eat at a nearby cafeteria. She discarded the idea when she considered that at that hour the old city would be dark and deserted, dangerous for any person walking alone. In the early days after the hurricane, the government had even imposed a curfew from 6:00 pm to 6:00 am, but they had already lifted it. She decided to leave early for the hotel and get something to eat there before meeting Linda.

By eight o'clock she was sitting in the lobby of the hotel. Jack showed up soon after, and, as they waited for Linda, Rita was able to fill him in on some of the things she had found out about Pat Colberg.

"I did some research on Lieutenant Colberg, Jack," said Rita.

"Great," said Jack. "You've been busy, looking into that in addition to preparing for this interview. Impressive. So, tell me."

"Well, Pat Colberg was a young nurse and a naval lieutenant who arrived in Puerto Rico on October 3, 2017, aboard the hospital ship USNS Comfort to assist in humanitarian relief efforts. She was twenty-five years old and single, a good-looking and vivacious redhead. The daughter of an Army NCO who retired as a First Sergeant, Pat was an Army brat who grew up in military bases around the world. An only child, her father had brought her up as a single parent after her mother died at a young age."

Shortly before eight-thirty, Rita saw a woman looking around. Confident that it was Linda, Rita went up to her and introduced herself. She was right—it was

Linda—and she brought her to the table where Jack stood up to greet her.

"Linda, this is Jack Hardy, my boss. Do you mind if he joins us?" asked Rita.

"Hello, Ms. Perkins, pleased to meet you," said Jack, getting up and shaking her hand.

"Were you able to talk to Fred? Is he coming?" asked Rita.

"No, he's out of town. He flew back home to Arizona to take care of family business. He's supposed to return this coming Saturday."

"So Fred is from Arizona. What about you, where are you from, Linda?" asked Jack.

"Born and raised in Maryville, Tennessee, Mr. Hardy. Graduated from the University of Tennessee."

"Good school," he said.

"Thank you. Yes, it is."

"Can you tell us anything about that night at The Islander?" asked Rita.

"I don't know how much you know, apart from the fact that Fred and I were the ones who found Pat the following morning."

"Not much," said Rita. "That's why we're here talking to you, so you can tell us what happened."

"Fred and I were both interviewed by the police and by the district attorney the same morning that we found Pat, and later by people from the NCIS and the FBI. For our initial interview with the police and the district attorney on the day of the incident we were together, but we gave separate statements to the others, the NCIS and the FBI," said Linda.

"That shouldn't be a problem if you were truthful and consistent," said Rita.

"Well, I know that I was truthful and consistent in answering the questions that they asked me. I hope that Fred was as well. I know that he was in the two interviews by the policeman and the district attorney.

He must have been in the others. In truth, however, I'm concerned about certain things that weren't brought out, at least in the first two, and about which I knew nothing until later."

"What is it, Linda, what are you concerned about?" asked Jack.

"The thing is that as Fred and I both said, we went back to the hotel the night that we met Pat and her two friends at The Islander. They asked us to come with them to the beach party, but we declined. Well, I later ran into one of those friends, Ann Miller, and she asked me why I hadn't gone to the party with Fred. That is the first time I ever heard that Fred had gone to the beach party."

"He didn't tell you that he went to the party?" asked Rita. "Not even after you found Pat's body, or when you were both interviewed by the police and the district attorney?"

"He has never mentioned it. Although why would he? It's none of my business."

"I thought you and Fred were a couple," said Rita.

"We're not. We are co-workers and friends. Maybe nothing happened, and he doesn't think that it's important."

"That's one way to look at it," said Jack. "Except that it puts him in the same place where Pat was last seen. Perhaps he was trying to conceal his presence there."

"I think you should tell the FBI," said Jack. "My wife will be back tomorrow from Rincón. She is good friends with special agent Frances Day. If you want, she can call her and explain what you've told us. She would then want to talk to you in person. Do you remember the name of the agent who interviewed you?"

"No, I don't."

"Did Ann Miller say anything else?" asked Rita.

"No, and I didn't belabor the point. She is also Fred's coworker and friend, and I didn't want it to get back to him that I was asking questions."

"Do you know where we can find Ann Miller?" asked Rita.

"She is staying here in La Concha. I don't know the room, though," said Linda.

"Is there anything else you want to know? I'm meeting up with some friends," said Linda.

"No, that's it for us," said Rita. "Thank you very much."

After Linda left, Jack told Rita that he would go to the front desk to see if he could get information on Ann Miller. He came back a few minutes later and said that they wouldn't give him her room number, that if he wanted, he could leave a note for her.

"What do you think, Rita? Why would Fred not mention that he returned to the beach party?"

"Could be anything from he didn't want Linda to know, to he didn't want anyone to know," said Rita.

"Well, I hope that Ann Miller will call us back. We can get more information from her about what happened at the beach party, and why Fred went back there without Linda if he did."

"How are you getting home, Rita? Can I give you a ride?"

"No need, Jack. I live too far for you to drive out there this time of night. I'll call Uber."

Chapter Thirteen

"I've found some information about Pat's ship, the Comfort," said Joyce. She and Andy were working on finding out as much as they could about the lieutenant. The ship was an important part of her life, so Joyce had done some research.

"The USNS Comfort is one of twin hospital ships in use by the United States Navy," she said. "The other one is the USNS Mercy. They were both built as oil tankers and are the largest hospital ships in use on any of the world's oceans. Either of them would be the second largest hospital in the United States, the fifth largest on the planet."

"The designation USNS stands for United States Naval Ship and means that they are non-commissioned ships owned by the United States Navy, and operated by the Military Sealift Command with a primarily civilian crew," she continued. "When either of the ships is deployed, uniformed naval hospital staff and naval support staff are embarked. This support staff consists of naval officers from the Medical Corps, Dental Corps, Medical Services Corps, Nurse Corps, and Chaplain Corps, as well as naval enlisted personnel with Hospital Corpsman or administrative and technical support ratings. As a non-combatant vessel, naval personnel from the combat specialties are not assigned as regular crew or staff. Their presence on board is limited to official visits, helicopter or tilt-rotor flight operations, or as patients."

Joyce and Andy were working on their assigned task of finding out about Pat's life aboard the comfort. Joyce had found information about the ship, and they had been able to contact some of the crew who knew Pat.

"According to Ruth Jaspers, a shipmate, Pat was very excited about coming to Puerto Rico," said Andy, adding that Ensign Jaspers had been very helpful.

"She told me that a group of the were up on deck as the Comfort entered San Juan Bay," added Andy, "that it was on a Saturday morning, and the ship came in under a blue and cloudless sky. According to her, as they entered the bay, the ramparts and sentry boxes of the old Spanish fort, El Morro, were on the port side, and beyond them, the city looked beautiful under the bright sun."

"The ensign added that Pat had told them that, although she didn't know much about Puerto Rico before this deployment, she had studied up on the history of the country when she found out that they were going there," said Andy.

"According to Jaspers, there was a lot of free time aboard the ship, which seemed strange since they knew that there was a great need for medical assistance after the hurricane. They couldn't understand why the Comfort was not more involved in providing it," said Andy. "They all wondered why the ship had sailed down in the first place."

"Apparently, although there wasn't much to do aboard as far as taking care of patients those first few weeks. The Navy could, and did, find things for everyone to do other than taking care of patients, but there was still plenty of free time, and Pat and her friends enjoyed going out and exploring the old city.

68

They were cautioned to avoid specific areas, including a neighborhood known as La Perla which lies between the northern walls of the city and the Atlantic Ocean," said Joyce. "They were cautioned that law enforcement authorities considered La Perla to be the heroin capital of the country, and so not a place for navy nurses to explore."

"Rose, another of Pat's shipmates, said that she, Pat, wanted to see the neighborhood where Despacito had been filmed, and she had met some locals who offered to take her there, and that she had accepted the offer," added Joyce.

The day after Liz and the other three returned from their trip to Rincón; everyone met in the office where Joyce and Andy filled them in on what they had found.

"We need to know what, if anything, happened in La Perla. Who did Pat go with, and what did she do there? I just don't know how we go look into things down there without arousing the suspicion of dangerous individuals," said Jack.

"How about I go with Marcos. My Spanish is pretty good, and Marcos shouldn't have any problems," said Bill.

"Why?" asked Marcos. "Because of how I look?"

"Come on, Marcos, you know you don't have the country club look," said David. "Hell, would you even want to have it?"

"I guess not, Mr. Montes, but I don't like what's behind the remark, the assumptions this fucking gringo makes."

"I am sorry, Marcos, I didn't mean anything by it. Just referring to how you look and how others see you. We are what we are. I agree with David; you wouldn't want to look any other way. You don't want to look like a banker or a lawyer, do you? Look, I know I'm not your favorite person. You keep calling me a gringo, and you don't mean it as a compliment. That's fine. The question is, can we work together to help your friend?"

"I don't know, gringo."

"You see what I'm saying? I suspect you wouldn't like it if I called you names, right? Anyway, I'm willing to work with you if you're willing to try to work with me. Remember that we're all trying to help your friend."

Bill waited for an answer to his question, which never came. He decided to continue as if he had received it.

"Fine," he said. "Can we go there tonight?"

"Bill, it will be dangerous at night," Jack said.

"I know, Jack. What are we going to find out in the middle of the day? Anyone who knows anything will be there at night."

"That's true," said Marcos.

"I can go with you," said David.

"No, three of us would be a search party."

Marcos knew La Perla well, even though he had not visited there since before Hurricane María. He had family there, including an aunt, the sister of his mother, and three cousins, two men and one woman. His aunt was the widow of a sanitation worker for the city of San Juan, one of his male cousins was a parole officer, and the other one a firefighter. His female cousin was a public-school teacher in the mountain town of Aibonito. His aunt still lived in the old neighborhood, but her three children had moved out. After Hurricane Irma, she'd had to leave, and was staying with one of her sons when María came.

They entered from Norzagaray Street, walking down Calle Bajada Matadero, which roughly translates to Slaughterhouse Lows Street, a reminder of the fact that a few centuries back before they started building houses, there had been a slaughterhouse on the slope that led to the sea.

Marcos was stunned. "Everything is gone—roofs, walls, even houses. It looks like a war zone."

They walked on past structures that were now uninhabitable, past people who, with no other place to go, sat huddled under makeshift shelters, in the rubble of their homes. The electricity was out. Most people were using candles or gas lamps, some, not many, were using generators, and there were bonfires on various street corners. Everybody looked at Marcos and Bill with suspicion, as outsiders up to no good, until someone recognized Marcos. After that, they were ignored.

Marcos pointed to mounds of trash, and they came across many stray and sorry-looking dogs and cats scavenging for food. All that was left was scattered wood, and here and there the broken pieces of a life, picture frames, broken flower vases, chairs, religious calendars, and even a large copy of a painting of the Sacred Heart of Jesus, a fixture in many homes and venerated in this Christian country. These were the faithful who would never think to blame their God for sending the storm their way, and destroying their homes and neighborhoods, as ancient pagan gods may have done. Instead, they would thank Him for saving their lives. And as if to underscore the bleak tableau of despair and death, Marcos pointed to the carcass of a dead dog lying amidst the rubble.

They passed by what had once been a restaurant called La Garita, which had boomed after the success of the song Despacito. The building, made of cement, was gone, with only its kitchen left standing. La Perla, first a refuge for outcasts not permitted in early Spanish times to stay within the walls of the city after dark, then a slum, and later a thriving community, was down for the count.

"The end of the world," said Marcos

"The Apocalypse," said Bill.

They found what they were looking for when Marcos recognized a group of men sitting next to what had been a restaurant a few weeks before.

"What is that man doing?" asked Bill.

"He was the owner of the store that used to be here. He is selling beer and soft drinks out of the cooler," said Marcos. "Gringo, people here are used to dealing with adversity, they don't sulk. They will do whatever they have to do to survive—whatever they have to do."

Marcos asked Bill to stay back while he approached the men. They recognized him as he came closer, and he talked with them for a few minutes.

"They don't know her name," Marcos told Bill. "But a couple of them told me that they remember a good-looking American who came once to the neighborhood with Santos."

"I asked why they thought that Santos and the woman had come to a place where nothing was standing, and they said that they didn't know about the woman, but Santos was there for the usual reason: drugs."

"Were they buying drugs?" asked Bill.

"No, not that," answered Marcos. "Santos doesn't need to buy drugs; he has access to all the drugs that he wants."

"They say that Santos comes down here because he provides drugs to dealers here, in San Juan, and throughout most of the country."

"So he delivers the drugs to the dealers?" asked Bill.

"No, he doesn't. He takes orders, and his people later deliver the drugs."

"I don't think we need to stay around any longer," said Bill. "Let's head back."

"But, before we leave, do you think you can ask them one last question? How do they know the woman was an American?" Do they know her, did she speak, or did Santos introduce her?"

"That's more than one question, gringo. I'll ask."

Marcos went back to the group of men and spoke with them for another few minutes.

"They don't know her, and she didn't speak. They know by the way she looked that she was American."

"So, they don't know her, they don't know her name, and she didn't speak. She just looked American?"

"That's what I said."

"She was good-looking. Do you think they could be more specific?"

"They said she was very tall and good-looking, that's it."

"We're not going to find out anything more," said Bill. "Let's go back."

They walked on darkened and often narrow and crooked alleys, the result of haphazard and unregulated construction and expansion of private homes and commercial establishments until they were confronted by a group of between eight and ten young men—boys, —wielding bats, tire irons, and knives. They asked for their money, and when Marcos refused to give it to them, they attacked.

One of the bigger boys advanced on Bill and swung a pipe at his head. Bill was able to duck and at the same time grabbed the boy and hurled him to the side. Another one came towards Marcos swinging a two by four piece of lumber. Marcos punched him hard on the stomach; the boy doubled over in pain and out of air. The rest of the gang then advanced on them. Bill and Marcos were able to fight them off, but not before one of the boys plunged a knife into Marcos's stomach.

Cellular reception was still very spotty, and it took Bill a few precious minutes to contact help. Given Marcos's condition, there was no question of moving him. Bill shouted for help and a few neighbors came and tried to assist.

Bill had nothing to stop the bleeding, so he took off his shirt and pressed it against Marcos's stomach. A neighbor brought a towel and gave it to Bill, who pressed it on top of his shirt, which was soaked with Marcos's blood. It was all useless, and by the time emergency responders arrived Marcos was barely alive. He was placed in an ambulance to get him to a hospital, and Bill insisted on getting in the back with him.

A paramedic gave Bill something to put on as he was shirtless. By then the police had also arrived. They insisted that Bill get down from the ambulance to answer their questions, but Bill refused. A crowd had already gathered, and they started to shout at the police to let Bill go. The patrolmen decided that they could question him later at the hospital. Marcos did not survive.

Chapter Fourteen

All of them, but especially Bill, were devastated by Marcos's death. The young man had lived a short and difficult life. They all felt that he was starting to connect with them, beginning to let his guard down.

David reminded everyone that if Marcos was working with them it was because he wanted to help his friend Robert, so they should set aside their grief, continue with the job at hand, and perhaps also find Marcos's killer.

They asked him what he meant about perhaps finding Marcos's killer, and he said that he didn't think that anyone in La Perla would attack Marcos, who was well known there, almost a local boy.

"I think that there is more behind this than an attempted robbery. If someone knew why Marcos and Bill were down there, could that be why they were attacked? A message not to go around asking questions? To stay away?" suggested David.

"Stay away from what, David?" Liz asked.

"I don't know. Asking too many questions about Santos, about Pat? I don't know what message."

"We're only interested in Pat Colberg's murder. Do you mean that the killer is warning us off?" asked Jack.

"The killer or somebody else who might feel threatened by our snooping—drug dealers, smugglers—who knows."

"Liz, I think you should be talking to Frances, don't you?" Jack asked.

"Yes, I'll give her a call right now."

"Before you do that," interrupted Rita, "Ann Miller called, and I asked her when we could meet."

"Who is Ann Miller?" asked Liz, her mind still on Marcos's death.

"She is one of the women who was at The Islander the night before Lieutenant Colberg's body was found. Fred Roger's colleague, who introduced her to him and Linda Perkins," said Rita.

"Oh, oh, of course. Call her and set it up, please."

Liz went to her office and called her friend, Agent Day.

"Frances, I'm sure you know about the young man killed in La Perla."

"I do, Liz, and that he was working for you."

"That's right. Look, I don't think it was a robbery. I think they meant to beat Marcos and Bill up to send a message and things spiraled out of control."

"That could well be, Liz. Whether killing him was intentional or not, it could have been intended as a message. But why else would someone stick a knife in the boy's stomach if they didn't mean to kill him? Of course, they wanted to kill him. Whether it was intended as a message remains to be seen. But what do you want me to do? The FBI doesn't investigate murder; you know that."

"I think you're right; the killing was intentional. As to the FBI investigating, this may be connected to the murder of the lieutenant, and you do have jurisdiction over that," said Liz.

"We do. Let me see what I can find out."

"Another thing, Frances: you need to look at a person called Fred Rogers. He knew Pat Colberg, was in Rincón when she was killed and has been untruthful about what he did the night before her body was found."

"I'll look into that as well. Thank you."

Later, Rita was able to talk to Ann Miller.

"It may be difficult to get together unless we do it on my day off," said Ann. "I work interviewing people throughout the island to determine their needs. My day off is Sunday. I can't meet on a weekday or a Saturday because on those days I'm in some small town in the mountains where conditions are still dire, and by the time we make it back to San Juan it is very late."

"We understand," said Rita. "I don't think there would be a problem setting up a meeting for a Sunday, but I would hate to ruin your day off. If you don't mind and would prefer, we could meet on a weekday, no matter how late. We could come to your hotel."

"Sounds good. A weekday would be fine, but no earlier than ten in the evening. Would that be agreeable? You know that I'm at the La Concha. Could we meet this Thursday at that hour in the lobby bar?"

They agreed, and that Thursday Liz, Rita, and Jack were sitting by 9:30 pm at the lobby bar waiting for Ann Miller. Close to 10:00 pm, an attractive young woman walked to their table, the only one not occupied by men only. She was a beautiful blonde in her thirties, of medium height, and dressed in slacks and a gray t-shirt.

She introduced herself as Ann Miller, and excused herself for her casual get-up, explaining that her job was exhausting and the last thing she wanted to do when she got back to her hotel late at night was to dress up.

A server came to the table, and Ann ordered a gin and tonic. Rita introduced Liz and Jack, and after they all exchanged some personal information, asked her about Pat.

"I met Pat at a party in an Old San Juan apartment, near the Catholic Cathedral. After the party, a group of us went to a nearby hotel, El Convento, across from the cathedral. Pat told us that before becoming a hotel, it was a religious convent. She said that it was the first one for nuns of the Carmelite Order in the Americas, open for more than 200 years. I asked her how she knew, and she told me that she always studied up on the places that she visited. She was amazing."

"The hotel is beautiful and has a nice indoor garden with an al fresco restaurant. Pat and I hit it off right from the beginning. I work with the Red Cross, and since she was a nurse, we had some common ground. We also had similar backgrounds, both having grown up in small towns. Pat went to nursing school at the University of Pennsylvania, I attended Temple, also in Philly."

"You went to Rincón together on the weekend that someone killed her, correct?" asked Rita. "Why did you go, it's kind of out of the way, isn't it?"

"My idea. I had heard about Rincón and its beach and surfer culture and was dying to visit. As it happened, Pat and I had a few days off that week, so we went. Another friend who had been to Puerto Rico before, and had friends in that area, came with us."

"We drove down on a Wednesday. By the time we arrived it was late in the afternoon, just as the sun was setting, so we drove to the nearest beach and watched the show. It didn't disappoint."

"Ann, you were with Pat the night before she was found dead, you went down to the beach with her. Do you have any idea what happened?" asked Liz.

"I don't. I'm sorry."

"We know that you met Linda Perkins and Fred Rogers at The Islander that last night. Did any of you three women know anybody else in town? I believe you said that your other friend did." Continued Liz. "By the way, Fred is your co-worker, right?"

"Yes, Fred is my co-worker. Our other friend, Sandra Martinez, has family and friends around Rincón. She was born in Puerto Rico, but her parents moved to Chicago when she was three. Sandra returns to the island often and has many friends here. One of them is a man called Santos. I don't remember his last name. She pointed him out to me, and I saw Pat speaking with him that night as we left for the beach party. I had a bad feeling about him. He made me uncomfortable."

"Why did this man make you uncomfortable?" asked Liz.

"His looks. He is a big, intimidating man, full of tattoos. I know that many people today have them but believe me, not to the extent that he does. They seem to cover his entire visible body. Plus, he is a member of a biker gang, Sandra told me."

"I guess I know what you're talking about. We met Santos, and it wasn't a pleasant experience," said Liz.

"Can you tell us what happened at the beach party?" asked Rita.

"After Linda and Fred left we went down to the beach. Pat stopped to talk to Santos for a few minutes before she joined us. She told us that Santos was upset and had decided to leave. I asked her why he was upset, but she wouldn't say."

"We believe that Pat and Santos already knew each other. What do you think?" asked Liz.

"She never said that she did, although it did seem strange to see them arguing."

"So, Santos was not at the beach party?" asked Jack.

"We didn't see him there."

"Do you know whether Pat and Santos were romantically involved?" asked Liz.

"I don't know."

"What do you think?"

"I don't know and won't guess."

"Why not?" asked Liz. "Anyway, what else happened at the beach party?"

"People were drinking. Some were smoking pot. A few were pairing off and walking farther down the beach."

"Did you see Robert Montes there?" asked Rita.

"I don't know who Robert Montes is. Maybe my friend Sandra does, she knew quite a few people there."

"Did anything else happen?" asked Liz.

"After a little over two hours, I was ready to leave. I told Sandra and Pat, and Sandra left with me. Pat said she would stay a while longer."

"Did you see Lieutenant Colberg later that night or the following morning?" asked Jack.

"I never saw Pat after we left her at the beach."

"Was she with anybody when you left?"

"She may have been. I'm not sure."

"Was she with Fred?" asked Jack. "He did go to the beach party, right?"

"Yes, he did, and they may have spoken to each other. I wouldn't say that he was with her. There were many people there and I saw both speaking with a few of them."

"One last question: did you see Fred leave, or did you leave before he did?" asked Liz.

"I didn't see him leave. He may have. I wasn't paying attention to what he was doing."

"Do you know whether Fred is back? He stays at the Vanderbilt, doesn't he?" asked Rita.

"Yes, he does. I don't think he's back yet. He flew home to Arizona. I think he'll be back Saturday or Sunday."

"One more thing. Do you know whether this was Lieutenant Colberg's first visit to Rincón?" asked Liz.

"I think so, why?"

"Nothing, it's only that from what someone else has told us that may not be the case."

"Well, that is a surprise."

"Thanks. We'll get in touch with Fred later," said Liz.

Chapter Fifteen

"Hello, Frances, how are you?"

"I'm well, Liz, how are you?"

"To tell you the truth, not good at all. Everybody here is heartsick over Marcos. He was hard to approach but he had a rough life and he was helping us. He didn't deserve what happened to him. His death is the reason I'm here."

Liz again told her friend about their suspicions regarding Marcos's killing, how they thought it had been meant as a warning because they were asking questions that made someone uncomfortable.

"We don't think that it's only about Lieutenant Colberg, although it could be related. We think that this is about drugs, weapons, and people smuggling."

"Why do you think that, Liz?"

"Because one of the persons that we ran across as we were looking into the murder may be involved in that sort of thing."

"What do you want from us, Liz?"

"We want you to take a look at this guy, if you haven't already."

"What's his name?"

"Santos Otero."

"We'll check him out. There's something else that I need to tell you. We're releasing Robert Montes. I can't justify holding him. We have looked into Lieutenant Colberg's case, and although Montes continues to be a suspect we have not discovered any solid evidence tying him to the murder, and we're also looking at other people. We don't have enough to arrest him and will have to let him go."

"I suppose that's good news if the other agencies feel the same, and if we can keep him safe from harm from others who may think he knows something," said Liz.

"As far as other agencies picking him up, I don't think that they would. They are all in the same position we are. As to his safety, that's something else, and he'll have to find a way to stay out of harms' way."

"Can you wait for me to come to get him with his father?"

"Sure, today?"

"Yes, in a couple of hours."

"Call me when you're ready."

Liz returned to her office; on her way she called David Montes to give him the news about his son. They agreed to meet to go pick him up.

She couldn't get Marcos out of her mind. She could see how Bill would be attacked by robbers. But Marcos, the victim of a robbery in La Perla? No, it didn't make sense. She couldn't come up with an explanation but she intended to find the answers.

When she arrived at her office, she told everyone the details of her meeting with Frances Day. The question now was whether, with Robert Montes no longer the prime suspect, he and his father would want Diaz and Hardy to continue representing them?

Bill argued that even if David and Robert Montes decided not to continue to be clients of the firm, and even if it was true that Marcos had been killed working for Robert, he was also working for the firm, and they couldn't leave things in the hands of the police.

"Look," he said. "I think that we owe this to Marcos, and besides, let's get real, the police have their hands full with all the stuff that's been happening since María. We all know that crime is off the charts, and even if it wasn't, the death of a young man from the projects with a police record wouldn't be high on their list of priorities. Hell, it won't even be on the list. Either we take this on or it doesn't get solved. I don't know about all of you, but to me that is unacceptable, and I'm not going to allow it to happen."

"We all agree with you, Bill," said Jack. "We can't let this fall through the cracks. The question is whether David Montes wants us to continue representing his son and investigating Lieutenant Colberg's death. If he wants us to do so, Marcos's death is part of that investigation. But even if he doesn't, we will get to the bottom of Marcos's murder."

When David arrived at the office, he reminded them that he too was upset about Marcos. He had a close relationship with the young man because of his son and felt responsible for what happened. He didn't think that they should drop the investigation.

"Robert is still a suspect, isn't he?" asked David. "He could still be arrested and charged, no? Besides, he is still in danger because of the things he may know."

"We agree, David. Robert is not out of the woods, and Marcos's murder is somehow tied up with the Colberg case," said Liz.

"This is what we think we have to do, and what we suggest to you." She continued, "We need to go pick up your son, and then we need him to help us get to the bottom of things by providing us with information. Then, and soon, you need to get him out of the country for a while."

"I agree," said David, "and I want to make sure that we find out who killed Marcos."

"Let's go get Robert."

Liz and David picked up Robert and told him that although he was still a suspect, the FBI didn't have sufficient evidence to hold him. They also broke the news to him that Marcos had been killed. Robert was shocked.

"Who did it? How did it happen?" He asked.

When he heard that it had been a robbery attempt in La Perla, he said that there was no way that Marcos would be robbed, much less killed, in La Perla.

"Even though I have no idea who killed Marcos," said Robert. "I do know that it wasn't anybody from La Perla. It was the same people who will come after me. I'm sure they killed Marcos because they don't appreciate people snooping around their business."

"Why would they come after you?" asked David.

"Dad, because they think I know who they are and what they're doing."

"Do you? Do you know who they are and what it's about?" asked Liz.

"I think I know what it's all about. I know that drugs, weapons, and people are coming into the country by boats that land on beaches around Rincón. I think that because I hang out with Santos and his friends they suspect that I know that they are involved."

"Why, are they the smugglers?" asked Liz.

"I think they are. I don't know for sure."

"You've been friends with Santos for a long time, haven't you? Why would he have a problem with you now?" asked David.

"The last time I saw Pat Colberg, the night before she was found dead, she told me that she had been arguing with Santos, and the next thing I knew she was dead."

"Do you know anything else? Do you know why Pat and Santos were arguing?" asked Liz.

"No. What I know is that if whoever killed Pat thinks I know something, they will come after me too."

"Why do you think Pat was killed, what was the reason?" asked Liz.

"I don't know. I think it has to do with Santos."

"Why, because she told you that they had been arguing that night?" asked Jack.

"Yes, and because I know Santos."

Chapter Sixteen

When Liz, David, and Robert returned to the office, Jack was meeting with another client behind closed doors, and Rita had gone to court on an unrelated matter. Joyce was doing research on Fred Rogers, while Bill and Andy were sitting in the conference room commiserating over Marcos's murder. Liz and the other two went to the conference room, and the conversation turned to whether Robert should leave Puerto Rico. The consensus was that he should.

The power went out and everyone grunted. They were all annoyed, but nobody was surprised, as even two months after the hurricane power went out regularly. At least they had power most of the time. In some inland areas it had still not been restored.

There was enough light coming through the large windows of the conference room, and because the offices were in an older building, they could be cranked open for ventilation. In newer buildings occupants would be sweltering behind sealed windows, buildings constructed on the assumption, it appeared, that power was a natural resource that would always be available. But power did go out often enough in the best of times, and interruption of the electrical supply was a major problem after the hurricanes.

Jack was finished with his client but the elderly woman was unable to leave because the elevators were not working. He brought her water, and said to her and the niece that was with her that power should return soon, and to let him know if they needed anything while they waited. He then joined the others in the conference room. Liz brought him up to date on their conversation, and he agreed that Robert should leave the country for the time being. He also asked Robert whether there was anything else that he could tell them, not only about Lieutenant Colberg and Santos Otero, but also about Marcos.

"I don't know anything else," said Robert. "If you want to know more about Santos you should ask his aunt, Peggy. She owns the bar La Ola in Rincón."

"We know who Peggy is," said Liz, "and we visited her at her bar. From what she told us, she doesn't have much use for Santos. She said that she kicked him and his friends out of her place."

"Well, she may have kicked them out because it wasn't good for business, that's true, but I don't agree that she and Santos are estranged. She is like a mother to him," said Robert. "Peggy took him in and brought him up after she and Ricky split up. Santos's father, Primo Otero, was married to Ricky's sister, Claudia. He was a drunk and a gangster, and Claudia abandoned him and Santos when Santos was a young boy. She moved to Chicago and never looked back. I believe she passed away some years ago. Primo was a bastard to Santos, a real prick."

"So Peggy lied to us. Is that what you're saying?" asked Liz.

"If she told you that she broke up with Santos, yes she lied to you," said Robert.

"Talking about Marcos, do you know anybody who can help us look into what happened in La Perla?" asked Jack. "We don't have any contacts there, and I don't think that we will be able to find out anything unless we have someone who knows their way around the neighborhood and is trusted there."

"My friend who has the apartment in Llorens where we first met. I can call him for you, if you like."

Marcos's friend was called Carlos. When Robert called him and explained what he needed, he said he would help Liz and her people. Liz spoke to him and they agreed to meet soon. In the meantime power had returned, and Jack excused himself to check on his other client and see her off. He didn't want to take the chance of her and her niece getting stuck in the elevator by themselves if the power were to go out again, so he rode with them to the ground floor. He then waited on the sidewalk while the niece went for the car.

Jack returned to the office as David and Robert were getting ready to leave. They had reservations to fly to Boston in the morning. Robert would stay there with friends while David would return to Puerto Rico the following day. Nobody other than their attorneys would be told where they were staying.

After David and Robert left, Liz, Jack, and the others remained in the conference room. It was Friday afternoon, and looking out through the large windows they could see that it had started to rain hard, as it often does in Puerto Rico, except that now any heavy downpour made people uneasy.

There was a cruise ship docked in one of the tourism terminals, and vans, taxicabs and other vehicles were trying to discharge passengers anxious to get on board in time for dinner's first sitting. If it continued to rain as hard, many wouldn't make it.

It was already getting dark, and the streetlights had come on as well as the lights on the big ship and in the terminal. The rain was coming in almost horizontal sheets pushed by frequent strong gusts. Beyond the ship the bay was hardly visible through the rain. The ferry boats that regularly cross, going from San Juan to the town of Cataño on the other side of the bay, were shrouded by the rain as were the other boats trying to go about their business or their pleasure. The scene would light up sporadically with the lightning that was now striking with increasing frequency. The cracks of thunder that followed, startled even if expected.

The dark and rainy evening heightened the somber mood in the room. They had much to do, and nobody would be taking the weekend off. Jack said that they needed to speak to Fred Rogers who was supposed to return to Puerto Rico the next day. Beyond that, he wanted to find Sandra Martinez, Pat Colberg's friend, who had gone with her and Ann Miller to Rincón, and knew people in town.

"We need to clarify if, and why, Peggy lied about her relationship with Santos," said Liz. "This is crucial to our investigation. We need to find out whether Robert was right about Peggy and Santos's relationship."

"Hopefully she'll have other information that will help us understand what happened on the night that Lieutenant Colberg was killed, and maybe even what happened to Marcos," she said.

Chapter Seventeen

Rita reached Ann Miller on Saturday morning and asked her two questions: whether Fred was coming in later that day, and whether she could tell her how to get in touch with Sandra Martinez. Ann told her that as far as she knew Fred would be arriving early that afternoon. She gave her Sandra Martinez's number, and told her that Sandra was staying in the Vanderbilt, but had left Friday afternoon to visit friends in Añasco. Rita gave Liz the information about Fred's arrival. and told her that she would arrange to see Sandra as soon as possible.

"I would like to see her today, if she agrees. I can go to her." Rita said to Liz.

"You don't have to do that, you can see her next week in San Juan."

"I don't mind driving to Añasco. I think it's important that we get her story as soon as we can, without giving her too much time to think about it or even talk to others."

"You're right. Still, you don't have to do it today, especially if it's going to mean problems at home. If you go, however, take one of the others with you—Bill, Andy, or Joyce."

"Thanks, Liz. I'm going."

Rita called Sandra and explained that she was looking into the death of her friend, Lieutenant Pat Colberg, and that she had already spoken to Ann Miller, who had been very helpful.

"I want to meet with you today if you don't mind. We're kind of in a hurry," said Rita.

"Well, I'm not in San Juan this weekend. If I were, we could have arranged something. I'm visiting friends in Añasco."

"It so happens that I'm in San Sebastian, a short drive from you. I promise I won't take up much of your time." Rita didn't want to wait until after the weekend so she lied about being in San Sebastian.

Surprised, Sandra said that she was going to be in Rincón that afternoon.

"Even better. I love Rincón," said Rita. "Can we meet at La Ola around three thirty in the afternoon?"

"I don't know, how about The Islander around four?"

"Sounds good, The Islander over by María's, right?"

"Yes, that's the place."

"See you there at four."

Rita called Joyce and asked her to come with her to Rincón. She knew that Joyce was a newcomer to Puerto Rico and hadn't seen much of the island, and should welcome the opportunity. Joyce answered that she was happy to help in any way she could.

Rita then made a more difficult call. Her girlfriend, Sam, did not take it well.

"We had plans for the weekend, Rita," said Sam, "how can you upend everything and take off? This is not the first time you do this. I'm tired of it and your misguided priorities. Why would you do this and head out there by yourself?"

"Sam, it's important, and I'm not going by myself. Joyce, our paralegal, is coming with me."

"You're ruining my weekend and going to Rincón with another woman?"

"This is office business. Joyce is our paralegal. She's straight and she's twice my age."

"I'm sorry, Rita. If you do this I won't be here when you return."

"Sam, I love you and I hope you don't mean what you said. I have to go and I hope that you'll be home when I come back."

Sam disconnected the call without another word.

Both sad and angry, Rita knew that she had to put the matter out of her mind until she returned home tomorrow. She had to concentrate on the job ahead, otherwise it would all have been for nothing.

She picked Joyce up and they were on their way to Rincón by midday. She and Joyce were office acquaintances, nothing more. They weren't friends and they knew very little about each other's personal lives. They had come to work together thanks to the Miller case but Joyce and Andy were, in a manner of speaking, from one side of the family, the Philadelphia side that came to Puerto Rico with Jack, and Rita from the other, hired by Liz in Puerto Rico. They all got along and worked well together, but knew very little about one another across family lines.

On the way to Rincón they talked about the case for a while, then reverted to silence until Rita started to talk about what was on her mind: her conflict with Sam. She told Joyce how heartsick she was because she had fought hard to achieve some stability in her life after many difficult years growing up gay in Puerto Rico. She shared with Joyce how she and Sam had met, and how happy they were. Not that things were perfect, there was always the odd troglodyte around who disapproved of their living arrangements, but they had thrived as a couple. Now everything was up in the air.

"I know it's hard but worrying about it is useless, Rita," said Joyce. "You've made a difficult decision and now you have to live with it. Sam needs to make hers. Don't second guess her, Sam will do what she will do, and your worrying about it won't change anything. You will deal with it tomorrow."

"What if she's not there when I come home, Joyce?"

"Then you will be sad. Either she will come back or you will learn to live without her. I know it's hard, yet there it is."

"Look," said Joyce. "Every person is different, but we all go through similar experiences. My husband left me many years ago for another person and I suffered."

"Another person?"

"Another man."

"Oh."

"So, dear, if you live long enough, you survive and adapt to many things. In your case, maybe you won't even have to."

Before they knew it, it was three forty-five in the afternoon and they had reached The Islander. They walked to the only table where there was a woman sitting by herself and asked her if she was Sandra Martinez. She said that she was. Rita and Joyce introduced themselves and Sandra invited them to sit. She was having a piña colada, and offered them a drink. When Rita and Joyce declined, Sandra said that if they didn't want alcohol, hers was a virgin piña colada, and it was very refreshing. They relented and Sandra called the young woman who was serving them.

"Are you Sue?" Rita asked the server.

"Yes, why?"

"You know my friends. They were here the other day asking about the woman who was found dead on the beach."

"Yes, I remember. They asked about a few others."

"They did. Nice to meet you. My friend and I will have the same thing she's having."

"Virgin?"

"Yes, please."

"So, Sandra, we wanted to ask you some questions about Pat Colberg and what happened to her. Will you help us?" asked Rita.

"I don't know what happened. Pat, Ann Miller and I came to Rincón for the weekend and were having a great time. Then Pat turned up dead. We couldn't believe it."

"Do you have any idea or suspicion regarding what happened?"

"No, I don't."

"You were here, at The Islander, with Pat and Ann before going to the beach party, right?"

"Yes, the three of us were here."

"Did you talk to anybody else?" asked Rita.

"A few people, yes."

"Do you know Fred Rogers and Linda Perkins?"

"Not Linda, no, but Fred is a co-worker. We met Linda that evening at The Islander."

"Pat, Ann and you went to the beach party, right?"

"Yes."

"What about Fred and Linda?"

"No, they went back to their rooms, I think."

"Did you see either of them later at the beach party?"

"No, I told you that they went back to their rooms."

"I understand that you know many people around here. Is that correct?"

"I know some people here and in other parts of Puerto Rico as well. I come here on a regular basis."

"Do you know a place in Rincón called La Ola?"

"Sure, everybody knows La Ola. It's a bar in Rincón, by the town square."

"I figured you would, and I'm sure you know the owner, Peggy Ramos."

"Yes."

"You also know Santos, right"

"Yes, he's her nephew."

"Did he and Pat have a relationship?"

"Santos and Pat? I have no idea."

"Do you know if they were together on the beach that night?"

"I don't know if they were together at the beach. I did see them talking. As we were on our way to the beach, Pat stopped and spoke to him for a few minutes, then she joined us, and I think he left."

"Do you know whether Peggy and Santos get along?"

"I think they do. But why are you asking about Peggy and Santos? Do you think they had something to do with any of this?"

Rita explained that she was trying to get a full picture about what had happened at The Islander and at the beach that day, and that they had already spoken to Peggy, who had mentioned that she had a falling out with Santos. Sandra replied that she didn't know about any problems, but that knowing Santos it wouldn't surprise her.

"Sandra, was Pat with anybody at the beach party?"

"She talked to a few persons."

"Any one person more than others?"

"She spent more time with Robert Montes."

"Do you know Robert?"

"Yes, he's a nice guy."

"Do you think he killed Pat?"

"Can we stop now? I feel like I'm in court."

"I'm sorry," said Rita. "A few more questions and we're finished, okay?

"No, I don't think Robert killed Pat." she answered. "Why would he? I don't think he's a violent guy and they got along well."

"Do you know a place called Mi Sitio?"

"Yes, it's a biker bar. Santos and his friends hang out there."

"Have you visited the place?"

"Once, and that was more than enough. I wouldn't set foot there ever again?"

"Why"

"C'mon, you know the answer. Why would you ask? It's a terrible place. Nazi poseurs, white supremacists, and a strong odor of testosterone and unwashed bodies, if you know what I mean."

"What a nauseating image you conjure," said Joyce, who hadn't said a word since they arrived. "Effective, though."

Chapter Eighteen

Liz was sure that Pat Colberg was not the victim of a random act of violence, or that she was just in the wrong place at the wrong time. She had found out from law enforcement contacts that the autopsy confirmed that she had been killed by blunt trauma to the head, and that she had not been sexually assaulted. Robbery had not been the motive; a tote bag with her wallet, her cell phone, her keys, and other personal effects was recovered on the beach, although in another, more isolated area than where the body was found. The wallet contained cash, credit cards, and photo identification, including her Common Access Card, the standard ID for active duty military service personnel. So if robbery or sexual assault weren't the motives, Lieutenant Colberg must have been killed for something that she did, or something that she knew, saw, or heard.

Liz and Jack, as well as the rest of their people, agreed that they needed to find out more about who Pat Colberg was, and what her activities in Puerto Rico had been. It was now Monday morning. Rita and Joyce were back from their trip to Rincón and their interview with Sandra Martinez. They explained that everything that she had said coincided with what they already knew, except for her statement that she had not seen Fred after he and Linda had left The Islander, which was in contradiction to Ann Miller's statement that he had returned and gone to the beach party. Bill then said that he had tried to reach Fred over the weekend, and had been unsuccessful.

They had already learned much about Pat from the interviews that they had conducted of people who knew her, and Joyce spoke to her father when he came to claim his daughter's body. Stan Colberg told her that Pat's mother had passed away when Pat was young, and that he had been estranged from his daughter for the past few years. He wouldn't explain why. He said that he knew next to nothing about Pat's life after she had obtained her nursing degree from the University of Pennsylvania and joined the Navy.

Jack suggested that they try to retrace Pat's activities based on the information they had, in the hope that they could shed some light on the mystery of her death. They knew that Pat liked to visit Old San Juan and recalled one specific bar that Robert Montes had mentioned as the place where he and Pat had met, El Batey.

"Everybody who knows Old San Juan, or has visited it more than once, knows that place," said Liz. "Jack, we can go there tomorrow night. Remember tonight we're invited to dinner with Al and Betty."

"Bill, please keep trying to reach Fred Rogers. It's important that we talk to him," said Jack.

"I assume that if he's back, he's working today. I plan to go to the Vanderbilt at four o'clock this afternoon and sit in the lobby. I know a woman at the front desk who will point him out to me when he walks in," said Bill.

"Sounds good," said Jack. "Take Andy with you."

At four o'clock that afternoon, Bill and Andy were at the Vanderbilt. Bill spoke to his friend at the front desk, and she confirmed that Fred had returned

Saturday afternoon. She agreed to alert him when Fred entered the lobby.

Andy had never been to the Vanderbilt. They sat in comfortable chairs, admiring the luxurious appointments in the vast and beautiful lobby bar, and Bill told him that the Vanderbilt was the oldest luxury hotel in Puerto Rico. first opened for business in 1919, and was the oldest luxury hotel in Puerto Rico.

"It first opened in 1919, was closed in 1996, and reopened in 2013 after extensive renovations," said Bill.

"Many famous people have stayed here," he said, "President John F. Kennedy, President Franklin D. Roosevelt and his wife, First Lady Eleanor Roosevelt, Charles Lindberg, singer Carlos Gardel, actor Errol Flynn, and comedian Bob Hope, among many others."

After waiting forty-five minutes, Bill received a text message from his friend telling him that Fred was walking in. He glanced at her and she signaled toward a man about to pass in front of them. Bill got up and stopped him. Fred was taller than him by about an inch. He looked to be in his early thirties, and a scar on his upper lip reminded Bill of the actor, Stacy Keach.

Bill identified himself and asked the man whether he was Fred Rogers. Instead of answering, Fred asked Bill why he wanted to know. Bill told him that he worked for the attorneys who represented a suspect in the death of Lieutenant Pat Colberg and wanted to ask Fred Rogers some questions; was he Fred Rogers? Fred hesitated, but admitted who he was and agreed to give them a few minutes.

"Fred, you and Linda Perkins discovered Pat Colberg's body at the beach in Rincón, is that correct?" asked Bill.

"Yes, we did."

"Did you know Lieutenant Colberg?"

Fred was silent for several seconds before answering that he and a friend, Linda Perkins, had met

Pat Colberg at a bar called The Islander the day before they discovered her body on the beach.

"We were down there for the weekend. She was there with two colleagues of mine, Ann Miller, and Sandra Martinez," he said.

"You had never seen or met Pat Colberg before?" asked Bill.

"That's right; I hadn't."

"Did you see her later that night?"

"No, I didn't. I never saw her again until Linda and I discovered her body the next morning."

"You didn't see her at the beach party?" insisted Bill.

"I didn't go to the beach party."

"I ask because someone told us that you returned alone to The Islander after you left with Linda, and went to the beach party."

"I don't know who told you that. Whoever did is lying, and I'm too busy to sit here and listen to their stories." With that, Fred left.

When Liz and Jack left the office that evening, they walked uphill to the center of the old city, up Calle del Cristo to El Batey.

"I never get tired of this place," said Liz as they walked into the dark interior of the bar, a seedy-looking throwback to the Old San Juan of the 1960s when it first opened for business.

To Jack, the bar had a run-down charm. For Liz, it brought back memories of the times when she visited Puerto Rico in her youth and roamed the old city with friends. The bar had not changed at all in all those years and was an iconic landmark for men and women now in their seventies and eighties who perhaps first came there in their late teens.

Liz knew that the Rolling Stones, among other well-known celebrities, had been there, had sat having drinks, and maybe even played pool in this bar that looked today as it did fifty years ago.

El Batey was still in its original location on the steep incline of Calle del Cristo, up the hill and not far from the place where Ponce de Leon lay entombed in the Saint John the Baptist Basilica and Metropolitan Cathedral.

The bar was to their right, as Liz and Jack entered, and a few regulars sat there nursing drinks, some looking like throwbacks to the 60s. Liz was tempted to ask them whether they had been patrons since those early days, but restrained herself from doing so.

The pool table was in the back, and the clacking sound of the billiard balls punctuated the rock music that came from the old jukebox, the kind that took quarters. This was a bar that had never been spruced up to attract the tourist trade. The walls still seemed to sweat with moisture and were covered with the graffiti scrawled by patrons through the years, some more eloquent than others. And yet, despite its lack of pretension and ostentation, or maybe because of it, El Batey continued to be renowned and often written up in contemporary travel magazines.

They sat at the bar and asked the bartender, Craig, for two rum and cokes. Nursing their drinks, they relaxed for a while taking in the atmosphere. When the bartender returned, Jack asked him whether he had a moment to speak to them. He asked what it was about, and Jack said to him that it had to do with a navy nurse killed on the beach in Rincón, Pat Colberg.

"I saw that in the news," said Craig.

"Do you mind if we show you some pictures?" asked Liz.

"Not at all. Hurry, though, before the crowds get here and I'm unable to look at them."

Liz fished some photographs from her purse and laid them side by side on the counter. Craig, an amiable, middle-aged man with a well-groomed beard, told them that they should remember that many people came to the bar, and he probably wouldn't recognize their pictures, but that he would give it a try. Liz was showing him some photographs taken at The Islander that she had borrowed from Ann Miller. They showed her and her two friends, Pat Colberg and Sandra Martinez.

Craig looked at the pictures and told them that he recognized Pat Colberg.

"I've seen this one before. She's a frequent customer, although she hasn't been here in the last few days."

"She is the woman that was murdered in Rincón, Pat Colberg," said Jack.

"My God, no. I had no idea it was her. Now that you mention it, sure, I knew that she was in the Navy and was an officer, but I didn't make the connection with what happened in Rincón. Wow, I'm sorry to hear that. She was a nice lady."

"Do you recognize anybody else?" asked Liz

Craig again looked. He said that he didn't recognize the other two, but that he did see someone in the background who looked familiar. Although the person had his back turned to the camera, Liz knew that it was Fred Rogers. She was surprised that the bartender at El Batey would recognize him.

They would have to look more closely at Mr. Rogers. With every new revelation, it seemed that he was much more than a surfer who had gone to Rincón with a friend and found himself in the middle of a murder inquiry.

"Do you know that person's name?" asked Jack.

"No, I'm sorry. I'm sure, though, that he's been here before."

"With Pat?" asked Liz.

"That I don't remember. Sorry."

"Don't be. You've been a great help," said Jack.

"I do remember that Pat would sometimes play pool with another man. Not this one. A rough-looking character with a ponytail, tattoos, and a leather vest. Sorry, I don't know his name."

"She would come with him, or meet him here?" asked Jack.

"No, it was only a couple of times, and they didn't come in together," Craig answered.

"Do you know that person's name?"

"No, although I've heard things about him," said Craig.

"Such as?" asked Liz.

"That he's into bad stuff.'

"What bad stuff?" asked Jack.

"I have no idea. I stay away from that kind of people."

"Did it surprise you that Pat Colberg was with him?" asked Liz.

"Yes, it did. Who people hang out with can be surprising and unexpected, but it's none of my business. Also, I'm not sure that they were together, only that they were playing pool."

Liz and Jack left and decided to take a walk down Calle del Cristo. As they walked towards the small chapel, Capilla del Cristo, that gives the street its name, they went by the cathedral on their left, the oldest in the United States and the second oldest in the Americas, and the El Convento hotel on the right. They crossed the street and sat on a bench in the small park facing the cathedral, with the hotel on their left, to enjoy the view, watch people walk by, and talk.

"Old San Juan is a remarkable place," said Jack.

"It reminds me of the French Quarter in New Orleans. There too, despite all the tacky souvenir shops and tourist traps, you can still find places like El Batey, say the Acme Oyster House in the French Quarter. Most are, sad to say, anachronisms on their way out. At least that is the case here in Puerto Rico, as entrepreneurs seek them out and try to adapt them to attract a wider variety of tourism, in the process making them bland and inoffensive, or perhaps offensive, caricatures of the original. Of course, they end up killing the qualities that made the places unique and attractive in the first place."

"Do you mean an El Batey franchise? God forbid," said Liz.

"Well, I suppose that if it has survived intact for more than fifty years, there's hope," said Jack.

Chapter Nineteen

"Pat Colberg seems to be in the middle of everything," said Liz. "We know she was in El Batey often enough for the bartender to know her name, that Santos was also there with her at least twice, and that she met Robert there. We have to find out whether she was also the woman seen in La Perla with Santos on an occasion when he was transacting business, and if it was her, whether she knew what he was doing."

"And we know that she was seen arguing with Santos at The Islander the night before her body was found," added Jack. "So, Santos looks like our main suspect, don't you agree?"

"Maybe, but we have nothing solid. We also need to find out how he ties into Marcos's death. We know that it wasn't a robbery," said Liz.

"That death is for us to solve. The police, the FBI, and everybody else is looking to solve Pat's murder, but I don't think that any of them are going to devote much time or significant resources to investigate Marcos's death, unless they think that it's related to Pat's murder, or any other matter that they consider important."

"It has to be related if we believe that Marcos's murder was not the result of an attempted robbery," said Jack.

"That's what I'm saying," said Liz.

"I think that we're going to have to do our digging in two places at the very least. We need to go back to La Perla, and we need to go back to Rincón," said Jack.

"By going back to La Perla I mean that someone has to go there to start snooping around, and talking to people," he added.

"Who?" asked Liz. "It can't be any of us. We'd stick out like sore thumbs— at least you and Bill would—and I'm not sending Rita down there."

"Nor are you going yourself," said Jack.

"Why not? I've been in dangerous places before. You seem to forget that I used to be a special agent with the FBI before we met."

"Right, let's assume, for argument's sake, that you go. Who would you go with?" Said Jack.

"Carlos, of course."

"Carlos? Who is he?"

"He's Robert's friend from the Llorens housing project, remember?"

"Is he the guy from the apartment where Robert Montes was staying, the one who agreed to help with our investigation into Marcos's murder?" asked Jack.

"Yes, I can give him a call."

"What about the Rincón angle?" asked Jack.

"I think we may have to be more surreptitious there. We've already asked many questions. I think that we need to start surveilling people, following them around, and I think Bill is the person to do that, maybe with Rita or Joyce. What do you think?"

"I agree. We need to talk to them about it."

"And we will, first thing tomorrow back at the office."

They continued walking down Calle del Cristo towards the small chapel at the end of the street. Liz asked Jack whether he knew anything about it. Jack replied that he did not. He said that he knew of the chapel, had seen it from outside since it was impossible to miss as you drive or walk down Cristo street.

"Well," said Liz, "this street ends right at the top of the old walls of the city, on the side that faces the bay. Centuries ago, the celebrations held to commemorate the patron saint, San Juan Bautista (St. John the Baptist), included a horse race down the street. They say that one year a rider in the traditional race lost control of his horse as it galloped at full speed to the end of the street. It was a young mare that was running the race for the first time and may have been spooked by fireworks. According to different versions, rider and horse either plunged over the wall or stopped short of it. Either way, the rider survived in what was deemed to be a miracle in answer to urgent pleas for holy intercession."

"And the chapel?" asked Jack.

"The young rider—now I remember his name, Baltazar Montañez—built the small chapel on the exact spot where the street ends, and he was saved. The altar is covered with silver and gold leaf and is surrounded by paintings by eighteenth-century Puerto Rican painter Jose Campeche. The chapel is today much the same as it was back then, another of your authentic places. It is adorned with silver ornaments brought by believers seeking a miracle, each representing ailing parts of the body, legs, arms, hearts, and others."

They turned left on Fortaleza Street, named after the governor's mansion. La Fortaleza (The Citadel), was built in the 16th century and is located on one end of the street, at the top of the hill, overlooking the bay. After making several turns along narrow side streets, they arrived at the parking garage in front of their office building, retrieved their car, and drove home.

Despite the hour, Liz decided to call David Montes, who she knew had returned from his trip to Boston.

"David, how are you, and how did you leave Robert?" she said.

"I'm fine and so is Robert, but he's not happy about being in Boston this time of year."

"Can't say I blame him," said Liz.

"Pretty cold up there," said David.

"Indeed," replied Liz. "Remember, though, that he's there for safety, not comfort. The reason I'm calling is that we need your help. We think that Pat Colberg's murder in Rincón, and Marcos's in La Perla, are related, and that Marcos's was meant as a warning to deter people from looking into the motive for Pat's. We think that some people might be afraid that they, or their activities, are exposed. We're convinced that Pat was mixed up with something or someone, maybe both, that got her killed."

"I see," said David. "Where do I come in?"

"We need to look deeper at the La Perla side of things. We will need to do the same with Rincón, but La Perla is where you can help us. Robert told us that Carlos Palou, his friend from the Llorens housing project, was available. We want to use him. But we don't want to send him out there on his own, nor put him in charge of anything. We want you to be involved."

"What do you want me to do?" asked David.

"I want you to go to La Perla and look around. We can talk more about what we need if you wouldn't mind coming to our office tomorrow morning."

"I'll be there. What time?"

'Ten o'clock?"

"Sounds good. See you then."

"Would you mind calling Carlos and asking him to come in at eleven?"

"l would have to pick him up, he doesn't have a car and public transportation is still a nightmare. Do you mind if he comes in with me?"

"No, I don't. When you come in, though, we will want to talk to you first."

"That's fine. See you in the morning."

The next morning they discussed the Rincón surveillance first. Bill told Liz and Jack that after thinking it through overnight he was convinced that it was best to bring an outside person to help him, someone who had experience in that sort of thing. He reasoned that if the work entailed following people, or getting close to them, such as Santos Otero or others in the Rincón area, it would have to be someone other than him because he would be recognized, at least by Santos and his men, after the incident at Mi Sitio.

"I can be the backup, do electronic surveillance and anything that doesn't involve getting up close and personal, which is what I would otherwise be doing. We need someone with experience to do that, and I want to bring in Harry. You remember, we used him in our last case."

"Sounds good, Bill, and it makes sense," said Jack. "I remember Harry, last name Rivera, comes from Colorado, right? The question is who will pay his fees. In our last case we had Al who paid for you, Harry, and the others. He could afford it. David Montes isn't in the same league. Remember that he's already paying for our services."

"David will be here soon. We'll run it by him," said Liz. "I'm sure we can work something out. He and Carlos are helping us with the La Perla end of things, hands-on, not with money, and are going in at some risk to themselves. I think that the firm can pay for a substantial part of Harry's fees. You can go ahead and see if he's available."

"I took care of that last night. He is."

110

Chapter Twenty

David and Carlos were at the office by ten o'clock in the morning. Carlos waited in the reception area while David went inside to meet with Liz, Jack, and Bill. Andy offered him coffee or something to drink. He declined. Although it was clear that he would have preferred to be someplace else, he was at ease waiting in the reception room for Montes, who was in the conference room telling everyone that Robert was okay in Boston, but freezing his butt off and wishing that he was back in Puerto Rico.

Bill explained what they needed: "Someone has to go down there, to La Perla, to look for information about whether Lieutenant Pat Colberg was the woman who was seen there with Santos Otero, and, if possible, why she was there. Also, if it was her, whether her presence had anything to do with what happened in Rincón, and, vice-versa, whether her presence in Rincón the night she was killed had anything to do with whatever she was doing in La Perla. We want to understand her relationship with Santos Otero. We think that you and Carlos can get that information through Carlos's contacts."

"Can you work with him? asked Bill. "We know that your son and Carlos were friends despite there being a not insignificant age difference between them. What about your relationship with him?"

"It's the other way around, Bill," explained David. "Carlos and I are both former Marines, although he is much younger than I, about twenty years. We both did one stint, four years each, in active service. Once a Marine, always a Marine, Semper Fi."

"I see," said Jack. "How did you ever meet? You weren't in active service at the same time."

"We both had our problems after we were discharged, mostly related to alcohol abuse. I can't break his confidence, but I can say that I am an alcoholic and have been attending AA meetings for many years."

As a recovering alcoholic himself, Jack felt the urge to share his own experiences with David. He refrained from doing so because he believed it would redefine their relationship. Liz understood what was going through her husband's mind, as he had shared his story of loss and redemption with her before they were married.

"He looks up to you, correct?" asked Jack.

"I don't know that he looks up to me, but he trusts me. He and I met, and having our military service, our problems with alcohol, and, more importantly, our recovery and redemption, in common, became good friends. Carlos is a good man who's had some problems and is starting to get his life back together. He has a job, which I helped him get, and is living for the time being in Llorens because that is what he can afford. It hasn't been easy living there, although despite public perception many decent, hard-working people do."

"He met my son through me, and I think he considers him to be a younger brother. My son does look up to him. When Robert found himself in trouble because of what happened in Rincón and with no place to go, he turned to Carlos who opened his door without considerations of personal risk."

"So, believe me," he continued, "Carlos will do whatever he can for my son, and I trust him completely."

"I can understand why on both counts," said Jack.

They asked Andy to bring Carlos to the conference room. When he came in, they all noticed the single tattoo on his right arm, the Marine Emblem, Eagle, Globe, and Anchor. They introduced themselves and explained why they needed him, that David Montes spoke highly of him. When they asked whether they could count on his help, he said that David Montes could rely on his support and so could Robert, and made it clear that he was in it for them only, and that he would do whatever they needed him to do.

"Thank you," said Liz. "I don't think we have anything else. You know what we need, and I'm sure that you know what to do. If you need us, let us know. We hope to hear from you soon."

"One last thing," said Bill. "I want you to know that although we're involved in this matter on a professional basis, this is also personal to us. We feel that we lost one of our own with the death of your friend Marcos."

"I appreciate that, sir," said Carlos.

"We should go down there while it's still daylight, don't you think?" asked David.

"Yes, I agree, and I suggest that rather than announce our presence to everybody, we should use the back door. I mean, everybody will know soon enough that we're there. We don't need to hide; we have nothing to fear. But it would help if we can buy some time under the radar," said Carlos.

"If by the back door you mean going through the cemetery, I agree," said David. "What should we do? Who should we see?"

"I thought we could go and see Gilberto Acosta. He's a good man and has his hand on the pulse of the neighborhood."

"Do you think he's still there, even after the hurricane? I know Gilberto. He's not a young man anymore, and he has a daughter in Morovis, where they're all from," said David.

"I think he's still there. If he isn't, we'll go find him in Morovis, or wherever he is," said Carlos.

"You think he's that important?"

"I would prefer to find him, although there are others that we could talk to if he's not available. But he knows everybody in La Perla, and what they're doing. He's been a community organizer for a long time, and everyone respects him."

"So, let's go."

They drove up towards La Perla, on the other side of Old San Juan, next to Morro Castle. The offices of Diaz and Hardy are on the southern side, next to the bay, while La Perla is on the north, by the ocean. It wasn't too far, and in theory they could have walked it. But they would have arrived drenched in sweat if they had because it is an uphill climb, sometimes quite steep; a hot and steamy climb under the bright, tropical sun. So they drove and were there in about ten minutes.

They parked on Norzagaray Street and walked down Calle Cementerio to the Santa María Magdalena de Pazzi Cemetery, one of the most beautiful cemeteries in the world because of its location next to the Atlantic Ocean. They went past the monuments, many of them ornate and beautiful, that mark the final resting place of many of Old San Juan's dead and some of Puerto Rico's most illustrious citizens.

From the cemetery, they crossed into La Perla and walked to the home of Gilberto Acosta. They were lucky to find him at home. Don Gilberto, as most respectfully addressed him, was a white-haired gentleman in his mid-seventies who had been involved in politics and community leadership for many years. He was a veteran of many battles with city and state governments and had been successful most of the time. He knew everybody in the neighborhood and all their secrets and was a powerful man in his community. No longer a young man, he now found himself in the middle of two difficult battles, one trying to cleanse La Perla of drugs, guns, and drug lords, the other raising his community from the devastation of two hurricanes.

"Don Gilberto," said Carlos. "You live here without any protection? I know you have enemies. You should be more careful."

"If someone wants to hurt me they know where I live. They also know that I have many friends, including you. They'll leave me alone."

"You don't have electricity yet?" asked David.

"No, I don't. I'm lucky to have part of my roof at least," Gilberto answered. "My community is destroyed."

Coming to Gilberto's house through the warren of crooked streets that is La Perla, David and Carlos had seen the destruction that he was talking about and that Bill and Marcos had witnessed the night that someone killed Marcos. They saw terrible desolation in incongruous juxtaposition to the magnificent views of the cemetery and Morro Castle to the west, and the Atlantic Ocean a few yards to the north.

"Don Gilberto, a good boy was killed here the other night. He was a friend of ours. I'm sure you knew him, his family once lived here," said Carlos.

"Yes," said Gilberto, who went on to explain that he knew who Marcos was and that his aunt lived in La Perla. He told them that after the hurricane she had gone to stay with family in another town.

"So many people had to leave when their houses were destroyed," said Gilberto. "I hope they all return, although I know that many won't. We don't get much help down here. I think that many people hope that we go away. But we won't because this is all we have, this is home."

"Marcos," he continued, "I know they are saying that he was killed in a robbery, but I hear other things."

"What things?" asked Carlos.

"Son, you know I have to be careful. As you say, things can happen to me if they think I talk too much. I know there is a man who is not from here who you should watch. I cannot tell you his name. He likes to go to a place in Rincón called something like Mi Casa."

"Mi Sitio?"

"Maybe, I don't know. So, you're leaving now. Be careful."

David and Carlos understood that their presence in Gilberto's house could be dangerous for him. They left as discreetly as possible, intending to use the same route they had entered by, the cemetery. As they made their way through the labyrinth of small alleys and the storm debris four men stopped them.

"What were you doing in don Gilberto's house?" one of them asked.

"He's a good friend, and we came to see how he's doing, and to ask if there's anything that he needs," replied David.

"What's your name?" The same man asked David. "You're not from here."

"I am David Montes, and this is my friend, Carlos. Both of us are friends of don Gilberto."

One of the men recognized David and told the other two that he was Robert Montes's father.

"And the other guy?"

"I'm Carlos, a friend of don Gilberto, of David, and of his son Robert. David and I were also friends of Marcos. Maybe you guys knew him. He was killed here in an attempted robbery, except that we don't think that it was a robbery, and we want to find out the truth. We came here to ask don Gilberto to help us. He said that he could not do so."

"'You're not from here, are you?"

"No, I'm from Llorens."

"Well, then you shouldn't be here. You're far from home."

"Leave them alone, Pachi, they're good friends of mine." It was don Gilberto.

"With respect, don Gilberto, this is none of your business," said one of the four.

"And I say it is. I told you that these are my friends. Besides, I don't think you want to mess with either of them, son. You could end up getting hurt."

"We don't want trouble," said David. "We were leaving."

One of the men pulled out a knife. Carlos immediately stepped between him and David, who happened to have brought his gun and was now pointing it at the man.

"Enough!" Shouted David. "I already said that we don't want trouble and are leaving. Now, get out of our way."

The man still threatened them, saying that they would be sorry, and Gilberto came up and whispered to Carlos that it was best if they left. As Carlos looked around, he saw that a small crowd was starting to gather. He looked at David, and they both began to walk away, leaving by one of the main streets feeding into the neighborhood rather than through the cemetery as they had intended.

Chapter Twenty-One

Bill and Harry decided to park near Mi Sitio to observe the people entering and leaving and take photographs of any who looked familiar, or looked suspicious. They had traveled from San Juan that morning in terrible weather. It was again raining hard, and there were flood warnings for several neighborhoods.

They stopped at Ramey Runway in Aguadilla for lunch. Gloria was a good friend, as had been her husband. Bill, Harry, and a few other former airmen who still lived in the area sometimes stopped by to say hello to her, and to see how she was doing. Not that they were checking up on her—she could, and did, take care of herself. They came because they were fond of Gloria, and she of them. It was also a way for all of them to feel some connection to a good friend and mentor. After lunch, they continued to Rincón.

"What a dump," said Harry when they got to Mi Sitio, as he looked at the one-story cement building. It had been painted many years ago in a color somewhat reminiscent of Pepto-Bismol, which would not have been flattering even when first applied. Now, many years later, it looked faded and dirty and was covered with crude graffiti. There was a double door in front that must have been painted sometime in the distant past in a color that may have been olive-green, and there were two windows on each side of the door. All four were covered with old grime that has one saving grace; it obscured the Neo-Nazi and white-supremacist posters taped to the windows from the inside. One flickering neon lightbulb hung over the door, and one lamppost illuminated the sandy area in front of the building that served as a parking lot. From that same lamppost swung a plastic sign bearing the name of the establishment, Mi Sitio, below which are painted two words: Comida Casera, home cooking. Perhaps in its early days, the place had been a restaurant. Bill and Harry doubted that anything that would qualify as home cooking had been served there for many years.

Sitting outside in their vehicle, parked on the street close to Mi Sitio, Bill and Harry saw Santos emerge from the bar and get on his bike. He left the parking lot heading in the direction of Rincón, and they decided to follow him. Santos rode to the center of town and parked on the street close to the town square. Bill kept driving while observing Santos to see what he would do. When he got off his bike and started walking, Harry got out of the car and followed him, and Bill parked and waited. Santos walked to La Ola. Harry waited a few minutes and followed him inside. He found an empty stool at the bar even though the place was already crowded, sat, and ordered a beer. He saw Santos enter the back room and emerge after a few minutes with a middle-aged American woman who Harry guessed was Peggy Ramos.

From the bar, Harry heard Santos say something about having to move some merchandise, that the buyer was supposed to have retrieved his stuff the day after they had brought it in and had not done so because there had been too much police activity in the area, both federal and local, after Pat Colberg's murder.

"We need to get this done. Our suppliers want their money and are not willing to wait any longer," said Santos. "I spoke to our buyers, and they said they would come tomorrow night. We need to be ready."

Harry paid for his beer and left ahead of Santos to wait in the car with Bill. Santos came out some ten minutes later, got on his bike, and headed back in the direction he had come. Bill and Harry followed him to Mi Sitio and parked their car out on the street some distance from their original spot.

"He went to La Ola and met with Peggy to talk about moving merchandise and complain about police activity? That's interesting," said Jack when Bill called to tell him what was happening.

"Peggy told us that they were estranged. It sure doesn't look that way. I'll let Liz know, and we will discuss it when you come back."

By then, night had fallen. After waiting around half an hour, they saw Santos again come out, this time with two of his men. They got into a van and drove off. Dark smoke came out of the truck whenever Santos hit the gas, and the engine knocked. Bill again followed, keeping his distance. They passed the town of Moca and continued toward San Sebastian. A few minutes later they turned left onto a narrow dirt road.

Bill did the same, shutting off his headlights and staying far enough behind so that they could barely see the van. The smoke helped keep it in sight, but the road was dark and climbed through dense brush, so Bill couldn't afford to fall too far behind.

Santos drove on, and when he stopped and parked in front of a run-down old house, Bill did the same, farther down the road, and he and Harry retrieved their night vision binoculars. They saw the three men enter the house and kept watching without leaving their car or coming any closer. They waited until the three came out, got in their van, and started to drive away. Bill started the car, turned it around, and left before the truck got close, and they were discovered. They waited ahead on the side of the better road until the van passed them. This time they did not follow.

"What do you think that was about?" asked Harry.

"I don't know. Should we go back and see?" asked Bill.

"Why not? I doubt they'll return tonight," answered Harry.

They drove back to the dirt road turnoff, went past the house, and parked some distance beyond it. The idea was that if someone decided to return, they wouldn't see their car, and therefore wouldn't expect intruders.

Bringing their guns and their night vision binoculars, they walked up to a window of the house and peered inside. A man was lying asleep on an old sofa, possibly drunk considering the empty bottles that were strewn on the floor. As they looked around the small living area, they noticed a door secured shut with a big padlock. They didn't see anything of value in the house.

"Why would they come here to this place with a drunk passed out on the sofa and nothing of any value visible?" asked Harry.

"Because whatever is of any value is behind that locked door, and it must be precious indeed for them to keep it there and feel compelled to come out here to check."

After a few minutes, they heard a vehicle approaching, and they moved away at once. They hurried up the road to get away from the house and hid behind some trees. From there they saw the same van coming back. This time they saw Santos and four men, the same two from before, and two others. They entered the house and came out a few minutes later carrying boxes which they loaded into the van. After bringing out several they got in the truck and drove off.

"What now?" asked Harry.

"Well, I don't think we should follow them. It's too dangerous. Who knows what they're carrying, but it could be guns, or drugs, or both. If so, they may have posted watchers on the road to make sure they aren't followed," said Bill.

"I think we should wait here a while, call Jack or Liz to let them know what's happening, and then go to Mi Sitio to see whether we spot the van. My guess is that they picked the stuff up in a hurry and that it wasn't planned. Why else would they have come to check, left, then returned to load the goods into their van and take them away? I think that they had to get the merchandise out and don't know yet where to store it. It will be in the van parked in the usual place until they figure things out."

They called Liz to let her know what was happening.

"I don't need to tell you to be very careful," she said. "If those guys are moving drugs, guns, or whatever, they will be very dangerous. Where are you?"

"We're still parked near the stash house," said Bill.

"Can you take pictures and send them to me?"

"Harry already did. They're on their way."

"We're leaving now for Mi Sitio to check out whether the van is there," said Bill. "We'll keep in touch."

"Again, be careful. Two people are dead. We don't want more," said Liz.

Bill and Harry drove to Mi Sitio, confident that they would find Santos and the van. When they got there, they didn't see the trailer, and most of the motorcycles, including the one that they had previously seen Santos riding, were gone. They decided that Harry would go inside to try to find out where Santos was or what had happened. He did and came out a few minutes later saying that Santos and most of the bikers were gone.

"There are only two guys left in there, and nobody's talking. What do you want to do?"

"These motherfuckers killed Marcos, and I'm not going to lose them. I think we should go inside and try to persuade the ones that stayed behind. Do you agree?"

"How do we do that?"

"Follow me," said Bill.

They walked towards the bar, and as they were going by the two bikes that were left, Bill kicked one of them over. Harry looked at him and did the same with the other one. Bill told Harry to go inside and say that there was a guy outside who had knocked over two Harleys. Harry did so, and he and the two bikers raced out.

Bill was by the car, and the two came after him. As they closed in, Bill turned around and kicked one of them in the groin. The man fell to his knees in pain. As the other one was about to hit Bill, Harry grabbed him from behind. Bill opened the trunk of their car, and they pushed the man inside. They got in the car and drove off while the other one was still on the ground, heading inland until they found a suitable, isolated place, where they stopped the car and pulled the biker from the trunk. It didn't take long for him to tell them what he knew, after which they drove away, leaving him stranded.

Chapter Twenty-Two

"Bill, for God's sake, what were you thinking?" asked Liz.

"I was thinking that I wasn't going to let them get away. Anyway, we let him go unharmed. They may try to come after me later, but they're not going to the police, you know that. And I did find out where the van was headed."

"Where, Bill?"

"You will be surprised. It's in the garage of a house in Rincón owned by Peggy Ramos."

"You are right. I am surprised. Do you think she knows?" asked Liz.

"I assume she does, but who knows? We will find out."

"It seems that we're getting into something other than finding out who killed Pat Colberg and Marcos."

"Liz, you know that it all ties in together. Santos is the central figure. If he is into drug trafficking and other things, I think we need to follow the van and maybe find some answers, or at least clues. I mean, why would someone split Pat Colberg's head open with a rock and why would someone have a knife stuck into Marcos? It has to be big, and this is big."

"I agree, Bill, but you're done with Rincón. Come back to San Juan and bring Harry. They know who you are. There's nothing more you can do, and you're both at risk. Come back to San Juan. We'll find another way to get to the bottom of this."

There was no sense arguing, and Liz was right anyway.

"Right, we're heading back. I think we should stop by Ramey Runway to talk to Gloria about what happened. She was the one who recommended Peggy to us."

"Fine," said Liz. "Leave right now."

"We will."

Liz told Jack what Bill had found, and what he and Harry had done.

"Jack, if the boxes that Santos loaded into his van contained drugs, guns, or whatever, there has to be a buyer, and that buyer must be getting impatient to receive his stuff, whatever it is. We need to find out where the delivery will take place so we can see who the players are," said Liz.

"Sure, Liz. I agree. How do we do it? Buyers and sellers will be on their guard, and it will be a perilous situation."

"We need to do it anyway, no matter the risk. Now, we've been concentrating our attention on Santos, following him around, and with good reason of course. However, there are other moving parts to this. Other people are involved, some of whom we may know. We need to find out who else might be involved," said Liz.

"They are pieces of the puzzle and could help us complete it," she continued.

"We know the names of other people who were present at The Islander or at the beach party the night before Pat Colberg's body was found. There were many other people there whose names we don't know and who may also have been involved, but there is nothing we can do about those, unless we can identify them," Liz continued.

"We know about Ann Miller, Sandra Martinez, Fred Rogers, Linda Perkins, and our client. Oh, and Sue," said Jack.

"Yes, those are the ones that we know about, in addition to Santos," said Liz. "Now, we don't have the resources to surveil all of them before Santos delivers his merchandise, so we have to make choices. I think we can be effective if we concentrate on two, and I think they should be Sandra Martinez and the mysterious Fred Rogers."

"Why mysterious?"

"Because he shows up everywhere and we don't know why. We know, for example, that he coincided in El Batey at least one time with Pat Colberg, but then says he met her for the first time at The Islander. Is that true, that they met that night for the first time? I think he bears watching."

"Right," said Jack. "We need to start doing that."

"I also think that we should take a closer look at Peggy Ramos. I know she's a friend of Gloria's, but she's also related to Santos and may have lied to us when she said they were estranged," said Jack.

"I agree. Bill should still be in the area. Let me call him," said Liz.

Bill and Harry were at Ramey Runway when Liz reached them. She told Bill to return to Rincón to take a closer look at Peggy, and that before they went, he should ask Gloria how well she knew her.

Chapter Twenty-Three

"I've known Peggy for a long time," Gloria said to Bill. "We have never been close friends, but I know her history, how, when, and why she came to Puerto Rico and Rincón. I know about her marriage, and about how she ended up owning La Ola."

She said that she had met Peggy's husband, Ricky, a long time ago, but hadn't seen him after he and Peggy divorced. She knew that Peggy had raised Santos, but didn't know anything about their present relationship.

"I know that Santos's father was a drunk and a bum and that his mother abandoned them both. Peggy took Santos in and raised him," said Gloria.

"Do you know anything about the father?" asked Bill.

"Only that his name was Primo Otero, that he was an abusive drunk, and that he lived in the countryside somewhere."

"Could that somewhere be near Moca, Gloria?" asked Bill.

"Yes, I think so."

"Harry, that must be the stash house. We need to go back and take another look at the place. Goodbye, Gloria. We don't know how Peggy ties into everything, whether she is a part of Santos's enterprise or is being used. We'll find out and will let you know when we do."

Bill and Harry drove back to the house in Moca. By the time they got there it was dark and there was no light coming from inside the house. There were no vehicles parked at or near it, so they decided to go in. Before they did, they looked through the window with their night vision binoculars. The door that had been locked was now ajar. The man that had been on the bed was now on the floor. They figured that it was Santos's father, Primo Otero, and decided that it was safe to enter.

They entered and saw that Primo was fine, just sleeping. There were no signs of violence on him or in the house, which they saw had two bedrooms, a small kitchen, a bathroom, and the room they were in. The house looked as bad inside as it did outside, maybe worse. It was a mess, dirty and abandoned. The kitchen hadn't been cleaned in years, and there were open containers full of decaying and rotten food all around. Empty liquor bottles were strewn on the floor and a small table in the kitchen, and there was one half-full bottle of cheap rum on a side table by the dirty sofa.

The room was now-unlocked, and although the boxes that had been stored in it had been removed, they still found powder residue on one table, which they collected. There was also one small box of ammunition that had not been packed into one of the larger boxes that were taken away by Santos.

As they were checking the room for more evidence, Primo came stumbling in. He asked who they were and threatened to hurt them. They disregarded him and went about their business, until Primo, who had left, came back wielding a bat. He swung it at Harry. He ducked, grabbed the bat from Primo and pushed him to the floor. They made him get on his feet, forced him into the living room, and had him sit on the couch.

"Are you Primo Otero?" asked Bill.

"Yeah, das me ... dis my housh ... ged oud."

"Do you know what was in this room?"

"Das my son Sano room," he continued to answer in the slurred speech of a boozer, very difficult to understand.

"Do you know what was in the room?"

"Das my son Sano room."

"Do you know where Santos is?"

"Das my son Sano room, you bede wash oud, he gona hurd yu."

They decided that it was useless to try to get any information from a boozer whose brain had been marinating in alcohol for a long time, and they left. By the time they did, Primo had slumped sideways and was half lying on the sofa, asleep again.

Chapter Twenty-Four

Frances Day called Liz and asked her to come to FBI headquarters to discuss an urgent matter. Special Agent Day and Liz were longtime friends. They met during Frances's FBI training at the academy in Quantico, Virginia, where Liz was an instructor and met up again during the former's first field assignment. The friends lost contact when Liz resigned from the Agency to establish her law firm, but coincided for the third time when Frances was re-assigned to Puerto Rico. Frances had helped Liz during her last case when she and her witnesses had faced real danger. She had gone out on a limb releasing to Liz, a witness who was in her custody. The local police were seeking the man on a trumped-up charge of murder. Frances put her job on the line and could have faced criminal prosecution by not turning the man over to police custody, but she was convinced that he would have been killed.

"Liz, how are you doing? Please sit down."

"Hello, Frances. It's always good to see you, even if this is work."

"Liz, you need to be careful."

"Why, am I in danger?"

"It's not about that—at least, not necessarily. I'm only authorized to tell you that you and your people are interfering with an important operation."

"C'mon, Frances, you have to give me more. What are you talking about?"

"In strictest confidence, Liz, the DEA has certain individuals under surveillance for illegal activities in the Rincón area, and they say that your actions may jeopardize their operation."

"We're only trying to do two things, clear our client's name, which may entail finding out who killed Pat Colberg, and find out who killed Marcos. We're not trying to interfere with the DEA's operation. If they want to warn me off any specific action, I'll consider it, but we will not stop doing our job. You know me better than that, I hope."

"I do. I was asked to deliver the message."

"What is it that we're doing that they consider interference?"

"As I understand it you risk revealing the identity of one or more undercover agents."

"What? How?"

"One of the agents and I don't know if there are more, says that it's by seeking him out and asking questions."

"Seeking him out. So, it's a he?"

"Figure of speech, Liz. Could be he or she."

"Or a slip of the tongue my friend. I'll assume it's a man."

"Up to you. I'll neither confirm nor deny."

"The second thing that I wanted to talk to you about, and I'm sure it ties in with the first, is that I did check up on Santos Otero as you asked me. What I found out is disquieting and is another reason why you have to be careful. He is suspected of being in the middle of many things, including drug trafficking, gun

131

running, among others. He is a dangerous person, and you should steer clear of him."

"I know who he is. We've already had a very unpleasant encounter with him in Rincón."

"But let's be clear," said Liz. "The only male that we have talked to regarding our investigation is Fred Rogers because he and Linda Perkins were the ones who discovered Pat Colberg's body. I assume that he is the undercover agent that you're referring to, although I'm surprised because as far as we knew he was here with the Red Cross. Anyway, whether it's him or somebody else, I have no interest in blowing anybody's cover or jeopardizing their investigation in any way, and I think that the solution would be for him to contact us so that we can arrange a discreet encounter."

"Let me look into this," said Frances. "If Mr. Rogers is the person, I'll propose your solution. If he isn't, I'll try to get authorization to tell you who the person is, because I do admit that it is ridiculous to ask you not to interfere without telling you how it is that you're interfering, unless you're expected to drop everything."

"Which I won't do."

"Which you won't do."

Frances asked Liz where Robert Montes was and Liz told her that he was traveling outside Puerto Rico, that he would return soon, and that if Frances needed him, he would cut his trip short and come back. Frances said that it wouldn't be necessary, for the moment.

"Liz, that's all I have. I'll try to get back to you soon on the matter we discussed."

"Thank you, Frances. By the way, I don't see you at the gym anymore. Is anything wrong?"

"Just taking care of some minor medical issues."

"Oh, anything you want to talk about?"

"Not today and not here, Liz. If you can, I want to meet somewhere for coffee."

"Of course. Why don't we do lunch, instead? How about meeting at La Mallorquina?"

"I don't know the restaurant. Where is it?"

"On Calle San Justo in Old San Juan. I know you'll enjoy it."

"Fine, is tomorrow at twelve o'clock good for you?"

"It is," said Liz. "See you there."

Liz returned to her office and discussed with Jack her conversation with Frances. They agreed that their best bet was Fred Rogers who had been so evasive with them. If he were doing undercover work for the DEA, it would explain that evasiveness.

"I'm having lunch tomorrow with Frances. Let's see what's on her mind," said Liz.

She went to her office to take care of other matters. The firm was doing very well. Everyone was busy, especially Rita. Liz was glad that she had hired her; she was an excellent attorney and a tireless worker, maybe too much so. She was aware that Rita was having problems at home. She had never complained but things get around, and Liz had heard rumors. She didn't feel that it was her place to mention anything to Rita about her personal life, but she could talk to her about work. She decided to call her in, but when she rang her office Rita didn't answer. She called Andy and he told her that Rita was attending a deposition in another attorney's office. Liz decided that she would have a talk with Rita as soon as possible.

The following day at the restaurant Frances remarked on the ambiance and asked what the name La Mallorquina meant.

"The woman from Mallorca," answered Liz. "Natives of the Spanish island of Mallorca, one of the Balearic Islands, opened the restaurant in the 1800s. I've read up on the area because part of my family came from there. It's an archipelago of islands located east of the Spanish mainland. Mallorca, where some of my ancestors came from, is one of the four largest islands in the group, together with Menorca, Ibiza, and Formentera."

"I know of Mallorca, Menorca, and Ibiza, but not Formentera. They are all popular tourist destinations, aren't they?" asked Frances.

"Yes, particularly Mallorca and Ibiza."

"The history of the islands is very interesting," said Liz. "The Romans controlled them in ancient times. They later became part of the Muslim Caliphate of Cordoba, until the so-called Reconquista, when the Moors were expelled," said Liz.

"At the time Spain did not yet exist as a country, and the Iberian Peninsula was home to a number of kingdoms. After many conflicts between European kingdoms, the Balearic Islands became part of the kingdom of Aragon. When Ferdinand II, King of Aragon, married Isabella I, Queen of Castile, they did not unify their kingdoms. Each of them continued to rule over their own. After their deaths, however, the kingdoms were joined under their son, Emperor Charles V, the same monarch who built Morro Castle. The unification of those kingdoms is seen by many as the foundation of the modern Spanish state, which included the Balearic Islands."

"Impressive. You have family there?"

"My grandmother was born in Mallorca. She would tell us stories. I guess that piqued my interest and I did some research. I have always been a student of history, so I've read as much as I could about her birthplace."

"Have you ever visited?"

"No. But I'll go someday to Mallorca, and to the small town of Soller, where she was born."

"But enough history. What about Fred Rogers?"

"What about him, Liz?"

"I don't mean to press you, my friend, but unless you can confirm that he is the undercover agent, and we come to some agreement where I can ask him some questions, I'll have to press on with our investigation until I find out who he is and what part he played in Pat Colberg's death."

"I'll see what I can do. Right now I still can't tell you if he is or isn't the undercover agent in question. I'll get back to you later this afternoon to let you know."

"Thank you," said Liz. "Now tell me what's going on with you."

"Liz, I'm sorry to burden you. I don't know where else to turn."

"What is it, Frances?"

"You know that the only family I have is my father. My mother passed away three years ago and I am an only child. My father does have a sister, and I have cousins, but we aren't close. Well, my father has been diagnosed with Alzheimer's disease."

"Frances, I'm so sorry."

"I'm overwhelmed. I'm all he has and he's all I have. Although his sister and my cousins mean well, I can't expect them to take full responsibility. He lives in Tampa by himself, and unless somebody lives with him he is going to have to move to a home. I can't let that happen, Liz, so I have requested a transfer to Tampa so that I can be with him."

"Of course. How soon?"

"I'm on vacation until the transfer comes through. I have been assured that considering the special circumstances it will be approved. Regardless, I'm leaving in two weeks."

"No. So soon? I do understand, but I sure will miss you."

"I'll miss you, and I'll miss Puerto Rico. I pray that we cross paths again someday."

Chapter Twenty-Five

"Cholo, we need to deliver now. Our buyers will be waiting for us in Llorens. They're already pissed-off, and I don't want to have a problem with them. I want you and Flaco to go to Rincón tonight, get the van, and go to Llorens to make the delivery. I'll have another person there to get the money. I don't want you bringing it back yourself. He knows what to do with it," said Santos.

"When do you want us to go?" asked Santos.

"They'll be waiting for you tonight at three o'clock in the morning. You and Flaco are dry until you come back tomorrow. No drinking and no taking anything else."

"You tell Flaco. He doesn't like dry, and I don't trust him. Why don't I take Jesse instead?" asked Cholo.

"Jesus? Yeah, that's fine. Go ahead and let him know."

They were all hanging out in Mi Sitio and Cholo went to where the others were playing pool to let Flaco know that he wasn't doing the run tonight, that Jesse would be going instead. Flaco was upset and asked Cholo why.

"Because you drink, Flaco, and you snort, and you smoke."

"Is that what you said to Santos?"

"Yeah, I did, because it's true. You got a problem with that?"

"I do you bastard," said Flaco as he took a swing at Cholo.

Cholo was able to move back but the blow still landed hard on his chest. This was a problem for Flaco because there was nobody in their group, or in Mi Sitio, stronger or meaner than Cholo, who proceeded to punch Flaco hard on the face and then grabbed him by the neck. He had no intention of loosening his grip and would have killed Flaco. It took Santos, with the help of Luis and Jose, to pry Flaco loose, already half gone. He fell to the floor where Cholo gave him two hard kicks for good measure, and would have continued kicking Flaco if Santos hadn't made him stop. Flaco tried to get up, slipped, and fell.

"Stay down, Flaco," said Santos.

The rest of them walked away. A few minutes later Flaco got up, and stumbled out of the bar. He was barely able to get on his bike. He was lucky that it had an electric starter as he wouldn't have been able to kick-start it, and would have been forced to walk.

Flaco rode to The Islander where he ordered a rum on the rocks, and had two of them before someone who knew him asked what had happened. By the time he answered, he was on his fourth drink, having put the first three away in quick succession.

"Santos is a pendejo because he trusts Cholo who is an even bigger pendejo. I told Cholo how I felt and beat the crap out of him."

"You look pretty beat up yourself, Flaco," said his friend.

"They all ganged up on me, Jaime. Cholo looks worse than I do."

"If you say so."

"Yeah, I say so. Is that a problem?" he asked. He tried to get up, but instead tripped over himself and fell back on his chair.

"Let's go," said Cholo later that night. He and Jesse got on their bikes and rode to Rincón, where they retrieved the van from the garage where it was parked. They checked the back and were satisfied that the cargo was there and untouched, then checked the van to make sure that everything was in working order, turn signal, headlights, and brake lights. The last thing they needed was to be stopped by the police for some simple infraction having to do with the van. Cholo would be driving. He was an impulsive and violent man, but a careful and safe driver who always observed the speed limit and all the rules of the road. He stopped at all stop signs, did not run yellow lights, let alone red ones, and always used his turn signals.

They left Rincón around midnight and encountered very little traffic all the way to San Juan, because of the late hour and because, since María, most people refrain from leaving their homes after dark. Many signal lights were still out, some roads remain difficult to maneuver due to storm debris and repair work, and, more important, people don't feel that the country is safe after dark. There are stories, many of them true, of carjackings, robberies, and other crimes. Movie streaming services and takeout restaurants are making a killing at the expense of restaurants and movie theaters.

By two o'clock in the morning they were on the freeway entering the outskirts of San Juan, and Cholo called the number provided by Santos for their contact in Llorens to let him know they were on their way, and would arrive within half an hour. The person at the other end asked for a password which Cholo provided. Cholo then asked the person to reciprocate, and she did so.

Cholo knew that the arrival of the van would be noticed by other groups in addition to Santos's buyers. Llorens-Torres is a community of one hundred and forty buildings and two thousand six hundred units. It is home to many law-abiding citizens, a majority of its population, but also to more than one violent gang. These gangs post sentries to monitor the neighborhood, as do self-appointed vigilante groups.

Cholo's trip was a success. He wanted to call Santos to let him know, but it was only five thirty in the morning. He would be in Rincón soon enough, so he decided that it wasn't necessary to call Santos. They stopped for breakfast at a fast food restaurant near Llorens and then left for Rincón. By eight in the morning they had reached the town of Isabela, on the way to Rincón, and Cholo decided to stop and visit a girlfriend. Jesse was not happy. He was tired and wanted to get home. It had been a long and stressful trip.

"Cholo, what am I supposed to do while you visit your girlfriend?"

"You wait in the van. Is that a problem?"

"Yes, it's a problem. We've been on the fuckin' road all night and I'm tired. Now I'm supposed to wait in the car while you stop and have a good time with your puta?"

"What did you call her?"

"I called her your puta."

"Where did you get the idea that you could talk to me that way, cabrón?"

"What, you're my boss now? Fuck you, maricón!"

Cholo pulled the van to the side of the road, threw open his door, and leaped out to come around the van and pull Jesse out. Enraged, he hadn't watched for traffic, and a pickup truck slammed into him. The truck hit Cholo at full speed, and he landed in the middle of the road, where he was run over by still another vehicle. Jesse remained in his seat, motionless.

The vehicles that struck Cholo stopped, and one of the drivers called 911 to report the accident. Ambulances and police soon arrived, but Cholo was beyond help. The area was cordoned off, and traffic started to jam heading west, because no cars could get through, and east because of rubberneckers. The police checked everyone's IDs and saw that Cholo and Jesse had police records. They checked the van's registration. The owner was a man named Primitivo Otero with an address in Moca.

"Where the hell are they?" exclaimed Santos to one of his men.

He was sitting at a table at The Islander waiting for a call that never came, and had tried to get in contact with Cholo, to no avail. When he was able to reach Jesse, he was shocked to find out about the accident.

"What happened, Jesse? Where's Cholo?"

"He's dead, Santos. We had an accident and he was hit by a car."

"What? Shit! Jesse, listen to me, because this can get ugly if you're not careful. You haven't done anything wrong, Jesse. Keep quiet, and whatever you do, no matter what happens, don't mention my name. Do you understand? Jesse, I need you to tell me that you understand. Tell me."

"I understand, Santos."

"Was there anything in the van, Jesse? You know what I mean."

"I don't think so. Everything's in San Juan."

"Are you sure?"

"Everything was in boxes, Santos."

"Did anybody open the boxes inside the van?"

"I don't think so. "

"No, no. Don't tell me that you don't think so. Think! Did anybody open any of the boxes while they were still inside the van?"

"No, Santos, nobody did."

"Stop repeating my name."

"Yes boss."

"They may ask you where you were coming from, what you were doing there, and where you were going. Say that you went to San Juan with Cholo, who wanted to check up on a sister who lives in La Perla, and that you were now returning home to Rincón."

"Cholo doesn't have a sister."

"Listen you, idiot. They don't know that."

"Sorry boss. What if they want an address?"

"Say you don't know. Cholo was driving, and La Perla is a confusing place. Hang up now, Jesse, and don't call me. I'll call you later."

Chapter Twenty-Six

Frances Day called Liz two days before she was scheduled to leave Puerto Rico to tell her that she would be able to arrange a meeting with Fred Rogers.

"Are you still interested in meeting with him?" She asked.

"Yes," replied Liz. "Just tell me where and when."

"Good. It has to be somewhere where he will feel safe, where his cover won't get blown," said Frances.

"Most of the El Yunque National Forest is still closed," she continued. "I can arrange to hold the meeting at the forest's visitor center. I would pick you up and take you there."

"That sounds perfect, Frances. I know that you're leaving in a couple of days. Do we have time?"

"If we do it tomorrow morning, Liz. Can you make it?"

"I can. Where do I meet you?"

"I'll pick you up in front of your building."

Frances picked Liz up early the next morning, as arranged, and they headed east, passed by the airport, and continued toward the El Yunque National Forest, with the mountain that gives the forest its name, El Yunque, visible ahead. It is one of the tallest mountains in Puerto Rico and the second tallest in the rainforest after Cerro La Punta.

As they drove up towards the rainforest's visitor center, they could see that some of the greenery was returning, although the forest canopy, so crucial for the species of plants and animals below, was still far from where it should be. Although the forest was recuperating, the estimate was that twenty percent of the trees would die.

When they arrived at the center, Fred Rogers was waiting, and he didn't look all that happy to see them.

"Mr. Rogers, this is Liz Diaz."

"Fred Rogers, you are a very elusive man," said Liz.

She was not about to be obsequious to this young man. As far as she was concerned it was he who wanted something from her, that she back off from questioning him to avoid blowing his cover. She would agree to do so, she thought, only if he was willing to answer some questions for her now.

"Ms. Diaz," he said. "I assume that Agent Day has told you who I am and that by having your people come looking for me you jeopardize my cover, my safety, and the entire operation that we're conducting."

"Look, Fred, I don't want to do any of those things, but I'm representing Robert Montes, a person who is a suspect in the death of Lieutenant Pat Colberg. You knew her, and you're a person who may have information regarding that murder, or of the events and the people surrounding it."

"You were with her at The Islander, and at the beach party the night before her body was found," she said, "and you were one of the persons who found her, together with Linda Perkins. So, although I don't want to do any of the things that you mentioned, my duty is to my client, not to you or your investigation, and unless you're willing to answer my questions, I won't be able to accommodate you."

"What do you want to know, Ms. Diaz?"

"We know that you went to that beach party. Why didn't you say so?"

"I didn't want Linda Perkins to know."

"Why not?"

"That is personal, irrelevant, and none of your business."

"I don't agree. I also don't want to argue with you over it. Let's move on. Did you meet Pat Colberg for the first time that evening at The Islander, or had you met her before?"

"I met her for the first time that night."

"Did you get together with Pat later at the beach party? Is that why you went back?"

"No to both questions."

"Do you know a bar in San Juan called El Batey?"

"Yes, I do."

"Do you know Santos Otero?"

"Yes, I do."

"How do you know him?"

"I can't get into that."

"Why, is he someone that the DEA is investigating? Is he a person of interest in the operation that you're involved in?"

"I can't get into that."

"Do you know Robert Montes?"

"I know of him. I don't know him."

"How do you know of him?"

"Because I know he is a suspect in the death of Lieutenant Pat Colberg."

"Do you know what he looks like? Have you ever seen him?"

"No."

"Was your presence in Rincón that weekend related to your operation? Were you on the job?"

144

"I can't answer that."

"Do you have any information that could help us prove that our client was not involved in the murder of Pat Colberg?"

"I don't think so."

"Well, we will try to stay away from you to avoid endangering you or your operation, but you leave too many unanswered questions. If we come across your name in our investigation, we won't disregard it. If you tell me how I can contact you I promise to come to you first with any questions I have."

"You will not come across my name, so I don't need to give you my contact information, and if you interfere with my operation, I'll make you pay."

"Fred, I have a feeling that we will see each other again. Goodbye."

Liz and Frances were silent on their way down from the visitor center until Liz said that she didn't have a good feeling about Fred Rogers.

"I don't like Fred, but that's irrelevant. What bothers me is that hr turns up in unexpected places and is untruthful about his activities. I don't think that we're going to be able to forget about him."

"Well, you're not going to get him to answer any more questions. You've already tried to without much success. I do agree that there is no reason for you to cut him any slack. I suppose that he's fair game."

"I don't know that he's done anything wrong, Frances, but we have received inconsistent information about his movements at The Islander and the beach on the night that Pat Colberg was killed."

Frances dropped Liz off in front of her apartment and said goodbye to her friend who would be leaving Puerto Rico the next day. Liz thanked her for her help on this case and the previous one, and waved as she drove away.

Chapter Twenty-Seven

A friend of Carlos had taken pictures of Cholo's delivery at Llorens, using a digital night-vision camera, and Carlos had recognized the Llorens men that appeared in them, and asked to borrow the photos. His friend transferred them to Carlos's camera, and he, in turn had sent them to David, to Jack, and to Bill.

"That's Cholo, and that's Jesse," David said to Jack when they met the following morning "I know them from Mi Sitio," he continued. "But I don't recognize anyone else."

"So, we already knew that Santos was doing business in La Perla. Now we know that he supplies Llorens. That information brings us closer to knowing what happened to Pat Colberg, and why Marcos was killed. It means that Santos had a motive, self-preservation."

David told Jack that Robert was returning to Puerto Rico and perhaps could help.

"He knows more people in Rincón, Jack, including Santos and his friends," said David.

"He will be in danger," said Carlos. "Wasn't that one of the reasons why he left?"

"It was, but he wants to come back and help, not only to clear his name but to find out why Marcos was killed," said David.

"Given the danger, I don't understand why he would want to be involved," said Carlos.

"When does he return, David?" asked Jack.

"Tonight, and he wants to go back to Rincón."

"That would be a big mistake. Can you bring him here tomorrow morning so that we can talk about it?"

"I'll let you know."

"I'll tell Liz, and we'll all discuss it tomorrow. In the meantime how can we make sure that Pat Colberg was the woman who went with Santos to La Perla?" asked Jack.

"I think we can only do that by showing her picture to the people there who saw them. If it wasn't Pat, it might be difficult to find out who it was," said Carlos.

"So, how can we get it done?" asked Jack.

"The last time David and I went to La Perla we were not very successful. Maybe I can try it on my own," said Carlos.

"Too risky. There has to be another way," said Jack.

"What other way?" asked Carlos. "Someone has to go to La Perla, and it might as well be me. I do know people there, even if we had problems the last time we went. I can go and ask don Gilberto to help me out. We can show Lieutenant Colberg's picture around, and maybe we can get some answers."

"Fine, but I still wouldn't want you to go there by yourself. Take Harry with you, tonight, if you can. In the meantime, David will be picking his son up at the airport, and we can all meet here tomorrow morning."

Carlos called Gilberto and they agreed to meet at a bar on San Sebastian Street not far from La Perla at

6:30 that evening. When they arrived Gilberto was waiting for them with two younger men.

"This is Andrés, my nephew, and this is his friend, Perico," said Gilberto. "They both live in the neighborhood. Considering the problems that you had the last time you went, I thought it would be wise for you not to go back there alone. What is it that you want to do this time?"

Carlos explained that they wanted to show Pat Colberg's picture to people who knew Santos, to see whether she was the woman who had gone with him to La Perla.

"You can either go with my nephew and his friend, or you can give them the picture and let them show it around. I think that it is safer for you, and for them, if you let them do it by themselves. You and your friend can wait here and have a few beers until they return."

Carlos and Harry agreed to let Andrés and Perico take care of it. They gave Andrés the photograph, and he and his friend left for La Perla. Carlos went to the bar and got a Coke for himself and beers for don Gilberto and Harry.

"Don Gilberto," he asked, "will La Perla recover?"

"We all want it to recover. It won't be easy, but I think we, the people who live there, will do it. We are a community and we want to stay together. The government isn't helping much. Sure, they offer to find us housing elsewhere, but they don't seem to be interested in reconstruction. I suspect that others may be interested in doing something else with the land. Maybe they will change their minds and help. You never know. If they don't, we will put up a fight."

"Do you know Santos, don Gilberto?" asked Harry.

"I do. He is scum who comes from outside and poisons our young people. We have enough bottom-feeders to deal with without men like him. He doesn't make it any easier for those of us who want to rescue our youth, and make our community a safer place."

"Well, he poisons my community too, Llorens. I don't know how he does it. Who his suppliers are? Maybe if we knew that, we could do something about it."

An hour and a half later Andrés and Perico returned.

"Did anybody recognize the lady?" asked Gilberto.

"Yes, they did," answered Andrés. "She has been down there with Santos."

"There's your answer, son. Anything else we can help you with?"

"You've done plenty don Gilberto, thank you. I hope you're successful in bringing La Perla back. And thank you, Andrés and Perico," said Harry.

The next day Liz wasn't happy with the way things had gone at La Perla, how the identification of Pat's picture had been carried out.

"You two didn't go to La Perla to show Pat's picture?" Liz asked Harry.

"No," he replied, "don Gilberto sent a nephew and his friend and they showed it around. They came back and told us that the people to whom they showed it identified Pat Colberg."

"So we have our confirmation," said Jack.

"Yes," said Liz, "but I wish we had done it ourselves and not through a couple of kids."

"Agree, it would have been preferable," said Bill, "but she was identified and it stands to reason that if Santos took her with him to La Perla, he also took her to Rincón. Someone must have seen them. Right now all we know is that they were seen talking to each other for about fifteen minutes the night before she was found dead. There must be more, don't you think? If he trusted her enough to bring her to La Perla while he transacted business they were more than passing acquaintances."

They decided that someone had to go back to Rincón that same day if possible. The question was where in Rincón to go. Two places came to mind where they might find answers, The Islander and Mi Sitio.

Robert wanted to go, but Liz talked him out of it.

"Not yet, Robert. Everyone in Rincón knows you and it would make it more difficult to get our answers. Our inquiries need to be more discreet. Your day will come. We can talk about that later."

"Harry, I think that you and Carlos should make this trip," said Liz. "Maybe you can avoid going to Mi Sitio and find answers at The Islander. If you don't, you can then decide what to do next, short of going to that biker hangout. If there was no other way and you have to go there, at least you have the advantage of anonymity as you are the only ones, other than Jack and Andy, who haven't been to Rincón."

They left immediately after lunch and were at The Islander by five. Harry asked for Sue and another server told him that she would be there soon. They ordered a soft drink for Carlos, a beer for Harry, and a conch fritter appetizer. When the woman came with their drinks, they struck up a conversation, and asked her whether she knew Santos. She said that she did.

"Did you ever see him with this woman?" asked Harry, showing her a photograph of Pat Colberg.

"That's the woman who was killed here on the beach, isn't it?" she remarked. "I remember seeing Santos with a young woman. It looks like her, but I'm not sure. I can't say that it was her."

Sue arrived soon after, and came to their table. Harry and Carlos identified themselves and asked her the same question.

"I don't have to see her picture," she said. "No, I never saw her with Santos other than that night."

"Did you ever see him with any other woman?" asked Carlos.

"I can't remember."

Chapter Twenty-Eight

When Jesse returned to Rincón he went straight to Mi Sitio, where Santos was waiting for him. After hearing what he had to say about what had happened, Santos asked him whether he was sure that the van was clean.

"It is clean, I'm sure, boss." said Jesse.

"Did they ask you any questions?" asked Santos.

"They took my statement about how the accident happened and they let me go. I guess they were too busy dealing with Cholo lying dead in the middle of the road, questioning the drivers and occupants of the two vehicles that hit him, and handling the traffic."

"Why did Cholo stop, Jesse?"

"I already told you, boss. He wanted to go to a girlfriend's house in Isabela and have me wait in the van while he visited. I said no but he insisted. We got into an argument and you know how he gets. The next thing I know two cars hit him and he's lying dead in the middle of the road. I couldn't believe it."

"Shit. The goddam idiot could never control himself," said Santos. "We can't take any chances. Get rid of the van. Take it to the junkyard, remove any paperwork, and ask Joe to crush it right away. Tell him that right away means right now, yesterday."

"But boss, how can he do it yesterday?"

"I can't believe this. Listen, you idiot, see if he has another van that we can use. We need two for tomorrow night. I will see you in a couple of hours when I come back from Rincón."

Santos drove to La Ola to meet with Peggy and bring her up to date on things, including the coming operation and Cholo's death.

"I think you're taking an unnecessary risk by going ahead with that job tomorrow. This business about smuggling illegals is not good. Too many things can go wrong and you're putting us all at risk," said Peggy.

"I can't stop it now. Everything is in motion. It's too late," he said.

"Well, I don't like it. I've told you often enough that smuggling people into the country is riskier than our other business. Those people that you 're bringing in can talk if they're caught. How much do they know? Maybe a lot, maybe not. They can at least talk about how it's done, where they came in, and who knows what else. They may even be able to identify someone. All that the feds need is one loose thread that they can start pulling on and they will unravel everything. I don't think that our other friends would appreciate that."

"Maybe not. So what? I'm not their employee. I am an entrepreneur, and I can have as many businesses and investments as I want. If you're not comfortable with what I do or how I do it, you can always pull out."

"You forget that I brought you into the business," she replied. "Don't get too far ahead of yourself."

"You were doing me a favor? You only brought me in because Primo was too drunk to do it anymore and you needed someone to take his place."

"Don't be impertinent. I see that you've decided to go ahead with your plans for tomorrow no matter what. Will you at least think about what I've said?"

"There's nothing to think about," he said. "If you don't like how I do things, or what I'm doing, I'll buy you out. It's up to you."

"Why are you here if you don't care what I think?" said Peggy.

"I wanted to let you know that our last delivery to San Juan was successful. There was, however, a problem. Cholo was run over by a car on the way back, and he is dead. Jesse was with him. The police came, but they didn't search the van. I have scrapped it anyway just in case."

"And, despite all of that you're going forward with your plans for tomorrow. That is reckless."

"Too bad you feel that way. We have nothing else to discuss. Goodbye."

"You bastard," she said. "You know that this is all down to your father and your uncle. This wasn't the life that I was looking for when I moved to Puerto Rico. I came lured by the beaches and because I made the mistake of falling for your good-for-nothing uncle. Everything was so beautiful in the beginning. Rincón was such an incredible and exciting place back then. It still is. We bought La Ola with money that my father lent us, and it would have worked, but your worthless uncle couldn't keep it inside his pants. To him, the bar became a place to drink, meet girls, and have a good time. I finally got tired and kicked him out. He signed the bar over to me but by then we were too deep in debt, and the bank started to foreclose."

"That's when the other bastard, your father Primitivo Otero walked into the picture. He was worse than your uncle because he was a gangster and a drug dealer. He saw an opportunity and took it, offering to lend me the money to pay the bank. More fool me for taking it. I understood what would eventually happen. I knew that there are no free rides in life and that Primo would someday call in his marker. Sure enough, he came one day and asked me to take custody of a van for him. All that I had to do was keep it in my garage. I knew that this was the hook."

"That's all on you, Peggy. What does any of it have to do with me?" asked Santos.

"Don't play that card with me. You well know that as your father descended into the hell of his addictions, I got increasingly involved in his affairs," she said. "In the end, I found myself at the head of his illegal businesses, and in charge of his son, you Santos, when your mother got tired of being abused and abandoned him, and you. Your father turned into the husk of a man that he is today and became a recluse. I had him moved to the small house in Moca, saw to it that he got his liquor and his food, and Primitivo Otero, the onetime feared gangster, lives there, away from the outside world and the business that is no longer his."

"Then the third bastard walked in, you, selfish, ungrateful villain that you are. You took over operational leadership of the enterprise and escalated the business from dealing drugs to smuggling them into the country. It didn't stop there; you began smuggling weapons when you recognized that there was a market for them in the violent world of the drug gangs that you did business with, and you began smuggling people when you saw the numbers that wanted to enter the country and the potential profits that could be realized."

"You will land us all in jail," she said.

"Crazy old bitch. Just stay out of my way," he said and stormed out.

Peggy was afraid that Santos would be caught and she would be discovered. She was fifty-four years old and did not want to spend the rest of her life in maximum-security federal prison. Watching the program Orange is the New Black on television made her shudder. What could she do? Santos wouldn't listen to her, and even if she decided to quit she would still have to answer for her part in everything that had happened during the past number of years. She could leave Puerto Rico, but that would mean that she would live the rest of her life in hiding and looking over her shoulder.

She decided that she had to look after herself. If Santos wouldn't listen to her, that was his problem. He wasn't family anyway. It was a big step that she was about to take, and once she took it there was no turning back. She couldn't know how it would all play out once she crossed the line, but she knew what her future would be if she didn't.

Still, she wasn't prepared to pick up the phone and call the police or the FBI. She decided instead to call Gloria. They weren't close friends, but Peggy knew that she could put her in contact with people who could help her do what she had decided to do. Gloria was surprised when she called and asked whether she could come over. She agreed to see her the following day.

Chapter Twenty-Nine

Robert told his father that he hadn't returned from Boston to sit back and do nothing. He was going to Rincón, or to Llorens, or to La Perla, or to any other place where he could be of help. He said that more than anything he felt responsible for Marcos's death and wanted to help find the culprit. David suggested that he speak with his friend Carlos.

"I know that you're among friends in Llorens. Why don't you go there?" said David.

They were sitting in the living room of David's house in Santa Rita, a middle-class neighborhood in Rio Piedras, the seat of the main campus of the University of Puerto Rico.

Robert did not attend school in the Rio Piedras campus. He wanted to be a civil engineer, so he went instead to the School of Engineering in the city of Mayaguez, near Rincón. He didn't last long. He preferred surfing and the beach over going to class, and eventually dropped out of school, and became a beach bum.

"Fine," said Robert. "I'll go visit Carlos in Llorens. He'll help me figure out what to do next."

Traffic was a mess. There had been another power outage, and all the lights were out. He took several shortcuts that any other day would have worked, except that everybody else was doing the same thing. It was aggressive driving, as is normal n Puerto Rico, but made worse by the lack of traffic lights and the absence of any meaningful police presence. A trip that should have taken forty-five minutes ended up taking over almost two hours. When he arrived in Llorens, the housing project and Carlos's apartment were also without power. No matter, he was grateful to be there. He climbed the stairs to the apartment and found Carlos with two mutual friends. Carlos gave him a cold beer that he pulled from an ice chest and took a Coke for himself. Robert took it, sat back, and relaxed. Before opening it, he placed the cold can on his forehead to cool down.

When Robert started to talk about Marcos's death, Carlos told him to save it until later, and when one of the other friends asked him where he had been, Robert answered that he was visiting family in the States. As it started getting dark outside, the two friends took their leave. It was better to avoid being outside after dark, even more so if the power was out.

Robert was going to spend the night, so he wasn't worried. He and Carlos went to the small balcony and looked out into the night. They could hear the loud noise of gasoline generators, and see the headlights of vehicles inching their way forward on the Baldorioty de Castro highway. They stretched for miles, a river of light through the surrounding darkness.

"What's going on, Carlos? I want to find out who killed Marcos. How can I help?" asked Robert.

"I don't know, Robert. Things are getting complicated. Santos is the name that keeps coming up. You know that he was at The Islander the night that Pat Colberg was killed. He was seen with her in La Perla while he was there transacting business. I saw his men coming here the other night to make a delivery. I think that Marcos was killed because Santos knew that people were asking questions in La Perla."

"So you think that he killed the lieutenant," asked Robert.

"Maybe. I'm not sure. It's only one theory. Similar to some people saying that it was you because you were with her that night."

"We know that it wasn't me, right?"

"Well, I wasn't there, so I have to take your word for it," said Carlos.

"I need to go to Rincón," said Robert. "I know that Liz doesn't want me to, but I'm the only one who can get close to Santos. I wouldn't call him a friend, but I've hung out with him and his group. I'm going."

"You shouldn't, Robert, not if your lawyer doesn't want you to."

"I'll call her and let her know."

"If you go, I'll have to go with you. I'm not letting you go by yourself."

Robert called Liz to let her know what he was doing, and why.

"Liz, I can get close to Santos. He has no reason to mistrust me. I know him."

"I thought you were afraid that someone might try to hurt you?" said Liz. "Don't go. Even if you're not concerned for your safety, you can still end up getting in the way of what we're trying to do."

"How, Liz? How am I going to get in the way of anything? You haven't gotten within ten feet of Santos or his boys."

"Fine, Robert. If I can't talk you out of it, at least be careful. Are you going alone?"

"No, Carlos is coming with me. Nobody there knows him."

"When are you going?"

"Tonight. Do me a favor. Call my father and let him know."

"Right away. I'm sure that he'll call you right back."

"I know. I won't answer."

As they were getting ready to leave, Robert received a call from David, which, as he told Liz, he didn't take. He should have expected what came next. Carlos's phone lit up, and he could not do the same. David was more his friend than Robert. He took the call.

"David, I couldn't talk him out of it. He says that Marcos is dead because of him."

"David, he's a big boy. Do you think you could have talked him out of it? The best I can do is go with him. No, he won't come to the phone. You're welcome, goodbye."

The drive from Llorens was difficult and slow until they were able to get out of the city. They made good time once they did, and the journey became somewhat monotonous.

Making conversation, Carlos asked Robert how he had gotten mixed up with Santos.

"I don't know, Carlos. It happened. We would see each other in the same places, Rincón is a small town. We knew many of the same guys, most of them American surfers, some from San Juan. We were locals, and we spoke Spanish. It happened over time. I wasn't aware, at first, of what he was involved with. Even now, I hear talk. I've never seen anything, and I was never part of his notorious bike club. I know that they're all into this Nazi and white-supremacist crap. I never was. Yes, we remained friends, that's what I hope will give me an in, let me get close to him."

By the time they got to Robert's rented house, it was one o'clock in the morning. They were glad they had the foresight to buy groceries and other essentials before they left San Juan, as there was nothing to eat or drink in the place. The cupboard and the refrigerator were not empty, but thanks to the constant black-outs most of the food in the fridge was spoiled. There were a few bottles of beer, a few soft drinks, and one bottle of white wine.

"Who owns this house?" asked Carlos.

"I think Santos's aunt, Peggy, does. She owns quite a bit of real estate in Rincón, in Añasco, and in other towns as far away as San Sebastian. We used to live in San Sebastian when I was a boy. My father worked in the sugar mill there, Central Plata. We moved from San Sebastian after the mill closed. We moved to San Juan, where I met Marcos and other kids from Llorens. We lived there for two years, then moved to Rio Piedras."

"I remember going to school in San Sebastian," he went on. "I remember playing in the town square—the plaza, as we call it in Spanish. I remember the yearly patron day festivities and the fiestas patronales. They were held in the town square in front of the church. The entire town participated. Everybody went, young and old, men and women."

"We kids enjoyed the rides that were set up all around the town square, the plaza. There was a Ferris wheel, a Carousel, among many others. Everybody enjoyed the food; the men enjoyed the drinking, sometimes too much. Besides the rides and the food stalls, there were other stalls where people would throw baseballs or shoot small rifles at targets to win prizes. I remember one stall where they had small metal horses running in circles around a track, and you would bet money on one or more. The church, Saint Sebastian the Martyr, had a stall in the yard where ladies from the parish sold different foods and desserts, all prepared by them and other townspeople."

"I know they still have those in most towns. Things have changed, though, haven't they?" remarked Carlos.

"Yes, they've changed. The fiestas became a mess as the years went by, fights broke out, and worse. They ended up being moved to the outskirts of town, where they were never the same, at least in San Sebastian."

Carlos got busy preparing an omelet with some of the ingredients they had brought, ham, cheese, onions, and mushrooms. It turned out to be quite tasty. Robert washed it down with the white wine and Carlos with a Coke, and then they turned in.

Chapter Thirty

The next morning they slept late, until around ten, and by the time they left the house to get something to eat it was past eleven. They walked to a place called Café 413, on the other side of the town square from La Ola, where they had brunch.

"We should find Santos in one of two places this afternoon, The Islander or Mi Sitio," said Robert.

"Don't you have his cell or know where he lives?" asked Carlos.

"Yes, I know where he lives, but he won't be there. I do have his cell, but if I call he will not pick up. If he does, he will make up some excuse not to see me. Either way, he'll know that I'm looking for him. Our best bet is to run into him in one of those two places. If we don't I'll call him."

"Makes sense," said Carlos.

They would go first to The Islander, hoping to avoid going to the biker's clubhouse.

It had started to rain while they were at the 413. The water, driven by strong gales, was coming down hard on the square and the surrounding buildings. As always, it brought a smell of fresh earth. Everyone caught outside scampered to find shelter. Some had umbrellas, but most were holding newspapers over their heads and walking fast, shrugging their shoulders, a reflexive action that didn't seem to serve any useful purpose. In many buildings, most of which were not air-conditioned, people were closing the windows and doors that faced the coming squalls, while leaving open those on opposite sides to allow in some air.

The rainstorm stopped as fast as it started, and bright sunlight soon dried the streets, erasing any evidence that it had rained. The only sign that it had was the oppressive humidity that followed as the standing water evaporated.

Carlos paid the bill and they left to find their car. On the way they passed in front of La Ola, on the chance that Santos might be there, but the place was empty. If they had gone by a few minutes earlier, they would have seen him and Peggy arguing.

A few minutes later they were in front of The Islander. The sky was starting to turn gray again and the sea was choppy. Many surfers were in the water taking advantage of the unsettled sea; others were sitting in the restaurant getting something to eat or having a beer. Some recognized Robert and waved to him. Others did not acknowledge him, perhaps not wanting to be associated with a suspected murderer.

They found an empty table and soon one person came over, Flaco. Robert wasn't aware of the problem between him and Santos and asked how they both were doing.

True to his name, Flaco was a thin man. He wore horn-rimmed glasses, had long, sinewy arms with strong hands, dark hair combed straight back from his brow, and a pencil mustache.

"I fought with Santos, Robert. I guess it was lucky that I did because if not I would have been with Cholo instead of Jesse when Cholo was killed."

"What accident? Is Cholo dead? asked Robert.

"You didn't know?"

"No, I didn't."

164

Flaco glanced at Carlos, who he didn't know.

Robert noticed and introduced them.

"Flaco, this is my good friend Carlos from Llorens Torres. Carlos, this is my good friend Flaco from Rincón."

"Flaco, Carlos is a brother. He helped me and gave me a place to stay when they were looking for me. I trust him, and so can you. He is a good man."

"I understand. They're not looking for you anymore?"

"No, they're not. I'm not all the way off the hook; I'm still a suspect, but at least nobody's looking for me right now. I'm no longer number one on their list."

"Do you know who killed her, the nurse?" asked Robert.

Flaco remained silent.

"You're not covering up for Santos, or Jesse and the others, are you?"

"Why would I do that, Robert? They're not my friends."

"Do you think that Santos will be coming here today?"

"I don't think so. He's planning something big for tonight."

"What would that be?"

"C'mon, Robert, I can't tell you."

"Why not? Santos isn't your friend. He got rid of you."

"Yeah, you're right. I owe him nothing. It's not that I'm protecting them, only that I'm no snitch."

"I think you're wrong, but I guess I understand. You want a beer?" asked Robert.

"Sure."

After a few beers, the conversation turned back to Santos.

"So now that you no longer run with the gang what are you doing?"

"Nothing. Santos screwed me."

"That's not good, Flaco, friends don't do that to friends," said Carlos.

Flaco looked at him for a long minute, then said that Santos didn't have friends.

"All he cares about now is money, and maybe his gringa."

"He has an American girlfriend?" asked Carlos.

"I think so, in San Juan."

"He cares for Aunt Peggy doesn't he?" asked Robert.

"I don't think so. I think he's getting ready to screw her over."

"How?"

"I don't know, Robert, but they're not good anymore."

Carlos got up, went to the bar, and came back with two beers and a Coca-Cola.

"Thank you, but I can't have another beer. Wouldn't mind a rum and coke, though."

"No problem, Flaco. I think I'll have one too," said Robert.

"I'll go get them," said Carlos. "Don Q rum, right?"

"Of course, is there any other?"

"I guess not. Same for you, Robert?"

"Sure, thanks."

"Flaco, so what the hell is Santos going to do now without you and Cholo? You two were his top men," said Robert.

"That's right," said Flaco, who, after having polished off a few beers, was now on his second rum and coke.

"I don't give a shit what that bastard does. He thinks he can get all those people on the beach without Cholo and me, that's his problem. I don't wish him anything bad, but if something happens, it's his fault."

"He made a mistake getting rid of you," said Robert. "Listen, Carlos, and I have to leave now. Can we see you tomorrow?"

Flaco gave Robert his number and Robert promised to call him. They paid the bill and left The Islander.

"Well, that was more information than I expected," said Carlos. "Do you think we should still go to Mi Sitio?"

"I think so. It's still early, and we know that something is going down tonight. We might as well see what we can find out."

When they arrived at the bar, Robert recognized Santos's bike among others that were parked out front. There were also three cars among the bikes, plus two vans on one side of the building. They parked the car and went inside.

Santos was sitting at a table with Jesse, now his top lieutenant, Luis, and Jose Luis. He looked up when Robert came in but remained seated. Robert walked to his table.

"How're you doing Santos? Haven't seen you in a few days, I think since the night of the beach party at María's Beach."

While Santos didn't get up, he did offer Robert his hand.

"You're right, how are you doing?"

"I'm sure you heard that I was in custody for the murder of that lieutenant. I guess I'm not their main suspect anymore because they released me."

"I'm glad to hear that, Robert. I wonder who they're looking at now. Do you have any idea?"

"No, they didn't tell me anything. Do you know who killed her?" asked Robert.

"No, why would I?"

"I don't know. You were talking to her that day at The Islander, so you knew her."

"Yeah, I talked to her for a few minutes, then I left. Are you saying that I had something to do with her death?"

"No, Santos. Why would I say that?"

"I don't know, but you're starting to piss me off. I think you and your friend back there should leave."

"You mean Carlos?"

"If that's the moron's name, then yes, I mean Carlos. Now, both of you get the hell out."

"I was trying to be friendly, Santos."

"You heard me. Get out."

"Why? You can't throw us out."

"Watch me," he said as he and his three friends rose from the table.

"Easy, Santos, we're leaving."

Chapter Thirty-One

"So what do we do now?" asked Carlos. "Maybe we should call Liz or Jack and let them know what's happening."

"If we do that they'll ask us to go back to San Juan. I think we should stick around and follow these guys. We know that something's going down tonight," said Robert.

"You're right. Let's wait and see," said Carlos.

"You agree?" asked a surprised Robert.

"Yes, I do."

"I don't think we'll have to wait long. Even though whatever is going to happen won't take place until around one or two in the morning, they'll want to set things up much sooner than that. They'll want to make sure that the police aren't watching them," said Robert.

"Sure, that makes sense."

They waited almost one hour before Santos, Jesse, Jose, Jose Luís, and two other men emerged from the bar. Santos and Jesse got into one of the vans, Jose and the other Jose in the other, and the two other men mounted their bikes. They all headed north towards Rincón and then continued past the town on Highway 413. After they reached a fork on the road, they veered left onto 4413, went past Maria's Beach, and continued on towards Domes Beach, turning right before they got to the old nuclear plant site and the domed structure that gave the beach its name. They went around the dome and parked the vans and the bikes on the other side, far from the old site, in a wooded, unpopulated area close to the beach.

Domes is a beautiful beach, with powdery, light, tan, sand, and bright blue waters. It is a surfing beach, with rough seas and big waves, not the place to go looking for a placid, tranquil experience, and there are no facilities, restrooms, or concessions. It is as close to an unspoiled, pristine beach as anyone will find in Puerto Rico.

Robert and Carlos followed far behind in their darkened car. Once they saw that Santos and his men had parked, they did the same and continued on foot, as silently as they could . It was rough going because Santos had picked a dark, moonless night, suitable for his purposes. Robert and Carlos did not have the night vision equipment that had been so helpful to Bill and Harry, and it was hard for them to see what the others were doing. They got close enough to get a general idea of what was happening, but far enough to avoid detection.

Everyone was silent, Santos and his men ahead, Robert and Carlos farther back. Santos's people were pros. They had their established and effective way of communicating with hand signals. Robert and Carlos had nothing similar and had to stop themselves from whispering to each other.

For a very long time—interminable, as far as Carlos and Robert were concerned—the only sound that broke the silence, apart from the sounds made by their bodies, was that made by pounding surf. After a while, Robert became aware of another sound. He tapped Carlos's shoulder and pointed at his ear. The sound, soft at first, grew louder. It stopped when two boats came close to the beach, stopping short of reaching ground. From their vantage point, Carlos and Robert saw four of Santos's men run down from the area where their vans and motor-bikes were concealed. They watched as twenty men and women jumped from the boats into the shallow water and waded the final few feet to the beach. The two boats turned around and disappeared into the night.

Santos's men herded the arrivals into their vans to get them off the beach. They drove them a short distance, past where Carlos and Robert were crouching, to an area behind the reactor dome site. Two or three vehicles were waiting there for the visitors. Santos and his men unloaded their human cargo and left in the direction of Rincón. Not all the men and women had someone waiting for them. Those that didn't walked away looking for the nearest road. Law enforcement would round up most of them in a few hours as nearby residents reported their presence.

"Fine," said Carlos. "Santos smuggles illegals. How does that help us find who killed Pat or Marcos?"

"I don't know, Carlos. I'm not the strategist here. But having this information can't hurt, don't you think?"

"As we all suspected, Santos is at the center of everything. Let's go home, nothing else is happening tonight," said Carlos.

By the time they got back to Robert's house it was almost five in the morning. They sat back and discussed what they would do the following day.

"I think that we need to sleep in a little, not too late, then call San Juan and tell them what we found out. They'll tell us what to do next," said Carlos.

"I agree," replied Robert.

The next morning they woke up at eleven o'clock. After having gone to bed exhausted at close to six in the morning, five hours of rest wasn't enough, but there were things that they needed to do, and there was no time to waste. They went back to Café 413 for breakfast, went La Ola and saw that Peggy wasn't there. They found out that she was in Aguadilla with Gloria when they called Jack later and he let them know.

"Liz, Rita, and Bill are on their way there at Peggy's request," he said.

"I wonder what that's all about," said Robert. "Do you think we should go there as well?"

"No. Peggy knows you, and who knows how she'll react when you walk in. No, come back to San Juan. Liz and the others will be here by early evening. We can all meet in the office."

"We're on our way."

"By the way," added Jack. "It was on the news that six refugees were picked up by the police near Domes Beach. Know anything about that?"

"We'll talk when we get to San Juan, Jack," said Robert.

"Yes, I had a feeling that you guys might know something."

Chapter Thirty-Two

"Gloria, I don't want to go into details with you. I've been mixed up in bad things, and I'm in trouble. I need to talk to your friends."

"What's going on? It can't be that bad."

"It is. The less you know, the better, there is real danger involved. I have been living a double life, that's all I can tell you."

"So, who do you want to talk to?"

"The people that you sent over to see me."

"Oh, Peggy. Don't tell me that you're mixed up with that."

"With what? With what happened to the lieutenant? No, not that, thank God. Other things."

"I'm sorry," continued Peggy. " Can you call your friends before I get cold feet and change my mind?"

At Peggy's insistence, Gloria called Liz. When she told her that Peggy wanted to talk to her, Liz asked whether she wanted to give her information about Pat Colberg's murder.

"I don't think so, Liz. It seems to be about something else."

"Can you let me speak to her?"

"She says that it isn't anything that she feels comfortable discussing over the phone. I think you should get over here."

"I can't drop everything to go to Aguadilla."

"I think you should. Bring Jack with you."

"It's that urgent?"

"I think it is."

"Fine, we'll be there this afternoon."

Liz spoke with Jack, and he agreed that if Gloria thought it was urgent, they should go as soon as possible. He told her that he couldn't go with her because he had to be in court.

"Take Rita and Bill," he suggested.

"Good idea. Rita needs a distraction anyway. She's having a hard time ever since she broke up with Sam. I know that she blames herself. She told me that Sam walked out on her, upset at the hours she has been working, but that she couldn't see herself doing anything different. It became a real dilemma for her. In the end, she realized that she would not be able to meet Sam's expectations, but I'm sure that being able to analyze it rationally doesn't make her feel any better. I'll ask her to come with me."

Rita wasn't in the mood for a road trip to Aguadilla. She tried to beg off, saying that she had too much work to do in the office. Liz told her that they were going to talk to Peggy Ramos, that nothing was more important at the moment. Rita thought to herself that having ended her relationship with Sam because of her commitment to her job, she needed to be consistent with that decision, and that meant going to Aguadilla.

They were at Ramey Runway by mid-afternoon. Gloria let them use her office so that they could talk to Peggy in private. Peggy found it hard to get started, but once she did, she told them everything, beginning with the early days with Primo and ending with the latest developments. It took her a considerable amount of time to tell her full story as Liz, Rita, and Bill sat and listened in astonishment. The information that they received did not provide the answers to the questions about who had killed Pat or Marcos, or why, but it did suggest many possibilities, including motives.

"Ms. Ramos, what do you want us to do?" asked Liz.

"I want you to tell me what to do next."

"Did you have anything to do with the deaths of Pat or Marcos, or do you have any information relevant to either of them?" asked Liz.

"No, I don't know who killed them or why. Whether any of the things that I know may be relevant is not for me to say."

"So, the first thing that I would advise you to do is to get an attorney," Liz again.

"Who?" Peggy asked. "Can't you represent me?"

"I suppose we could, as long as you didn't have anything to do with what happened to Pat or Marcos. The thing is that we don't represent people involved in drug trafficking unless they didn't do what they are accused of doing, which we know wouldn't be your case. We could help you find another attorney to do that, and if you and that attorney agree that you want to talk to law enforcement, we could help with that if you want us to."

"Would you be there when they interview me?"

"No, but we will get someone for you. You won't be by yourself," said Rita.

"You do know, however, that if what you're telling us is true, you may already be in considerable danger," said Bill.

"Yes, I understand that I am in danger now because of my last conversation with Santos. I know that he feels that I know too much and he may not want to take the risk of me doing what I'm doing right now."

"That's right," said Rita. "Do you think you can go back to Rincón?"

"I think I have to. I have a business to run. I can't walk away from La Ola and my life."

"You may have to do that sooner than you think," said Bill.

"I realize that, but I still have time to make some arrangements, don't I?"

"Very little time," said Liz.

"Look, if you go back, you have to be careful to act your normal self. Follow your routine," said Bill. "You do what you have to do in a couple of days, then you call us, and you leave. Say you're taking a few days off, whatever. If you think that you are in imminent danger you call us right away, understood?"

"I will, but I have to go back right now or I'll be missed."

"Gloria, sorry to put you through this, and sorry that I'm not the person who you thought I was."

"I'm sorry too, Peggy."

Peggy drove back to Rincón, nervous and distraught. She had intended to go straight to La Ola, but decided to stop at her house first. She needed to be by herself for a while to settle her nerves and think things through. At her home, she served herself a glass of wine and turned on some soothing music. She sat for around half an hour considering her alternatives, and concluded that she had done the right thing.

When she returned to La Ola, Santos was waiting for her.

"Where were you, Peggy? I've been here for a while waiting for you."

"I was visiting an old friend, then stopped by my house, why? I had no idea that you were waiting for me. You should have called. What do you want? I didn't think that there was anything else to talk about."

"Maybe not. It depends. I came to let you know that everything went well last night, without a hitch. I hope that you've had a chance to think and are no longer worried. I can handle the business, Peggy. Look how well it went last night. There's no need to worry.

176

You know that I didn't mean it about forcing you out. I was upset because of Cholo getting killed and everything. Forgive me."

"Sometimes you scare me, Santos. You have ever since you were a boy."

"You didn't complain when I defended you from Primo, did you?"

"You're right; I didn't."

"Look," said Santos. "I don't want to argue. Let me buy you dinner tonight. It's already about that time. I'll take you to La Copa Llena; you always liked that place."

"Look at me. I'm not dressed to go anywhere."

"Go home and change. I'll swing by to pick you up in half an hour. Be ready."

"Fine, but I need forty-five minutes."

She went home, baffled by Santos's changed attitude. She didn't trust what he said, found it hard to believe that his previous blow-up was meaningless, and that all was forgiven. She knew that he was up to something and was sure that it did not bode well for her, so she gave Liz a call. They discussed what had happened and Liz put Bill on the line.

"Santos is a very dangerous man always, and more so right now," he said. "He is worried as he must feel that everything is on the line for him. You've already told him that you don't approve of what he's doing, yet he comes back to you all sweetness and forgiveness without even waiting for you to recant."

"That's right, Bill. I never said I was sorry or that I had changed my mind. He said that he hoped I had thought things over, but he never gave me an opportunity to say whether I had or not."

"I think you should get out before he comes to get you. You are in danger, Peggy," said Bill.

"Where do I go? I have nowhere to go."

"Come to San Juan and check yourself into a hotel. Call me when you're in your room. We will come to you. Peggy, you must leave right now. If you go with him, you may never make it to the restaurant. Do you understand?"

"Which hotel? I don't know what to do."

"Leave now. We can discuss this while you're on the road. The important thing is that you get out before Santos comes to pick you up. Go now."

"Whatever you say, I'm on my way."

Chapter Thirty-Three

"Have we heard from Peggy?" asked Jack.
"Yes, she checked into the Marriott," answered Bill.

"She needs to decide what she wants to do. Give her a call. Tell her that we're coming to see her tomorrow morning. Ask her to meet us for breakfast at the restaurant downstairs by the pool. Rita, can you come with us?"

"Sure, Liz. Should we meet there?"

"Yes. Bill, I hate to ask you, but can you pick me up at my place? Driving with so many signal lights out is such a nightmare."

"I can do that."

"Thanks. Rita, go ahead and call Peggy. Tell her to meet us at the restaurant at eight tomorrow morning."

Rita called Peggy's number but got no answer. It worried her that she wouldn't pick up. They decided that it could be that she didn't recognize Rita's number.

"Let's give it a few minutes and I'll call her. My name will come up when I do," said Liz.

"Do you think she can get us any closer to finding out what happened to Pat Colberg, and to exonerating Robert?" asked Jack.

"Or to finding out what happened to Marcos?" asked Bill.

"We'll find out, won't we?" answered Liz. She then tried to reach Peggy and also got no answer. Now they were all worried.

"We need to go to the hotel right now," said Bill. "Can you come with me, Carlos?"

"Call us as soon as you get to talk to her or find out what's happening," said Liz.

It took Bill and Carlos half an hour to get to the Marriott. They were slowed by the heavy traffic that plagues that area of town. The Condado hotel strip is home to a combination of high-end hotels and restaurants, tacky souvenir shops, and a sprinkling of street prostitution. The area is patrolled by a large police contingent watching out for the large number of tourists who were already returning to San Juan, if not to other parts of the country, including essential eco-tourism areas such as the rainforest and others outside of the city, which were not ready to receive them.

Bill called Peggy's number; again there was no answer. He and Carlos went to the front desk to ask for assistance. They too called Peggy, to no avail. Bill asked for someone to go up to the room and check on the guest because he was worried that something might have happened to her. The woman at the desk called security and they went up to the room with Bill and Carlos. When they got there, the door was open, and the room was empty. There was no sign of Peggy, but her luggage was still there. There was no way to keep the police out of the matter now. Hotel security called them. Bill and Carlos left before they arrived, without leaving their names.

Later, in the office, they were trying to make sense of what had happened. Although they all knew that Santos must have been involved, they didn't think that he could have taken Peggy himself.

"How would he know where she was? He would have had to follow her from Rincón, but she left before he came to pick her up. So, unless he got there as she was leaving, it could not have happened that way," said Bill.

"She could have called someone," said Jack.

"I don't think that she would have done that," said Liz. "Called someone to tell them what? No, if anything, she would have called Bill or me."

"So what, then?" asked Rita.

"The only plausible explanation is that Santos called her from Rincón when she was already at the Marriott and she took his call. He could have asked her where she was, and it is conceivable that feeling safe three hours away she may have let slip the information," said Bill.

"That would have been stupid of her," said Rita.

"I agree, Rita. Stupid yet possible. They may have gotten into a serious argument. She may have blurted it out," answered Bill.

"He's three hours away. He wouldn't have had time to drive to San Juan," said Jack.

"Don't you think that she would have at least called us?" said Rita.

"Sure. She might not have been in a hurry to do it, though, knowing that he was still in Rincón," said Liz. "Which means that there must have been a third person involved who was able to get to her sooner."

"How would they have gotten her out of the hotel without her making a fuss?" asked Rita.

"Someone she trusted, someone she knew, which seems far-fetched, or it was a figure of authority," said Bill.

"All that may be true, but we're still guessing," said Jack, "and things are about to get more complicated now that the police are involved. It may take them some time, but they will make it back to

Rincón. Somebody will start to put the pieces together—Peggy, Santos, Pat Colberg, and the people who have been asking questions, us. So we need to get back to Rincón before they do, right away. We need to shadow Santos and his men. We also need to get moving here in San Juan, go back to El Batey, which we know is a possible point of contact, and back to La Perla, which is another."

"Harry and Andy should go Rincón. Santos doesn't know them. Carlos, do you think you could do La Perla, maybe take Robert with you? I think you can reach him at his father's house. We don't want to send another gringo or me."

"Sure, I think he or his father will be glad to help."

"Rita, maybe you and Joyce can get together with Ann Miller," said Liz. "I want to talk to Linda Perkins. I think she knows more than she's letting on."

"Bill and I can swing by El Batey right now," said Jack.

"Another thing, take copies of the pictures we have of everyone involved. You may want to show them around."

Harry and Andy left right away for Rincón. On the way they discussed whether to go to the biker place and assuming Santos was there, follow him.

"I think that we should go straight to Primo's house, see what's there," said Harry.

"Primo?" asked Andy.

"Yes, Santos's father. An old drunk who lives alone in a dilapidated old house out in the sticks near the town of Moca. Santos uses the place as his stash house."

"But, Harry," said Andy. "If Santos is in Rincón at all, he will be in Mi Sitio, not in Moca, don't you think?"

182

"You're right, but let's go to Moca first, anyway. We can then go to the nasty place."

Chapter Thirty-Four

There were only a few people at El Batey when Jack and Bill got there. As soon as they sat at the bar, Craig, an experienced bartender who knew how to work his tips, recognized and greeted Jack.

"Glad to see you again Jack. Where's your beautiful wife? This guy with you tonight is a poor substitute," he said, smiling at Bill and offering his hand. "Welcome to El Batey, sir. My name is Craig."

"Craig," said Jack. "You remember that rough-looking guy that we talked about last time, the one that you said was into bad things? Let me show you the pictures again. Have you seen him since?"

"Yes, he's been back."

"Alone?"

"No, he came with a woman."

"Was it the one with whom you told us he had been playing pool? Here, look at the picture. That is Pat Colberg, the nurse that was killed in Rincón. Was it her?"

"No, not her. Let me see again."

Craig again looked at the picture.

"It was this one," he said, pointing to Linda Perkins.

"No, you must be mistaken. That's Linda Perkins. She and Fred found the body. It must have been Pat Colberg."

"No. the lieutenant played pool with this man a few times. It was this one who later came with him," he said, pointing at Linda's picture.

"Fuck me," said Bill. "Excuse the profanity."

"Man," said Craig, "look around you. We're used to worse, no need to apologize."

"How about him?" asked Jack, pointing at Fred. "Has he come back?"

"Yes, a few times."

"With anyone?" asked Bill.

"No."

"Has he been here at any time when this woman, Linda Perkins, was here?" asked Jack.

"No, but he saw her coming in once and asked me if there was a back door he could use."

"Is there?" asked Bill.

"Of course. All of these old buildings are warrens with passageways, courtyards, and many doors."

"So he was able to leave without her seeing him?" asked Bill.

"Yes, he was. At least I think so."

"Have you seen any of them tonight?" asked Jack.

"No, I haven't."

"Thank you for your help," Jack said to him. "We would appreciate it if you did not let any of them know that we have been asking questions."

They ordered a couple of beers, non-alcoholic Clausthaler for Jack, Corona for Bill, and sat talking until they saw that the pool table was free. Although neither of them was good, they decided to play. To their surprise, Jack turned out to be better than the Bill. They played two games of Eight Ball. To Bill's feigned chagrin, Jack won both.

"I thought you military guys were good at this sort of thing. You're awful," said Jack.

"I don't know Jack; there's more to you than meets the eye. Does Liz know this side of you?"

"What, does she know about the many hours that I spent in dark rooms playing pool and drinking? All too well, my friend, all too well."

They paid their bill, and as they were leaving, they ran into Fred Rogers, who stopped them and invited them for a drink.

"I think we need to talk," he said. "Let me buy you both a drink. Craig mixes a great rum and coke. By the way, some trivia. Did you know that this is one of the places featured in The Rum Diary?"

"I knew," said Bill. "But I don't think Jack knows what you're talking about."

"The Rum Diary is a novel written by Hunter S. Thompson about Puerto Rico in the 1960s. It was later adapted into a movie starring Johnny Depp," said Fred.

"I'll have to look it up," said Jack.

"I'm sure Liz knows it," said Bill.

"I'm sure she does," replied Jack.

"I know we may have all gotten off on the wrong foot," said Fred, "but I don't think that it has to stay that way. I suspect that you think that I was involved with the death of Lieutenant Pat Colberg because of what others have told you about the night when she was killed."

"Do you find that strange?" asked Jack. "You haven't been straight with us, and we know that you've been untruthful about your activities that night."

"Maybe this will help. At my request, my superiors have authorized me to work with you because I have convinced them that you might be able to assist us."

"We don't know anything about your investigations. All that we're interested in is finding out what happened to Lieutenant Colberg, and who killed our friend Marcos," said Bill.

"We have our theories, which I won't share with you now because it would get us nowhere, but you may soon come to believe as we do," said Fred.

"I don't ask that you trust me or confide in me, not yet anyway," he continued. "All I want at this point is to meet with you two, and with your wife Liz, Jack. Nobody else, for the time being. I know that she doesn't like me, but do you think we could do that?"

"I don't see why not. Let me call her."

"I assume that you know that Santos is involved in alien smuggling, in addition to his drug-running business," said Bill.

"That's why we need to talk."

Jack called Liz, who was in the apartment with her daughter, who was home from college for a few days. He told her what Fred was suggesting, but she interrupted him.

"Jack, I'm dealing with a situation here. Cris has informed me that she wants to take a year off from NYU to travel in Europe with a boyfriend."

Liz sounded worried. Cris was a level-headed young woman, and the news had taken his wife by surprise. She wasn't aware that her daughter had a boyfriend, let alone one with whom she was planning to spend a year in Europe.

"Oh," said Jack, "don't worry, we can talk later."

"No, I'm sorry. What's going on?"

"I wanted to let you know that we ran into Fred Rogers at El Batey. We've had a fascinating conversation, the upshot of which was that he wants to meet tomorrow with you, Bill, and me. Only us three. He wants it to be outside the office. I think we need to hear him out, Liz."

"Whatever you say, Jack. Where should we meet?"

"I was thinking La Bombonera in Old San Juan."

"Yes, that's fine. Seven thirty tomorrow morning?"

"He says that's fine. See you later. Wait, have you ever heard of The Rum Diary?"

"Of course, the book about Puerto Rico that was adapted into a movie starring Johnny Depp."

Chapter Thirty-Five

They met the next morning at La Bombonera, an iconic Old San Juan restaurant which first opened its doors in 1902. It features stained-glass windows and marble table-tops, the waiters wear bolero jackets and bow ties, and the delicious coffee is still brewed in a magnificent, bronze, Royal brand, espresso machine.

"Thank you for meeting with me," said Fred. "As a preliminary matter, please understand that whatever information I share with you should be kept confidential."

"As I was telling your husband and Bill last night," he continued. "Santos's activities smuggling drugs, guns, and people into Puerto Rico are bad enough. There are other things also happening as a result of all that federal money floating around. Many outsiders are coming to this island, most but not all well-meaning and scrupulous people. Some are involved in illegal activities, diverting supplies, including controlled substances, to sell on the black market, for example. That is the focus of my investigation, not Santos's activities, although they may have a bearing on things."

"Large quantities of relief material are coming in, but much of it isn't reaching those who need it. Many have signed lucrative contracts, and many of them without following proper vetting procedures, because of the dire needs that must be addressed. Everybody knows about the multi-million-dollar contract for the repair of the country's electrical grid that was awarded to a stateside company with fewer than five permanent employees, but there are many others. Money makes the world go 'round."

"So, what were you doing in Rincón with Linda Perkins the weekend that Pat Colberg was killed?" asked Liz.

"I was doing my job."

"Which was?" asked Bill.

"I was looking for connections."

"What do you mean, looking for connections?" asked Liz.

Fred told them that he was concerned about all of Santos's illegal activities, but that his primary concern was that he was involved with the diversion of relief supplies that were being brought into Puerto Rico to meet legitimate needs, including controlled substances, which he was then selling on the black market.

"I'm sure you know that there are still many isolated communities without power, which also lack many other necessities, including medical care and supplies," he said. "Well, as I started to say, apart from the million dollar contracts, some people make a killing when they gain unlawful access to supplies that are being brought in by the government and by NGOs. They appropriate a small percentage of the goods, although they grow bolder as they get away with it."

"We think that Santos has connections that provide the diverted supplies to him. He then takes care of distribution."

"Who?"

"We had our suspects, including Lieutenant Colberg. Then she was killed."

"Pat Colberg?" asked Liz.

"Yes, we were keeping an eye on her."

"What do you want from us, Agent Rogers? I don't see how we can be of any help," said Jack.

"Simple. I want you to tell me what you have found out about Santos's operation. I know that you have questioned people, and may have found out things that could help us. You know what he's doing, and you know that he's involved in other things that we never knew about."

"Listen," said Liz. "We can't say yes to you without talking it over among ourselves. Another thing, we can't keep this from the other members of our team—at least not our core members and our employees. It's a matter of trust."

"You, your attorneys, your employees, I can live with. Your clients and their friends are another matter because neither you nor I know very much about them."

"And what do we get in exchange?" asked Jack.

"My help as a DEA agent, if you ever need it."

"Fair enough," said Jack. "We'll be in touch."

Fred asked for his check but was told that Jack had taken care of it. He thanked him, adding that it was best if they didn't all leave together and that he hoped to hear from them soon. He then got up and left.

Liz, Jack, and Bill stayed and ordered more coffee. They watched as Fred walked out of the restaurant, and turned left on San Francisco Street.

"Intriguing proposition. I don't know that I trust him. What do you guys think?" asked Liz.

"He's with the DEA. I think we have to give some weight to what he said," said Jack.

"Yes, of course. I wish Frances Day were still in Puerto Rico so we could bounce it off her," said Liz.

"Do you know anybody else there?" asked Bill.

"FBI? Nope."

Twenty minutes later they too left the restaurant and walked to their office near the cruise ship terminals. At the foot of San Francisco Street they made a right in front of Plaza Colón, with the statue of Cristopher Columbus in the center, and continued past the Tapia Theater. Built in 1824, the Tapia is one of the oldest drama stage buildings still in use in the United States.

Back in the office, Liz asked Rita to join them in the conference room to discuss the morning's events. After hearing Fred's proposition, she too was suspicious about his motives.

"Why does he need us?" she asked. "He is a DEA agent with every resource at his disposal, including other agents and money. Why come to us? What do we have to offer? No matter how you answer that question, it doesn't put him in a good light. For whatever reason, he's not being truthful with us."

"So I don't think that we're ready to accept his offer, correct?" asked Jack.

"I agree with Rita, as of now we don't need him, and I too am suspicious of his motives, so yes, we should at least wait on making a decision, " said Liz. "Besides, we have more pressing matters right now."

"I think we all agree that we need to wait. We can revisit this later," said Jack.

"Fine," said Liz. "I'm off to find Linda Perkins. We'll stay in touch. Rita, you and Joyce need to go ahead and get together with Ann Miller."

Chapter Thirty-Six

Peggy was locked up in a room, that's all she knew. She didn't know where because she had been brought in blindfolded. She was taken from her hotel room by two men. She couldn't believe that she had been stupid enough to open the door when they knocked announcing that they were hotel maintenance. Once she opened, they grabbed her without saying a word. She was sure that the room where she was being kept was somewhere in San Juan because the ride hadn't been very long. That was all.

The windows had iron bars. She could look out from them and tell that she was in a building, probably on a third or fourth floor. She could shout at people below, asking for help, but that would alert her captors; who knew what might happen then? Looking at the surrounding buildings, all of identical construction, she guessed that she was being held in a public housing project. She couldn't figure out which, never having been inside one. Even if she was right, it didn't help. There are hundreds of public housing projects in the country, most of them in San Juan, but many in other towns.

She had been there almost one full day; had arrived the previous night, and she guessed that it was now the middle of the following day. She could hear quiet voices outside her room, but it was hard to make out what they were saying. She thought she could make out one female and two male voices. One voice sounded familiar, but she couldn't place it. It was probably her imagination, she thought.

Someone had come into the room that morning to bring water and food. The person wore a balaclava and did not speak. Still, it was evident to Peggy that it was a woman. When later on Peggy knocked on the door and asked to go to the bathroom, the guard tied a blindfold over her eyes and led her out, then waited outside the door for her. There were some personal effects in the bathroom: three toothbrushes, shampoo, and soap in the shower stall. The medicine cabinet had a bottle of prescription reflux medicine for a person named Eduardo Perez, filled out in a drugstore located in Isla Verde. Well, one mistake, thought Peggy, who was now guessed that she was being held at the Llorens-Torres housing project.

After a few minutes, the person outside knocked on the door. Peggy answered that she was almost finished, flushed the toilet, washed her hands and stepped out. Her captor again placed the blindfold over her eyes and led her back to her room. Once inside, she removed the blindfold, and left the room, locking the door behind her.

Peggy still couldn't figure out why she was being held. There was no way for her to know that she had been taken in a moment of panic by people afraid of what she knew.

In Rincón, Sergeant Lopez from the local police station, the same policeman who had responded when Pat Colberg's body had been found, came by La Ola the day after Peggy's disappearance to ask questions. The woman tending bar told him that she hadn't seen Peggy since the previous day.

"The last time I saw her, she was sitting at that table talking to her nephew, Santos. She left here to go home and get ready because Santos was taking her to dinner. I think I heard them mention La Copa Llena."

"Have you spoken to either of them since?" asked Lopez.

"No, sir, I haven't."

"Has Santos been here today?" he asked.

"No, he hasn't."

"Do you have keys to open the bar?"

"Yes, I always open. Peggy comes in later."

Lopez drove to La Copa Llena. He spoke to the manager, asking her if Santos and Peggy had been there the previous night. She told him that they hadn't. The sergeant then decided to swing by Mi Sitio. He didn't want to go by himself, so he stopped at the station and picked up a patrolman.

When they arrived there were a number of bikes parked outside. Lopez and the other cop went in and saw that Santos was sitting at a table with two others. They walked over and asked him to please step outside. Santos complied and once outside asked what it was all about.

"It's about Peggy. She is nowhere to be found," answered Lopez. "The police in San Juan suspect that something may have happened to her."

"I don't know where she is. We were supposed to have supper yesterday, but when I stopped by her house to pick her up, she wasn't there."

"Have you heard from her since?" asked Lopez.

"No, I haven't."

"Have you tried to reach her?"

"No, I haven't."

"Are you worried?"

"No, I'm not. You know, Peggy and I don't get along that well, so I'm not involved in her life, or are interested in what she does, or, frankly, what happens to her. She lives her own life."

"Well, let us know if you hear from her please."

"I'll do that, Sergeant."

As soon as the police left, Santos made a phone call.

"The police have been here. I think we need to get this resolved now. There's only one thing that we can do. Do it."

"That's right. Yes, I know she's almost family. There's no other way. Yes, I'm coming, but don't wait for me to get there. I have other things to do and will not be going to Llorens. I don't want to be seen there. Get moving."

Harry and Andy were parked outside Mi Sitio after having spent the night watching the house in Moca. When it was clear that nothing would be happening, they decided to try their luck at the bar. They saw Santos and Jesse get into one of the vans.

"We should follow them," said Andy.

"We will," answered Harry.

It was soon evident to Harry that Santos was not heading for Moca, or for anywhere else nearby. Before long, they were traveling east on Highway 2. It seemed that they would be going to San Juan. Following them would be exhausting. The trip would take more than three hours, with Harry having to take care all the way not to be spotted, and they could lose them anywhere along the way, or when they entered San Juan traffic.

Chapter Thirty-Seven

As an agent with the DEA, Fred was aware that controlled substances are stocked in all naval medical treatment facilities (MTFs), on land and in hospital ships such as the USNS Comfort. He knew that the drugs were supposed to be administered, monitored, and dispensed by a licensed pharmacist, on land or at sea, and that each substance is classified following federal law into one of five schedules. Schedule I are drugs with no acceptable medical use, and high abuse potential, Schedule II are drugs that have an acceptable medical use but also a high abuse potential, Schedules III, IV, and V are drugs that have an acceptable medical use, and have lesser degrees of abuse potential.

Heroin, marijuana, LSD, Ecstasy, and peyote are Schedule I controlled substances, cocaine, methadone, methamphetamine, oxycodone, Dexedrine, Adderall, and Ritalin are Schedule II drugs, Vicodin, Ketamine, anabolic steroids, testosterone, and products containing less than 90 milligrams of codeine per dosage, are Schedule III drugs, Xanax, Soma, Darvon, Darvocet, Valium, Ativan, and Ambien are Schedule IV drugs, Lomotil and Lyrica are Schedule V drugs.

Following the murder of Lieutenant Colberg, the pharmacist aboard the USNS Comfort had been required to run an audit of the inventory of controlled substances aboard the ship. The review revealed that a significant amount of Schedule I and Schedule II drugs were missing, and the pharmacist had reported her findings to her Commanding Officer. The possible theft was then reported to the DEA, as required, and it was the main reason why that agency had decided to participate in the investigation of the lieutenant's murder, assigning the case to Fred Rogers.

The NCIS had searched the lieutenant's living quarters aboard the ship. The hard drive of the computer that she used was removed for analysis, while investigators pored over her background for any signs that would help shed light on what had happened. Her co-workers, members of her family, and friends, present, and past, were questioned, as were her superior officers as well as the personnel that worked under her.

Fred told his supervisor at DEA headquarters that he was sure that Lieutenant Colberg was involved in the theft of controlled substances from the Comfort.

"She couldn't have acted alone, Fred," said his superior, Agent Ted Sanchez.

Sanchez had been transferred to San Juan from his hometown of Laredo, Texas, under the mistaken belief that because he had a Hispanic last name, he spoke Spanish. The truth was that Agent Sanchez's family had been in the United States for generations. An ancestor had been a Texan who died fighting Mexican general Santa Anna in the Alamo, defending Texan independence. Santa Anna's forces killed 189 Texan defenders in the Alamo. He later executed more than 342 prisoners. The Sanchez family's ancestor was one of the 189.

"Fred," said Sanchez, "even if she was involved, she could not have acted alone, either at the point of origin, the thefts, or at the point of distribution and sale. I've coordinated with NCIS to have their people look at other sailors while you and a couple of others work the shore side angle. We need to find out who is involved, how the operation is run. Why was the lieutenant killed? If she was part of the operation, it's hard to understand how such an important link in the enterprise ended up dead."

Chapter Thirty-Eight

The two men and one woman in the Llorens apartment were told that it was time to dispose of Peggy. She knew too much and couldn't be allowed to talk. They would have to wait until nighttime to move her. The instructions were to drive her to a remote location in the mountains, near the town of Barranquitas, where they were to dispose of her.

Around midnight, a man and a woman who Peggy didn't recognize came into the room. The man tied Peggy's hands behind her back and placed a blindfold over her eyes. They led her out of the apartment and down the stairs to the ground floor, a difficult task because her movements were restricted, and she couldn't see where she was going.

"C'mon, walk," said the man, who was holding her by her arms.

Peggy could hear a car with the engine running and expected to be placed in the back seat. She soon realized that they were about to push her into the trunk.

"I'm an old woman," she said. "I'll suffocate if you put me in the trunk, or I'll have a heart attack."

"So much the better," said the man as he pushed her in. "It will save us some trouble."

The road to the town of Barranquitas winds its way through the mountains, with frequent, often sharp turns. Every one of those turns slammed Peggy against the sides of the car.

In the passenger cabin, the woman sat in front next to the driver. The second man sat in the back. This second man would be Peggy's killer. He was in his early twenties, already a cold-blooded killer, a hit-man, an assassin. He had dead eyes, without expression, sympathy, concern, even without hate. He was a man doing his job. Even among drug lords and hardened gang members, there was respect and fear for this man.

As with most mountain roads in Puerto Rico, the drive was perilous. Making it worse, now it had started to rain hard.

"I hate driving these twisting country roads at night in the rain," said the man that was driving. "There's nobody else around, the lights from distant houses. That and the smell of the wet vegetation and soil always remind me of cemeteries and death."

"Shut the hell up," said the young killer in the back seat. "Where did you get that from, one of the telenovelas that you watch with your fat wife? Shut up."

The driver did not say another word, didn't even look at the boy's reflection in his rearview mirror.

He had to keep his eyes on the road. In these inland mountain areas, the rains and of the two hurricanes had caused mudslides and avalanches. Storm debris often obstructed the roads, and there were few lights, as vast swaths of the countryside were still without electricity. They needed a remote area to do what they intended to do, away from the ears and eyes of neighbors, but it was that remoteness that made the roads more dangerous.

They were heading uphill, with steep mountains rising on one side of the road and descending on the other. With the rain coming down hard, the way was slick with a mixture of rain and motor oil. The driver was moving at deliberate speed. He did not anticipate any traffic, so he was keeping to the middle of the road, flashing his high beams at every turn as a signal to any vehicle approaching from the opposite direction. The heavy rain made it hard to see the way ahead and the high beam signal, although necessary, made it even worse as the intense light was reflected by the rain ahead of the car. And even with the car windows up and the air conditioner going full blast, the windshield kept fogging up.

As they were rounding one of many sharp turns, they were suddenly facing a large Ford F-350 XL pickup truck traveling in the opposite direction that was also keeping to the middle of the road.

"He's going to hit us," said the woman.

They were no match for the giant truck that was on them in a split second. The truck veered to its right as its driver tried to avoid a collision. The driver of the car made a hard turn in the opposite direction, to his right, unfortunately heading toward danger. Although he applied the brakes, the vehicle slid on the wet surface, raced off the road and tumbled down the side of the mountain. It came to rest, wheels up, twenty-five feet below.

The truck stopped, and the driver jumped out. He ran to where the car had left the road, looked down and saw that it was resting upside-down, its wheels still turning. It was a dangerous thing to do, but he ran down the embankment, tumbling and sliding until he reached the vehicle. He looked inside the passenger compartment and saw that there were three persons inside, all of them bloody and motionless. As far as he could tell they were dead. He was getting ready to climb back to the road when he heard moaning close by. It seemed that as the car hurtled down the side of the mountain the trunk popped open and a badly mangled Peggy Ramos was thrown out, with her hands still tied behind her back. She was unconscious, bloody, and wet, but she was alive. The man called for emergency assistance, pulled Peggy farther away from the wreck, behind a large boulder, and stayed with her until help arrived.

It took the ambulance forty-five minutes to get there. The paramedics then had to wait another thirty minutes for the specialized personnel that would have to winch Peggy up on a stretcher. They confirmed that she was the only survivor, secured her and pulled her up, unconscious, to the road above, where an ambulance waited. She was taken to the Puerto Rico Medical Center, was operated on for the traumatic injuries that she suffered, and was placed in the Intensive Care Unit, where she remained in a coma.

The bodies of the other three occupants of the car were also retrieved, as were their firearms. The police investigation revealed, in its preliminary stages, that although the woman and one of the men did not have criminal records, the young man in the back seat had an impressive rap sheet, including arrests for narcotics violations, home invasion robberies, kidnapping, and murder. He had served time in juvenile detention and later in prison. The juvenile detention was for narcotics-related offenses, as was the prison sentence handed down in his single adult criminal conviction. The other items listed were arrests and arraignments on charges that were still pending and had not yet been resolved, either by dismissal or conviction. They included serious matters such as the alleged kidnapping of a college student for ransom, two home invasion robberies, and murder.

Peggy did not have anything on her; not her driver's license, not her credit cards, and not any other document that could identify her; the police did not find any at the site of the accident, or in the car. The cops did conclude, based on the weapons found at the scene, on the fact that Peggy's arms were tied behind her back, and on the criminal record of the young man in the back seat, that they were dealing with a serious criminal matter. They needed to identify the woman in a coma as soon as possible, so they did the only thing that they could, considering her condition: took her picture and circulated it to local and federal law enforcement agencies, and took her fingerprints for biometric identification. Not knowing what they were dealing with they took the precaution of posting a guard in the ICU unit.

"Did our people take care of Peggy?" asked Santos.

"No, Santos," answered Jesse. "They were on their way to do so, but, according to our contact, there was an accident on their way to Barranquitas and your aunt was the only survivor. The other three were killed. Peggy is now in the ICU unit at the medical center in Rio Piedras. Our guy investigated when he recognized the photograph of her that was circulated. The police don't know yet who she is."

"We need to get to her, Jesse. If she talks, she will sink us all."

"Sure, Santos, but she's under guard, you know. How do we get to her?" asked Jesse.

"I need to think about that, Jesse. We'll find a way."

Chapter Thirty-Nine

Liz called Linda and arranged to meet with her away from her hotel. When she suggested her office, Linda said that she was working out in the field and that she wouldn't be in San Juan for the next few days.

"I'm in Morovis, Liz. Do you know that town?" asked Linda. "It's up in the mountains."

"I know it very well, Linda. I visited the area in connection with one of our cases. You wouldn't know about it, of course, since you didn't live here, but it was a big deal a couple of years ago. One of our principal witnesses, in fact, the one who set us on the right path at significant risk to his life, had family in Morovis, his parents, and we visited him. There is a restaurant there that we went to, some distance away in the outskirts on Highway 155. It's called Casa Alemania. Do you know it?

"I have heard of it, but never visited."

"It's kind of out of the way so we can chat there unobserved and undisturbed. How about meeting there for lunch tomorrow? If you don't mind, I'll bring my husband, Jack Hardy, and another of our people, Bill. Unless you have a problem with that."

"No, that's fine. What time do you want to meet?" asked Linda.

"Eleven-thirty?"

"Yes. See you then."

The next day Liz, Jack, and Bill left for Morovis early, making allowances for the usual lousy road conditions. They knew that the town in the hard-hit central mountains had been devastated by Hurricane María, which destroyed thousands of homes. Weeks later, there was still no gasoline, even for ambulances and other emergency vehicles. Most of the town was without power or drinking water, and local officials improvised and take over tasks that they were not equipped to do, such as trying to repair damaged bridges.

They knew that the same thing happened in many towns where outer communities were isolated from essential services after a bridge over a river on a connecting road was washed away, and where residents were often forced to ford rushing waters holding on to ropes that had been stretched across by neighbors.

Traveling through Morovis on their way to the restaurant, Liz suggested that they stop by the house of Arnaldo Ruiz's parents to see how they were doing. Arnaldo had been their witness in the power plant case. Jack reminded her that it was getting close to the appointed time for their meeting, so they decided to visit the elder Ruiz's after they finished with Linda.

When they got to Casa Alemania, they found her on the second-floor dining room, sitting by herself at a far corner table. She rose from her seat as they approached, nodding to Jack, who she knew from when he had interviewed her a few days earlier at the hotel.

"Linda, thank you for agreeing to meet with us. I am Liz; this is Bill. You already know my husband, Jack."

"Yes, I do. Hello, Jack."

"Quite a view," exclaimed Bill.

"Yes, it is. We were too preoccupied the last time we were here to appreciate it," said Liz.

"Yes, with Al Miller and Lieutenant Jorge Ramos ready to jump all over each other, and us not knowing who to trust," said Jack.

"Linda, what's going on?" asked Liz.

"What do you mean?"

"Strange things are happening, why would Fred Rogers avoid you?" asked Jack.

"When has Fred ever avoided me? We're friends."

"Look, Linda, as we go over what has happened since Pat Colberg's murder, we're starting to see a pattern. The same group of people keeps surfacing in the same places, Fred, Santos, Pat, when she was alive, and you. The four of you were at The Islander, while you have been seen in the same bar in Old San Juan and other places," said Liz.

"We think that you're somehow involved in what's happening," said Bill.

"Involved in what, Pat Colberg's death? Why would you say that?"

"Because we don't believe in coincidence and you're showing up in too many places," said Liz.

"Now, we have given this some thought, and have concluded that you're either with the bad guys or you're with law enforcement. The simple fact that we're talking to you is an indication that we don't think that you're with the bad guys, right?" explained Jack.

"Why have we reached that conclusion?" said Liz. "For several reasons. You haven't been in Puerto Rico long enough to have gotten involved in organized criminal activity, and Fred, who we don't trust, is avoiding you. Why would he be doing that?"

"On the other hand, you've been seen with Santos," said Jack. "So we could be wrong. If we are, we've made a terrible mistake by contacting one of the bad guys. But we don't think that's the case."

"Why would you even take the chance?" asked Linda.

"Because we're running around in circles, and we need to break out," said Bill.

"Look," said Linda, "this is a perilous situation. Terrible as the lieutenant's murder is, we're talking about a criminal enterprise that moves millions of dollars, and that is willing to do anything to defend their business."

"So we were right. Who are you?" asked Bill. "Who do you work for?"

"I shouldn't be sharing this, but I'm with the DEA. At first, I was assigned to investigate the possible black-market sale of controlled substances stolen from the Navy, but the scope of my investigation was widened when Lieutenant Colberg was killed. I was at The Islander doing my job the night that it happened."

"You were there with Fred Rogers. Why?" asked Bill.

"I can't answer that question."

"But he, too, is with the DEA, he told us so," said Liz.

"Yes, he is," said Linda.

"Are you and he working together?" asked Jack.

"Each of us is aware of what the other is doing. Let's put it that way."

"What about Pat Colberg, was she crooked?" asked Liz.

"We don't know the answer to that yet, Liz."

"Do you know who killed her or why?" asked Liz, again.

"Everything surrounding Lieutenant Colberg is still unclear. No, I don't know who killed her, or why."

"We are going to have to trust each other. We have already gone out on a limb reaching out to you," said Liz.

"And I by admitting to you who I am. Not only that, I'm doing so without my boss's permission."

"We doubt that. The minute we made our approach, you and your boss talked about this and decided what to do. Don't take us for fools; we know how you guys work. The point is, can we help each other?"

"I think we can," said Linda. "As a token of our goodwill, I am going to share some information with you. Peggy Ramos is alive. She is in a coma at the Rio Piedras Medical Center after having survived a car accident that, as it turns out, may have ended up saving her life."

Linda told them all that she knew, including that the consensus was that Peggy was on the way to her execution when the accident happened.

"By the way, Cholo, Santos's man, was killed in a separate traffic accident. I'm sure he's getting desperate," said Linda.

"Peggy is in danger," said Liz. "She was kidnapped, and it looks like they were getting ready to kill her. That means that someone, maybe Santos, has already decided that she knows too much. They will try to get to her," said Bill.

"I agree. I know that she's under guard in the ICU," said Linda. "The police found out who she was after circulating her photograph. What does she know that makes her so dangerous to Santos?"

"You need to talk to her about that, but I believe she has intimate and detailed knowledge of his operation. Having her under guard is not going to help, Linda. They will get to her if they think that she is dangerous to them. Can't your people protect her?"

"Yes, if my superiors believe that she has information that's useful to our investigation."

"So, here's where we help you, Linda. I figure that you have your suspicions about Santos. As I said, Peggy Ramos knows what Santos is up to. I can tell you that she has been part of his operation forever. As a matter of fact, it was her thing before it was his. She brought him into the business when his father, Primo, became a useless drunk."

"I'm sure you already know that I have befriended Santos."

"Yes, we know that you've been with him at El Batey. You're playing a dangerous game," said Bill.

"It's what I do. I'm not afraid of him."

"Maybe you should be," said Jack.

"Look, I know that I have to be careful. I can take care of myself."

"Can you protect Peggy?" asked Bill.

"I'll discuss it with my people and will let you know."

"In the meantime?" asked Bill.

"In the meantime, the ICU is under guard."

"You know that's not enough," said Liz.

"I know," said Linda. "All I can do is promise that I'll get right on this."

"I guess we'll have to live with that and hope that Peggy can too," said Bill.

"What about Fred, Linda?" asked Jack.

"I don't know anything about his personal life. Our relationship is entirely professional if that's what you're asking."

"Is he crooked?"

"I wouldn't know."

Chapter Forty

"Bill, where's Harry?" asked Liza.

"He should be in San Juan, I spoke to him earlier. He told me that he had followed Santos from Rincón but lost him in San Juan traffic."

"We need to get someone over to the medical center to check up on Peggy. I don't know that there is too much we can do. Still, she is in danger and we need to figure out some way to help."

"Right, I'll get on it."

Bill was able to reach Harry, who had returned to San Juan with Andy. It was already four o'clock in the afternoon, and they were both back in the office. Bill explained what the situation was with Peggy and told them that it was urgent that they both go to the hospital as soon as possible.

"Bill, this sort of work is right up my alley. It is what I have always done, you as well. But not Andy—he has been game and has helped us, including with our recent trip to Rincón, but I don't think it's fair to ask him to assume certain risks. I'm sure he'll do it if we ask. That is why we shouldn't."

"Of course you're right. Do you mind going by yourself, then?"

"Not at all, Bill. I'm on my way."

Harry was old school. Like Bill, he was an Air Force veteran who had served with the Air Force

Security Forces as a Warrant Officer, had extensive weapons training, and was an expert in one-to-one combat techniques. He could have retired from the military with full benefits after having served twenty years in active duty, but the Air Force was home. He decided to stay on. He later lost one eye while serving somewhere in the Middle East, retired with a disability and twenty-five years of service. Harry then returned to Puerto Rico, where he had been stationed for a short time at Ramey Air Force Base before its closure in 1973, and joined his old boss, Bill, in his private security business.

When he arrived at the medical center ICU, Harry found out that Peggy, still in a coma, had been airlifted to the USNS Comfort for medical care. He called Jack to tell them what had happened and raced to the port. Liz called Linda to ask her what was going on.

"Liz, you asked me to do something fast. The only thing that I could think of was to bring her over to where we could keep an eye on her."

"Did you consider that there could be people aboard that ship that don't want her to talk?" asked Liz.

"I know," Linda replied. "They could also hurt her at the medical center where none of us could do very much to help her."

"I understand, but we could at least get into the medical center ICU, whereas we will be completely shut out from the Comfort."

"I promise you that I will not let that happen."

"Dammit," said Liz after she disconnected. "This is like being inside a carnival funhouse with all the crazy mirrors. You can never trust what's in front of you."

"Why do you say that?" asked her husband.

"Because we have put all our trust in Linda Perkins, and now she has brought Peggy into the lion's den."

"What do you mean, Liz?"

"Linda had Peggy transferred from the Rio Piedras Medical Center to the USNS Comfort."

"So, that's a good thing, isn't it?" asked Jack.

"Yes, if we've judged her correctly. Not so much if we haven't."

"Not much we can do now," said Bill.

"There's one thing we can do. It's better than doing nothing," said Liz. "We can let Fred Rogers know."

"I thought he was the bad guy," said Bill.

"While I still think that he is, there's a chance that he isn't, right? I mean, we are, at best, making an educated guess on both Linda and him because we need to move things along. My thinking is that Peggy is inaccessible to us right now, so it's better to have Fred and Linda facing each other than run the risk of putting all our money on one of them. It's called insurance, hedging your bets, buying credit default swaps, or betting pass/don't pass at the craps table," said Liz.

"You play dice? I never knew that," said Jack.

Even if it was a dangerous move, they had to do something. They called Fred to tell him what was going on and that Peggy could be in danger. Bill also spoke to Harry to suggest that he try to get aboard the ship by saying that he was Peggy's nephew, and showing his retired military I.D. It was worth a try.

Harry walked up to the looming ship, a gigantic vessel whose proportions betrayed its origins as an oil tanker before the Navy converted it into a hospital ship.

The marines monitoring the gangplank asked Harry why he was there.

"Sir, do you need medical assistance?"

"No guys, I'm here to visit my aunt, who was in a terrible accident. She is in the ship's intensive care ward. She resembles my mother. I'm sure she must be scared, being here all alone. You see, she is deaf and has a touch of Alzheimer's," said Harry.

"I used to be one of you, put 25 years in the Air Force. Here, let me show you my card." Harry pulled out his wallet and showed them his retired military I.D.

"What do you say, guys, will you let me come aboard?"

The marine staff sergeant first looked Harry over. He then examined both sides of his I.D. card and then asked to see his driver's license. When Harry handed it to him, the sergeant compared both documents and again looked at Harry.

"What happened to the beard?" he asked.

"Shaved it when everybody else started growing theirs."

"Are you carrying any weapons?" asked the sergeant.

"No, I am not."

"Welcome aboard, sir. Hope your aunt recovers."

"Thank you. Can you tell me how to get to the ICU?"

The sergeant gave him directions but warned him that he would still get lost. He told him that when he did, he should ask any sailor for directions, gave Harry a visitor I.D. and waved him onto the gangplank.

Chapter Forty-One

Fred knew that Peggy had valuable information about Santos's activities that she would divulge once she recovered from her coma. So did Linda, and so did other people aboard the Comfort.

"Liz," said Fred. "The danger is that any military personnel involved in criminal activity have much to lose. You used to be with the FBI, I'm sure you know that all military personnel are subject to the provisions of the Uniform Code of Military Justice (UCMJ)."

"Yes, I know the UCMJ, and I know how it works," replied Liz. "Among other things, it describes those actions that constitute criminal offenses."

"So you know that the consequences under it can be quite harsh. A conviction for drug charges under Article 112(a) of the Code can result in the reduction of rank, forfeiture of all pay and allowances, confinement for up to fifteen years, and a dishonorable discharge," said Fred.

"And a person so convicted can also face charges for violations of State law, although not for a violation of federal law, as that could constitute double jeopardy," she continued. "So, someone facing those consequences would have an incentive to make sure Peggy doesn't talk, is that what you're saying?" asked Liz. "Well, I agree. That's why I'm worried, Fred."

"Being in a coma in the place where part of the illegal activity took place is not good. I can get people in there," said Fred.

Liz didn't tell Fred that Harry was already at the ICU. She had also decided not to tell Linda that she had spoken to Fred.

One hour later, Harry called the office. Jack took his call.

"Jack, you won't believe this. The Comfort is leaving Puerto Rico on the 15th, two days from now, so they want to transfer Peggy out."

"She just got there. Linda Perkins arranged it," exclaimed Jack. "Where are they sending her?"

"Back to the Rio Piedras Medical Center," said Harry. "One bit of good news: she is starting to come out of her coma. One bit of bad news: Santos is her next of kin. He wants to take charge of her and decide where she goes."

"Wow, is he her next of kin? Doesn't she have anyone else?" asked Jack. "Let me have Rita follow up on this."

"The only person who could tell us about Peggy's family would be Peggy or her ex-husband Ricky, wherever he is, or Santos, or Santos's father, Primo," said Rita.

"So that means that it would have to be Primo, who is in a perpetual drunken stupor. Rita, can you please get Bill for me? Thanks."

A few moments later Bill was in the office, and Jack brought him up to speed on what was happening.

"You can't be serious, Jack. The guy is out of it."

"He's our only hope. Otherwise, Santos gets Peggy. We need to get out there right now."

"Jack, let's think about this. Primo is always drunk. We won't be able to sober him up in time to do us any good. His brain is too far gone. If we try to withhold alcohol, it will take days before he is in any shape to help, assuming he doesn't go into withdrawal, gets hallucinations, and suffers Delirium Tremens. At best, he would be confused and unable to concentrate, with no memory. We would have wasted our time."

"What do we do?"

"When are they transferring Peggy?"

"Harry says tonight."

"The only other thing that we can do is keep Santos away," said Bill.

"I don't think he would dare go near the Comfort. He will try to assert his claim at the medical center, but I don't think that they would be comfortable with this continued jostling of a patient who is in delicate condition. I think that if he does prevail, it will only be once she is in a stable condition, which could take days. The risk is that something can happen to her in the meantime," said Jack.

"We need to make sure that she's protected."

By now Liz had joined them. She suggested that they talk to sergeant Lopez from the Rincón police station, who knew Peggy and had been making inquiries about her disappearance.

"I think that is a good idea. We should try to talk to him now. I'll call the station," said Bill.

Although it was past working hours, Lopez was still in his office. Bill explained their concerns, and as Lopez knew Peggy and Santos well enough, including Santos's local exploits, it didn't take much to convince him that Peggy could be in danger.

"I don't have jurisdiction in San Juan, but I do have good friends that might be able to help. I'll let you know."

Like much of what is happening in Puerto Rico with the response to the hurricane disaster, Peggy's transfers to and from the Comfort were further examples of disorganization and lack of communication between local and federal agencies. In this case, it had resulted in Peggy being sent back from the Comfort to the Rio Piedras Medical Center on the same day that she had arrived by helicopter. So was the departure of the ship so soon after it had come to Puerto Rico. Its response to the humanitarian crisis had been hobbled by red tape and regulations, things such as requiring that prospective patients present hard-to-obtain medical certification from a local doctor before they could be admitted to the Comfort. Petty bureaucracy was alive and well in the midst of a humanitarian crisis. Even presuming the best intentions, in the end, rules and regulations prevailed over common sense.

Peggy would be taken by ambulance from the Comfort to the Puerto Rico Medical Center, and Harry was able to talk his way into riding with her. When the ambulance arrived at the hospital, it was met by medical personnel and by two uniformed members of the police. They wheeled Peggy to the ICU followed by the two policemen and Harry. She was beginning to show hopeful signs, but the doctors explained that full recovery could take anywhere from months to years, and that some patients never progressed from a vegetative state. This meant that it could be some time before Peggy was able to provide any information regarding Santos or be well enough to face the consequences of her behavior. It could also mean that nobody had anything to fear if what Peggy knew remained locked in her head.

The USNS Comfort left Puerto Rico on November 15, 2017, to replenish and return, or so they said, but it never did come back. Its deployment lasted 53 days, beginning two weeks after Hurricane Maria slammed into the country. Although the Comfort had 250 hospital beds, it admitted an average of only six patients a day for a total of 290 admissions during the 53 days. In addition to those admissions, medical personnel on the ship treated 1,625 people as outpatients. So, on average, 30 persons were seen as outpatients, and five were admitted for hospitalization per day.

Against all prognostications, within two days of her transfer to the medical center, Peggy was recovering from her coma at a fast clip. In the beginning, she was alert for short periods of time, no more than a few minutes, but the periods of consciousness were increasing in duration. They informed Santos, her next of kin, of the good news, but the two policemen that Sergeant Lopez had arranged through a friend were still standing guard outside the ICU, and Harry was still allowed to come and visit.

Very soon, the FBI, NCIS, DEA, and Commonwealth police would descend on Peggy, and she would be out of reach for private questioning, lost to Diaz and Hardy who would have to look elsewhere for answers. It wouldn't matter, they had already concluded that Peggy did not have any information that could help them in their investigation into who killed Pat or Marcos. They would still keep an eye on her, for her safety and on the chance that she might remember something important. They would do their best to keep Santos away from her.

Chapter Forty-Two

"Whatever happens to Peggy, whether she recovers full consciousness, and when, we're in the same position that we were before we spoke to her. We're still trying to find out what happened to Pat Colberg and Marcos," said Jack as they all sat around the firm's conference table the morning after Peggy was transferred back to the medical center ICU.

"The information that she was going to share might have helped, but we can, and will, proceed without it," said Jack.

"Back to La Perla," said Liz. "I think that our best opportunity to find the truth is there. Rincón is important too. We can't forget Rincón, that's where the lieutenant was killed. Right now, we need to go to La Perla. I don't think that it can be Bill—he is the stereotype of an Anglo-American and would stick out like a sore thumb—or Jack, same thing."

"Harry Rivera is another story. He's Hispanic and that helped him pass as Peggy's nephew. He could do it, so could Carlos, and so could I," said Liz.

"Don't tell me that you plan to go to La Perla to ask questions yourself," said Bill.

"It seems that you two men forget my background. You do remember that I used to be with the FBI, where I was often in dangerous situations, that I was a personal defense instructor in the FBI Academy in Quantico, and that I am an expert Krav Maga practitioner. I am more than able to take care of myself, and you know it. I think I'm better prepared to face dangerous situations than either of you."

"Sorry, Liz. You are correct," said Jack.

"Thank you. I don't think that it's fair to keep asking Carlos to do stuff for us unless we can't do it ourselves. This I think we can do ourselves, so it's going to be Harry and me," she said. "But I think that we will need Carlos to set up the meeting. Don Gilberto doesn't know me at all, and Harry not well."

Harry wasn't with the rest of them in the office. He was coming in later because he had a long night at the medical center. When Carlos came in, they told him that they wanted him to arrange a meeting with don Gilberto for Liz, Harry and he, that they needed him to go to be there because Gilberto trusted him.

"I hope that will be the extent of your involvement this time around," said Liz.

At 3:30 that afternoon, Liz, Harry, and Carlos were waiting for Gilberto at Las Palmas on San Sebastian Street. The older man arrived a short time later, alone this time. Carlos introduced Liz, telling Gilberto that she was one of the attorneys representing Robert Montes.

"Liz, are you from Puerto Rico?" asked Gilberto.

"No, don Gilberto, I was born in New York, in the Bronx. But both of my parents were born here, and although I wasn't, I consider myself Puerto Rican. My lifelong dream was to live in Puerto Rico. Now I do. I am a lawyer, as Carlos told you. My office is right here in Old San Juan. I wouldn't live anywhere else."

"Hija, I understand you. So many of our people have had to leave their home for many years. Our peasants, jíbaros, country people, seventy years ago going to big northern cities, New York, and others. To a cold land where people spoke a language that they didn't understand, who had different customs and traditions, and who, in their great majority, didn't like them. They left behind their families, their warm lands, their campos because they had to feed their families. Tomateros, some of their countrymen called them with disdain because they were going north to work picking tomatoes."

"Now so many are leaving because of this diablo of a hurricane. María, how they could give it such a holy name I'll never understand. You say that you're Puerto Rican, and that is good enough for me, but, hija, I'll call you Isabel if you don't mind."

"I don't mind, don Gilberto."

"So, how can I help you?"

"Don Gilberto, we still don't know who killed our friend Marcos, nor who killed that lieutenant. Marcos was killed in La Perla, and although Lieutenant Colberg was killed in Rincón, we feel that there is a connection between those two murders. We believe that our understanding of what happened starts right here," said Liz.

"Don Gilberto," said Carlos, "the last time we were here, we brought some pictures that we wanted to show around in your neighborhood to see whether anyone would recognize the persons in them. You were gracious enough to have two boys do the work for us, and we're grateful for that."

"Yes, Andrés and Perico," said Gilberto.

"We now think that to understand what's going on, we have to go down there ourselves. No messengers this time," said Liz.

"Hija, you know it can be dangerous down there if you go around asking questions about sensitive matters."

"I know that, and I appreciate your concern. Even so, we need to do it. We were hoping that you could help us."

"I'll help you, Isabel, but it has to be only one of you. I can't protect two or three."

222

"Well, in that case, it will be me," said Liz.

"No, hija, not you. Send Carlos or Harry."

"He's right, Liz," said Harry. "Not you. I'll do it."

"Or I. I know my way around," said Carlos.

"Again guys? We have been over this. I'm getting tired of this over-protective crap. Excuse my language, don Gilberto. I am a grown woman capable of taking care of myself, yet these guys still see me as a defenseless girl. I can assure you that I am anything but defenseless."

"It's not that you're a woman. We know how capable you are, Liz. It's about you, or anyone of us, going down there alone asking sensitive questions—whether it's you, Carlos, or myself," said Harry.

"Don Gilberto," said Carlos, "you know what happened last time. You know that Harry's right. It's too risky for one person alone to go poking around asking questions. It needs to be at least two of us going down there. Many people in La Perla know me already. I can go with Liz."

"Carlos, we didn't want you taking any more risks. You've already helped us enough," said Liz.

"I want to see this through, Liz, not only because I want to help you or Robert, but because they killed Marcos, and I want to get the people that did it. He was one of mine."

"Very well, Carlos, you and Isabel," said Gilberto. "Let's go."

"I'll be waiting for you right here, guys. You call me at the first sign of trouble, agreed?" said Harry.

"Yes, thank you," said Liz.

Chapter Forty-Three

Gilberto insisted that it was safer if he came along. He was right. He still commanded a great deal of respect in his community, even if there were some who didn't care who he was, or even knew the work he had done. Liz told him that they wanted to double check on the identification that Andrés and Perico had obtained of Pat Colberg as the woman seen with Santos. Gilberto asked someone to find the two, and they brought them in minutes.

"Boys, the picture that this man gave you to show around: do you remember? You said that people that you showed it to had seen her with Santos. Who did you show it to?"

"The guys at the corner, don Gilberto. Please don't get us into trouble with them," said Andrés.

"Don't worry, we won't mention your names. Now leave, get out of here," said Gilberto.

He knew the corner they were talking about. It was the corner where outsiders came to get their drugs, where the dealers and other thugs hung out. It was a dangerous place, so they needed to tread lightly, making sure that the people they approached understood that they weren't at risk.

Although Carlos had been to La Perla before, Liz hadn't. She was overwhelmed by the destruction that she saw. This was November, and the neighborhood was still without power or water. Devastation was all around them, houses reduced to sticks and rubble, one after the other; most with makeshift shelters put up in place. People were still trying to live their lives in what used to be their homes. As they walked, a man came up to them, a civic leader who ran a sports program for the young.

"Good evening, don Gilberto. Beautiful day. God bless you and your friends. Tell them that La Perla is coming back. We're not leaving. This was a bad hurricane, yes, but living here near the ocean they're all bad. Yet we have survived them, all of them, all our lives. We're not going anywhere. This is home. We're not leaving," he said, pointing to a nearby jumble of sticks and stones that used to be his house.

"This is where my house will be. Right here by the sea. I enjoy the sound of the waves at night, and the smell of the ocean. Yes, I do," said the man.

"The spirit is there," said Gilberto. "It's going to be an uphill battle, more difficult than in most other places. I know that people in mountain communities are having a real hard time, but they will get help. Us? They see us as criminals, our neighborhood as a drug-infested slum. We suspect that people with money want to get rid of us so that they can build luxury apartments or hotels. But don't you worry, we will win. We will stay right here."

"They're right, of course, there is too much crime," he continued, "but they don't see that there are also decent, hard-working people here. Besides, the criminals will still be around, even if they operate out of other neighborhoods."

"We're on our own, Isabel. We will stick together. It will be hard work, yes, but we will get it done."

As they continued walking, they approached a small clearing where cars were driving slowly by and a group of young people was standing around. Expensive vehicles; blanquito vehicles driven by well-to-do people from outside neighborhoods who were there for one purpose only. These were the buyers, the consumers. As they slowed down, one of the youths approached, the sellers, the dealers, the suppliers, and they transacted their business.

The three of them, Liz, Carlos, and Gilberto, stopped a prudent distance away from one of the sellers. Liz and Carlos stood there while Gilberto went up to him. The young man gave Liz a withering look. He recognized Gilberto, however, and allowed him to get close.

"We're not looking for trouble, for you or for us," Gilberto said to him. "We want to show you some pictures. We know that you do business with Santos. That's your business, not ours. We're not here to interfere with that in any way. I want to show you some pictures. If you don't mind, my friend Carlos has them. May he show them to you?"

The man had not spoken a word. So far, it had all been Gilberto's monologue. He hadn't said no, either.

"Do you mind if my friend shows you what he has? Carlos, show him."

Carlos went to the man and showed him pictures, not only of Pat, as Andrés and Perico had done, but also of other people, including Ann Miller, Linda Perkins, and Sandra Martinez.

"Please," said Carlos, "have you seen any of them before?"

When he didn't recognize anyone, Carlos asked him to show the pictures to his friends.

"Can you show them to your other friends? We will wait right here. Take your time."

Three of the dealers approached Carlos. One of them pushed him hard on the chest.

"Get out before we hurt you," said the young man.

Carlos was getting ready to respond when Gilberto stepped in saying that Carlos and Isabel were friends of his who wanted some information, and did not want to cause trouble. At that point, another man, older than the others, came up and told the other three to back off.

"Sorry, don Gilberto, these guys don't know who you are. How can we help you?"

"Hello, Paco. We want them to tell us whether they recognize anyone in these pictures."

"Guys, look at the pictures and answer the questions. Hurry up, clients are waiting for you."

The three looked at the pictures. To Liz's surprise, although they did recognize Pat Colberg, they also recognized another person, Sandra Martinez.

"Are you sure?" asked Liz.

"He's sure," said Paco. "Now you have to leave."

"One more question, please. Who did you see her with?"

"With Santos," said one of the men. "I've seen them together many times."

"This one?" Liz asked, pointing to Pat.

"Her, too."

"Thank you. Let's go."

Chapter Forty-Four

"Sandra Martinez," said Jack. "Is there anybody in the Red Cross who isn't mixed up with this? I wonder whether Fred knows anything about Sandra."

"What about Ann Miller, is she also involved?" asked Liz. "I guess so, in the sense that she, Linda, and Sandra were at The Islander the night of the beach party."

"This is looking more and more like one of those closed-room mysteries by Agatha Christie. Everybody was at The Islander the night Pat was killed, and most of them have visited El Batey and La Perla," said Bill. "I think we need to talk to Flaco. You know, the guy that Santos kicked out."

"Let's see if we can find him before we make another trip down there," said Jack. "Who was it that spoke to him in Rincón the last time?"

"Robert and Carlos saw him at The Islander," said Bill. "I don't think that we should be sending Robert down there, considering his fear that someone may be out to hurt him, so I guess it's going to have to be Carlos again. We should at least call our friend Sue at the Islander and try to find out if Flaco is in the area. I'll call. The Islander is closed now, but I'll call later and ask her."

"What about Sandra Martinez, where is she? I know that she's with the Red Cross. But they're all over the island. Maybe Fred Rogers can find out," said Liz. "I'll give him a call. It'll be interesting to hear what they plan to do with the investigation into the missing drugs in the Comfort now that the ship has sailed."

"Hi, Fred, we need to talk," said Liz. "Can we meet at La Bombonera in half an hour?"

"Of course," replied Fred.

"See you guys back here around lunchtime. By then you should have spoken to Sue at the Islander, Bill, and we'll decide whether to return to Rincón."

Liz walked to La Bombonera. She got there before Fred, asked to be seated in the back, and ordered a café con leche and a Mallorca. These were traditional specialties of the house, coffee with milk and a cake-like pastry served the way she and many liked it, pressed and buttered. While she was sitting there her mind wandered and she found herself thinking about the turns her life had taken. She couldn't conceive of living anywhere else, difficult as things had been since the hurricane, and despite the many things that infuriated her on a daily basis, such as the traffic, the litter, especially on the beaches, and the stray dogs, among others. This was home. She knew that it was her place. These were her people. Most of them were friendly, as long as you stayed away from politics, a very big if. And, of course, there was the crime and the corruption, and she had seen enough of it up close. It was enough to ruin any paradise, and perhaps it would, in the end, ruin this one, if things continued on their present path. The people didn't deserve it, but neither did they put a stop to it. They needed to get together and vent their outrage, to demand honest and efficient government, and to throw out the bums and crooks who didn't deliver it, no matter their political sympathies. They hadn't done it, at least, so far. They preferred to vote them into office as long as they were from their political party and supported their preference for the country's political status, be that statehood, independence or don't rock the boat.

Shit! She thought to herself. Who killed Pat? She could see her, happy with her friends at The Islander. Pat, were you a crook too?

"Liz, Liz, hi."

She looked up, shaken from her daydream, to find Fred standing in front of her table.

"Where were you, Liz? I mean, where was your head? asked Fred.

"Sorry, Fred. Too many things on my mind. Please sit. How're you doing?"

"Fine, Liz. How about you?"

"I'm good, Fred. I'm worried about too many things. Too many questions, too few answers. No, not too few answers. Make that no answers."

"That bad?"

"I'm afraid so. By the way, what's going to happen with your investigation on the black-market sale of controlled substances from the ship?"

"Well, even though the Comfort is no longer here, I had already gathered enough evidence of what was going on, and we're going to shut that operation down, Liz."

"Glad to hear that. How about Pat, was she involved?"

"In a manner of speaking."

"What do you mean, Fred, in a manner of speaking?"

"In confidence, Liz, it means that she was working for us."

"Are you serious?"

"Yes, I am, Liz. Lieutenant Pat Colberg, rest in peace, was killed in the line of duty. She worked for the NCIS."

"But you had told us that she was a suspect," said Liz.

"I couldn't tell you the truth."

"When do you ever? That's why I feel that I can never trust you. You lie too easily."

"Anyway," she went on, "there's your motive for murder. Someone found her out."

"Maybe."

"Maybe?"

"Yes, Liz, maybe, but we are still not sure. We're not there yet. Not ready to reach that conclusion."

"Why not?"

"Because we do not know that she was found out."

"She must have been. What other motives could there be? Right now I'm very frustrated, Fred. I know full well that because we don't see another motive, it doesn't mean that there isn't one."

"Exactly."

"I still think that someone must have found her out."

"Who, Liz? People at NCIS knew about her undercover work, of course. Not so her fellow crewmembers aboard the Comfort. She was fully qualified to work as a nurse, and that is what she did. If anything, they would have thought that she was working the black market if they found out that she was under investigation. None of them knew of her real job."

"Could Santos have found out?" wondered Liz.

"Someone would have had to tell him. No other way, of course."

"I see two possibilities, Fred—both involving Linda Perkins, who we know also works with the DEA—one inadvertent. She could have told Santos directly, or she could have confided in Sandra Martinez, who then told Santos. We know that both of them, Linda and Sandra, have been seen with him. Now, as Linda was an agent, getting close to Santos may have been part of her mission. Sandra had no such excuse, as far as I know," said Liz.

"But we can continue talking about this later," said Liz. "What I wanted to ask is whether you can tell us where she is working, Sandra that is. We know that she's somewhere in the mountains, one of the hard-hit towns up there. Can you tell me which one?"

"I'll find out and call you within the hour, Liz."

"Thank you. Take care."

Chapter Forty-Five

"SO, your meeting with Fred went well?" asked Jack.

"Yes," said Liz. "He should be calling me very soon to give us information on where to find Sandra Martinez."

"Meanwhile I called The Islander and spoke to Sue," said Bill. "She told me that Flaco shows up at the Islander every afternoon around four, and warned me that if we wanted to have a coherent conversation with him, we should be there before he starts drinking, so no later than five. I've already spoken to Carlos, and he is on his way here. He is going with me to Rincón this afternoon. I want to be there by three forty-five before Flaco gets there so that I can buy him his first drink."

"Sounds like a fun afternoon for both of you," said Jack.

Liz received a call from Fred letting her know that Sandra Martinez was working in Orocovis, a town in the mountains that Liz, and some of the others, knew well.

"That's the town where the Toro Negro Preserve is, where Ramos had his cabin," said Bill.

"Yes, where we all came very close to cashing in all our chips," said Liz.

"Well," said Bill, "I suppose that some of us are going back there to visit Sandra Martinez."

"Yes," said Liz, "early tomorrow. Jack, you, me, and Rita are going to Orocovis."

"Sure. I'll let Rita know that she's going. We should be ready to spend the night."

"I would agree, except that I don't know that there are any hotels nearby," said Liz. "Jack, every town in Puerto Rico doesn't have a Holiday Inn, a Hampton Inn, or a Motel 6. The drive to Orocovis takes about an hour and a half, a good part of it on winding mountain roads. I think we can go there and return the same day. Don't worry; I'm driving."

"If we leave early we can be back before nightfall. I don't think that we need to spend that much time with Sandra Martinez," said Jack.

Bill and Carlos left for Rincón right after lunch and were at The Islander before four o'clock. Flaco wasn't there yet, but Sue assured them that he would arrive soon. They could see the ocean from where they were sitting. Several surfers were in the water. A few minutes later, Carlos saw Flaco entering The Islander. Carlos waved him over, but Flaco did not recognize him. He walked over to him anyway. Not many people waved at him lately, and he concluded that it must be a good friend.

"I know you," said Flaco.

"Yes, you do. My name is Carlos, and this is my friend, Bill. Don't you remember me? I was here a few days ago with our mutual friend, Robert Montes. Sit down, let me buy you a drink."

Flaco accepted Carlos's offer. After a few drinks, the three of them were good friends, Bill and Flaco bonded together by alcohol, Carlos, a recovering alcoholic, by Coca-Cola. Carlos brought up how Santos had betrayed Flaco, an old friend, and one of his two trusted lieutenants, along with Cholo. Now both of them were gone, Cholo killed in a traffic accident and Flaco banished.

"I don't know what he's going to do without Cholo and me taking care of things. It's his fault. If it had been me doing the last Llorens run with Cholo, he would be alive today. We made a good team, made everything run. Santos, he's a piece of shit."

"You owe him nothing," said Bill. "You gave more than you received, and look what it got you."

"Do you remember that woman who was killed on the beach?" asked Carlos.

"I remember, but I don't want to talk about it."

"Why not?" asked Bill.

"Because I don't know what happened."

"But did you know who she was?"

"Yeah, I know. She was Robert's girlfriend."

"Did you see her that night? Were they together?"

"I didn't see them because I wasn't there. When Santos came to the bar, he said that he had talked to her at The Islander, asked her what she was doing."

"Why would he do that?" asked Carlos.

"Robert didn't know that she and Santos were friends. We were going to do a job that night. He didn't want her around," said Flaco.

"Santos and Robert weren't friends, right?" asked Bill.

"No, they knew each other, but they weren't friends."

"Were they in business together?" asked Bill.

"No. Santos always thought that Robert was a loser."

"What was the job that night?" asked Carlos.

"Drugs and weapons. We were bringing them in later that night on María's Beach."

"Why was Santos upset?" asked Bill.

"Because he didn't know that there was going to be a beach party that night. By the time he found out it was too late to do anything about it. You know, the landing was going to be much farther up the beach from the party, and later, but Santos doesn't take risks. He likes things quiet and smooth. He was afraid that this time it wasn't going to be so. All sorts of things could go wrong that would be beyond his control."

"So what happened when Santos got to Mi Sitio that night?" asked Bill.

"Listen, friends. I don't want to talk about this anymore. It's not fun, and it's ruining a nice evening. Dammit, there goes the power again."

The Islander was used to frequent power outages, so the staff was prepared and fired up a generator that, although noisy, provided enough power to keep things going, including to keep a few lights on. They were out on the terrace with a view of the ocean and there was a breeze blowing from the water, so it was still a pleasant evening. Flaco was settling down to some serious drinking. Bill and Carlos figured that they would get no more information from him. Nevertheless, they would stick around a while longer in case something else came up.

Carlos, the sober one, would be driving. Bill was drinking at a much slower pace than Flaco, but even at a slower pace he would soon be impaired and useless. Trying to stay sober, he asked Sue to bring plain Coca-Cola whenever he ordered rum and coke.

They stayed until around seven o'clock, by which time Flaco was drunk beyond redemption. He hugged both of his new friends when they told him they had to return to San Juan, after giving Sue a hefty tip, and asking her to keep an eye on Flaco.

Chapter Forty-Six

"I don't think we're going to get anything out of talking to Sandra Martinez," said Jack to Liz the night before they were supposed to go to Orocovis. They were having a quiet dinner at Marmalade Restaurant, not far from their office. It was one of their favorite places to eat. The restaurant had first opened its doors in Old San Juan around thirteen years ago, but it had suffered considerable damage from Hurricane María and had closed.

"When did this place reopen?" asked Jack.

"It just did, last Friday. They were closed for almost two months."

"Well, I'm glad they were able to come back," said Jack.

They ordered the Jamón Ibérico appetizer, Pata Negra ham served with honey grilled pears, and Spanish Cabrales blue cheese followed up with the White Bean Soup, a perennial favorite. For their main course, Liz had the Alaskan Halibut Cheeks; Jack ordered the Sea Bass. As usual, they did not order wine or any other alcoholic beverage.

"I think that we have good reason to go to Orocovis. Sandra Martinez was one of the last persons to see Pat Colberg alive. She spoke to her, and she also knew Santos. We don't know what else she could tell us.

Any information that she gives us will be helpful. Don't you think?"

"I do. Rita is meeting us in the office at eight in the morning, so that we can get an early start. We'll see what the drive will be like once we get on those interior roads."

They ordered dessert and coffee, and the conversation turned to more personal matters.

"Jack, I don't know what to do about Cris," said Liz.

"What about Cris? Oh, sure, the boyfriend and the trip."

"Yes, the boyfriend, the year off, and the trip."

"Honey, even though I understand your concern, I think that there are two things that you should keep in mind—three. First, Cris is a responsible, level-headed young woman. Second, many young people are doing what Cris wants to do. She will gain much from the experience. Third, I don't know what you can do about it, other than trying to persuade her not to go, that won't end up making things worse."

"I suppose you're right. I find it hard to disregard the dangers out there. So many things can go wrong."

"And won't. There are dangers out there, just not around every corner, as everyone now seems to think. She'll be fine. Trust her, let her fly, she's ready."

"It's that it has been me and her for so long."

"She will always be your daughter. You have to accept that she has her own life now. For that matter, so do you. It's you and me now."

"It is, isn't it? You're right. Let's go home."

They finished their coffee and walked back to the office to get their car.

The next morning they were on the road by nine. The trip was uneventful. They ran into the usual traffic getting out of the city, and once they left the main highway and got on secondary state roads, such as 155 into Orocovis, they had to contend with some delays from storm debris obstructions and roadwork. When they arrived in Orocovis, they asked where they could find the Red Cross people. Someone directed them to an aid distribution center in a barrio called Cacao, where they found Sandra. This was one of many areas in the mountains that had suffered devastating damage. The residents were still without power or potable water. Many were living in severely damaged houses.

"Look at that line," exclaimed Jack as he pointed toward a group of people standing at the back of a truck from which workers were handing out bottles of water and other supplies.

Liz and Jack talked to Sandra. They knew that she had been to La Perla more than once with Santos, and Liz had decided to confront her with the information.

"Sandra, we know that your friends with Santos Otero and that you have been to La Perla with him more than once," said Liz.

"That's right. Why is it any of your business? We're friends; he took me to see the damage. After all, I am a relief worker."

"You remember that we're looking into the murder of Pat Colberg in Rincón, right? You were at The Islander the day that it happened, so was Santos. When I interviewed you a few days ago, you didn't tell me that you and he were friends. We were wondering why," said Rita.

"I don't recall that you ever asked me whether Santos and I were friends, and I never denied that I knew him. I think you asked me about how he got along with his aunt, Peggy, and I told you what I knew."

"Do you know Ann Miller and Fred Rogers well? Are you friends with either or both of them?" asked Liz.

"We're co-workers. I know them. I wouldn't say we're friends. Not like Santos, who I've known for a long time. You know that I visit Puerto Rico often," replied Sandra.

"You've known Santos for a long time?" asked Rita.

"Yes, for years."

"And you're his friend despite his Nazi sympathies, his white supremacist ideas which so turn you off that you don't go to his hangout," said Rita.

"Right. I assume you have friends with whom you don't discuss certain subjects because it would kill your friendship—say, if you don't agree with our current president, whom some of your friends adore?" said Sandra.

"Again, you're his friend even though he is a self-avowed Nazi?"

"Yes, I'm still Santos's friend despite abhorring that side of him."

"No small matter, that," said Jack.

"I think that they are mesmerized by the uniforms and the shiny helmets. They've never carried it beyond talk."

"They are prone to violence, Santos, and his friends."

"Yes, because they're idiots, not because they're Nazis."

They weren't going to get any more from Sandra Martinez, and they didn't want to tip their hand by letting her know that they were aware of Santos's illegal activities, so they decided to leave.

"Sandra, you know that our client is Robert Montes. The only thing that we're interested in is proving that he wasn't Pat Colberg's killer," said Liz.

"I understand," replied Sandra.

"So we would appreciate any help you can give us. Here is my card. Give me a call if you think of anything," said Liz.

"I'm sorry, Sandra, one last thing. Did you stay at the beach party until it ended?" asked Rita.

"Pretty much, yes."

"When did it break up?" asked Rita, again.

"Must've been almost two in the morning."

"Had Robert returned by the time you left?"

"Yes."

"How about Pat? We understand that they had gone for a walk on the beach. Did she come back with him?"

"No, he returned by himself and left the beach without speaking to anyone."

"And what time was that?" asked Jack.

"Shortly before the party broke up, maybe half an hour earlier."

"Did Pat ever return?" she repeated. "Not that I know."

"She had come with you and Ann Miller. Weren't you worried for your friend?"

"Yes, and we waited around as long as we dared. We weren't going to stay on the beach after everybody else left. It wouldn't have been safe. The Islander had already closed. It was late, and there was nobody else around. There was nothing else we could do. We thought that she would show up later."

"Except that she didn't. Not alive."

"That's right. By the time we woke up the next morning they had found her body."

"Thank you. Again, give us a call if you think of anything else."

Chapter Forty-Seven

"I know who Bill is. I know Carlos, too," said Santos when he was told that Flaco had been seen drinking with the two men at The Islander. A server had given their names to Jose Luis.

"That fool can't keep his mouth shut when someone buys him a drink," said Santos. "We need to pick him up and find out what he's been saying. Go find him, then take him to Moca."

Jesse and Jose Luis took the van and went looking for Flaco. They found him in the usual place, The Islander, sitting by himself.

"Come on, Flaco. Let's go."

"I'm not going anywhere with you, cabrones."

"Don't make trouble, Flaco, Santos wants to talk to you. We'll bring you back here afterward," said Jesse.

"Like Hell, you will. Pendejos."

Jesse and Jose Luis pulled him up from his chair and dragged him away. Sue saw them push him into the back of the van and drive off. She knew that something terrible was going to happen to Flaco if she didn't do anything, so she retrieved the card that Bill had given her and called him. Bill was on his way to San Juan with Carlos, already about two hours away from Rincón.

"Thank you, Sue."

"Santos has Flaco. I have a pretty good idea where they are taking him, to their stash house in Moca. If we don't do something, they'll kill him."

"Turn around, then. Let's go get him."

It took them two hours to get to the Moca house. They left the car at a safe distance and walked the rest of the way. When they were close, they saw that the van was parked outside. The house was dimly lit. They approached, trying not to make any noise that would give away their presence, and got close enough to peer through a window. They saw Primo sitting on the sofa, and Flaco, Jesse, and Jose Luis seated around a small wooden table. Had Bill and Carlos not known better, they would have thought that they were looking at four friends.

"What are they doing?" whispered Carlos.

"I think they're waiting for Santos," answered Bill. "He'll be here soon, no doubt, and not alone. So, if we're going to do something, we have to do it now."

"Did you see any guns?" asked Carlos.

"No. They could be armed, but I don't think so. They went to pick up Flaco and didn't expect any trouble that the two of them couldn't handle. Do you have your flashlight?"

"Yes," answered Carlos.

"They don't expect any trouble out here in the middle of nowhere. If we move fast, we'll surprise them. There's only one door so we won't be able to come from two directions. We both have to come in fast, making a loud noise and shining our flashlights in their faces. They are all sitting together, except for Primo, and we don't need to worry about him. I'm sure he's drunk. You grab Flaco and pull him out. If we move quickly enough, we'll be out of there before they can react. Are you ready?"

"I am, let's go," said Carlos.

"Wait. We go on the count of three," said Bill.

They approached the front door, which they assumed, correctly, was unlocked, and burst in shouting "FBI!" and moving to the table. As Carlos approached Flaco, Primo, who they had disregarded, rose from the sofa and came at him. Although Carlos pushed him away, the distraction was enough to shake Jesse into action. He jumped up and confronted Bill, forcing him away. Jose Luis too got up and threw a punch at Carlos.

Flaco realized that he needed to do his part. He got up, grabbed his chair, and smashed it over Jose Luis's back, knocking him to the ground. Bill made short work of Jesse and shouted at Carlos and Flaco to get out. He knew that Santos and others couldn't be far behind. They needed to get out fast before they came. They couldn't leave Jesse and Jose Luis free to follow them, so they made them crowd into the stash room and jammed the door closed with a chair. Even though they would soon break out, the few minutes gained should enable them to get away.

They ran from the house towards their car, hidden a short distance away. As they did, they saw the headlights of three approaching motorcycles and were able to get down low on the ground to avoid detection. They waited until Santos and his friends went by. They would soon run into Jesse, turn around and come after them. There was no time to lose as they ran to the car, got in, and sped away. Bill was at the wheel, and he could see the headlights of the three bikes and the van following some distance behind. He kept his lights off as he veered from the dirt road onto the paved state road.

"You okay, Flaco?" asked Carlos.

"I am now. How did you guys know?"

"Sue alerted us that you had been taken from The Islander," said Carlos.

"What do we do?" he asked.

"We go to San Juan, and you help us by telling us everything you know. No more misplaced loyalties. Do you understand?" asked Bill.

"Yes. I don't know what Santos would have done to me, but I don't think it would have gone well."

"We need to lose them. Flaco, you know the roads around here. Is there anywhere we can turn to get off this road?"

"Yes, you can make a hard right in about half a mile."

"Where would that take us?" asked Carlos.

"That is State Road 443, which will take us to Highway 2, and on to San Juan," said Flaco.

"Is it passable?" asked Bill.

"I think that crews have cleared the storm debris. We should be able to get through."

"I guess we'll find out. We can't continue on this road at this speed and with our headlights off. We'll get killed."

They made the hard right onto 443, hoping that Santos didn't follow, and kept their headlights off for a few miles until they were satisfied that they weren't being followed. They connected with Highway 2 without incident.

"Listen, guys, it's late, and I have nowhere to take you, Flaco, nor am I going to drop you off at your apartment in Llorens at this hour, Carlos. That means that both of you are coming home with me. Tomorrow we'll go to the office and figure out what comes next.

Chapter Forty-Eight

"Andy, please call David and Robert. Have them come to the office as soon as possible. If they ask you why, just tell them it's important," said Jack.

They were all again sitting around the conference table, everyone except Carlos and Flaco who were waiting in Bill's office.

"We need to bring Carlos in," said Bill. "He has become an important member of our team."

"I agree, Bill. We trust him. The thing is that he is not an employee of this office, and that could present a problem regarding confidentiality. Don't worry, though, we will bring him in as soon as David and Robert get here," said Liz.

"And Flaco?"

"Yes, we all need to debrief him," said Jack.

"In the meantime, this can't get any more complicated, can it?" asked Bill. "Everyone and their uncle seems to have been in or around María's Beach at the time of Pat Colberg's murder. She, Ann Miller, Sandra Martinez, Fred Rogers, Robert Montes, and Linda Perkins, to name a few, were at The Islander or the beach party, while Santos and his men were there later to conduct one of their smuggling operations. That means that any of them could have killed the lieutenant. How on earth do we identify the culprit?"

"Now that Flaco is ready to tell us all he knows, we will start by listening to what he has to say. I think he may feel intimidated talking to so many people, though. He trusts Bill and Carlos, who saved him. I think we should take him out to breakfast, so he feels more at ease," said Liz. "What do you say, Jack? One of us has to stay here, waiting for David and Robert. I can go with Bill and Carlos, or I can stay if you prefer, and you go with them."

"No, that's fine, you go. I think it should be you because of the language."

Liz and Bill went to get Carlos and Flaco, and after Bill introduced Liz, who greeted him in Spanish, they all walked to La Bombonera.

Once there, they asked to be seated at a table in the rear. They sat, ordered coffee and started to talk about Santos, about what Flaco knew of his operation, and about what had happened the night Pat Colberg was killed.

"Flaco—I know everybody calls you that. If you don't mind, I would prefer to address you by your real name," said Liz.

"Ms. Diaz, nobody ever calls me by my real name. As you say, everybody calls me Flaco. I'm sure most don't know that my real name is Antonio, Antonio Marchand. My mother used to call me Tony. You know how in school other students have nicknames for you? That's when everybody started calling me Flaco, even my mother."

"Can I call you Antonio, or Tony?" asked Liz.

"Tony is fine."

"So, Tony, what did you do for Santos?"

"Whatever he asked me to do."

"Did he pay you? Were you his employee?"

"He paid us whenever we did a job."

"What kind of jobs? What did he ask you to do for him?"

Flaco remained quiet, and Carlos chided him.

"You already forgot what almost happened to you? Do you think it couldn't still happen if Santos got his hands on you? Answer Liz's questions."

"Look, I'm sorry. I'm not a snitch."

"I understand, Tony, but you know that we're not the police. I'm not looking to put anyone in jail; I want to find out what happened to two people, Lieutenant Pat Colberg and Marcos."

"I don't know what happened to either of them."

"Fine, but you know things that could help us get to the truth," said Liz. "Why don't you go ahead and tell us, in your own words, without us asking questions, what happened the night that Lieutenant Colberg was killed."

"Well, a bunch of us were waiting for Santos," he began. "We knew that we were working a job that night, or early the next morning, so we needed to prepare. Two boats would be coming into María's Beach bringing drugs and weapons. Our job was to wait for them at the beach, unload them from the boats, load them into our vans and take them to Primo's house in Moca. The one that you rescued me from."

"Who brings the contraband in?" asked Bill.

"I don't know. Santos knows, maybe Cholo, except he's dead."

"Please continue, Tony," said Liz.

"We always get started early, to make sure that things are in order. So, although the boats won't arrive for hours, we are in place by eleven o'clock at night at the latest. That means in position, everything ready and waiting, maybe two or three hours ahead of the boat's arrivals. Even before that, we drive around to make sure that nothing is wrong, that there is nobody else around, so, say, that would be around ten."

The server came with their coffee and to take their orders. Liz, Bill, and Carlos put in theirs without delay, eager for Tony to continue. Tony, though, started to peruse the menu, taking his time doing so.

"Eggs, Tony, eggs. Scrambled, sunny-side up, over, poached, whatever," said Carlos.

"C'mon, Carlos, let him take his time. Don't rush him." Said Liz.

"Scrambled eggs, bacon, and home fries," said Flaco.

"Toast?"

"Yes, bring him toast," said Carlos.

"Rye, buttered," said Flaco.

"Maybe the caballero would prefer a Mallorca, toasted and buttered?" asked the server.

"Yes, that," said Flaco.

"May I have your menu, sir?"

When they finished their breakfast, Flaco continued telling his story.

"Santos arrived at Mi Sitio a little past eight thirty. He was agitated," continued Flaco. "He was cussing up a storm and asked why none of us had told him that there would be a party that night on María's Beach. Cholo said that nobody knew, which upset Santos even more. He asked Cholo whether it was a secret party. It looked like he was ready to take someone's head off. We all looked in different directions, trying to avoid eye contact which would lead to being singled out. The only one who could calm him down in those situations was Cholo because he was bigger and meaner than Santos. He was a real crazy man, you know, Cholo."

"The operation was already in motion. It couldn't be stopped. The boats would arrive at the pre-arranged time, party or no party. At least they would arrive in an area somewhat north of where the party was taking place. They hoped that by the time they got there, around two o'clock in the morning, the party would be over and everyone would be gone. We had to be extra careful."

"We were all waiting at our assigned positions. Everything was quiet. There was nobody else around until we saw a couple walking up from the party. As they came closer, we crouched lower behind the sea grapes, watching them, not knowing what we would do if they came too near. We looked at Santos; he put his finger to his lips signaling silence."

"As they approached I recognized Robert Montes, but not the woman that was with him. They stretched a blanket on the sand and sat down. After a while, they seemed to be arguing, though we couldn't hear what they were saying. After a few minutes, Robert got up and left, leaving the woman behind. She sat there. It must have been around one in the morning. Santos then got up, said he would be right back, went to where she was, and sat next to her. They talked for a while, then they both got up. She walked away from the beach, Santos returned to where we were.

"A few minutes later, I was surprised to see a man coming towards us. I didn't recognize him; Santos did and went out to meet him. They walked to where the vans were parked and spoke briefly. The man left before the boats arrived."

"Are you sure you couldn't recognize the man, Tony?" asked Bill.

"I had never seen him before in my life."

"Do you have any idea what he was doing there?"

"No."

"What happened next, Tony?"

"The boats arrived, we unloaded them, loaded up the vans, and drove to Moca. No problem."

Chapter Forty-Nine

They returned to the office, where David, Robert, and Jack were waiting. Robert was surprised when he saw Flaco and Carlos walking in with Liz and Bill.

"What's Flaco doing here?" he asked.

"Flaco is helping us, Robert, and we need to talk. He says that he remembers seeing you with Pat Colberg on the beach the night she was killed, that you argued and you left. He says that he also saw her with Santos, who later met with another man."

"Great," said David. "That means that Robert left her alive and someone else killed her later."

"Maybe," said Liz.

"What do you mean, maybe?" asked Robert.

"We don't know what happened. Her body was not found until hours later," said Bill.

"Robert, do you have any idea who that other man that Santos met may have been?" asked Liz.

"I wasn't there. How would I know?"

"We think that it could have been Fred," said Bill.

"David, when you looked at the photographs that Carlos took the night that Cholo made the drug delivery at Llorens you were almost positive that the money man was another one of Santos's men. Could it have been our mystery man, the one who Tony saw with Santos and the lieutenant?" asked Bill.

"Tony?" asked Robert.

"Sorry, Flaco," said Bill.

"Sure," said David. "It could have been the mystery man. It could have been anybody."

"How can we identify this guy?" asked Liz.

"We can try to enhance Carlos's photos to get a better look. We can also show them to other people who may be able to recognize them," suggested Rita. "What are the two places where everyone seems to be seen—El Batey and The Islander, right? We can show the enhanced photos to Craig at El Batey and Sue at The Islander."

"Great idea, let's do it," said Jack.

"Who can we get to enhance the photos?" asked David.

"Law enforcement has the right equipment. We can ask Fred or Linda."

"I don't know, Bill."

"Why not?" asked Bill.

"Well, I hope we can trust them, at least one of them. I'm not there yet, however, on whether we can trust both, one, or neither," said Liz. "There are too many questions."

"We don't need them, do we?" She continued. "I mean, there are so many apps and programs that can now do that work. Carlos, you must know. You're into photography."

"Yes. I think we can do it on our own. Let me find out."

"By the way, we're not any closer to finding out why Marcos was killed, and I don't think we'll know why until we find out the who. First who killed him and then who ordered the kill. Then we'll know why. We all agree that someone gave the order, that there was a reason more sinister than robbery," said Bill.

"Yes, I think we all agree on that," said Jack.

"So, the way I see it, La Perla being the tight-knit community that it is, someone with the right contacts should be able to find out who killed Marcos, himself basically a local boy," said Bill.

"We thought don Gilberto had those contacts. It looks like he doesn't," said Carlos. "Unless it wasn't someone from La Perla."

"Where from, then?" asked Liz.

"Rincón, maybe?" suggested David.

"That would make sense, wouldn't it? Santos operates in Rincón and La Perla. I'm sure he had something to do with it. The answer could be in Rincón." said Bill.

"How's Peggy doing? If she was in business with Santos she might be able to point us in the right direction, give us some names," said Liz. "Harry, can you head over there and see what you can find out?"

"Sure, right away."

"Take Andy with you," said Liz.

When Harry and Andy went to the ICU, they were told that Peggy was recuperating well and had been transferred to a semi-private room. Harry asked whether anyone had visited his aunt. The volunteer at the desk checked her computer and told him that his cousin had already gone up. Harry asked for the room number, he and Andy stuck the paper IDs on their shirts, and they hurried up. When they got to the room, Santos was standing by Peggy's bed.

"Hello," said Harry.

"Who are you?" replied Santos.

"I'm Harry, Peggy's nephew. Her brother's son. They sent me to check on her when we heard of her accident. Who are you?"

"I'm Santos, her ex-husband's nephew. Peggy brought me up."

"Sure, I've heard of you. Not good things, I might add. Some say that you were responsible for her accident."

"Who would be saying that?"

"I've been to Rincón, and that's what some people are saying."

"If you tell me who's saying that I'll set them straight."

"Why would I put anyone in danger by giving their name to a gangster like you?"

"What did you say?"

"You heard me."

Santos, his face red with fury, wheeled around and stormed out of the room.

"You sure got him wound up," said Peggy opening her eyes.

"Good, keeps him off balance," said Harry.

"But tell me, who are you?" asked Peggy, speaking with some difficulty, slurring her words.

"I work with Liz Diaz and Jack Hardy. We have been watching over you as best we can. So has Sergeant Lopez, who arranged for a friend to send two agents. We've told everyone that I am your nephew, your brother's son."

"We need your help," he continued. "We want to know whether Santos has anybody in Rincón who he might use if he needs to get something done."

"'Something meaning what?"

"Meaning getting rid of someone."

"I can't think clearly yet... But wait, there are two boys they are crazy enough to do that. I know Santos used them before, I don't know what for. They live in Añasco. Los Batman, people say Los Batman, for some reason."

"Batmen?"

"No, I know it's bad grammar, but that's what they call themselves, Los Batman, not Batmen."

"Okay, but listen, aunt Peggy, I assume you have enough money to afford a room in a private hospital in San Juan so that you can be safer. Am I right?"

"I do."

"I'm going to get that rolling. In the meantime, you should give instructions that only I, Andy, Liz, or Jack can visit you here, not Santos. I'll get the nurse to come over so you can let her know, and we will see you soon."

"What's your name? Tell me your name," said Peggy.

"I'm Harry, Aunt Peggy, don't you remember me? Listen, you'll be out of here by tomorrow, I promise. What's your cell number? I'll call it now so you can have my number."

"Is this your phone?" asked Harry. "I'll do it."

"You call me anytime if there's a problem, anytime."

"There's my call. I'll get it."

"Here it is, this is my number. Do you need anything before we leave?"

"No... thank you... I'm drained now... Thank you."

Chapter Fifty

"Flaco, do you know two brothers in Añasco that people call Los Batman?" asked Bill. "Harry called to tell me that they may have had something to do with Marcos's death."

"I don't, Bill, but I have friends in Añasco who may. I'll ask around."

"Be discreet, Flaco," said Jack. "We don't want them to know that someone is looking for them."

"If Flaco can tell us where to find them, so much the better. If he can't, we need to get out there and find them ourselves," said Bill. "I'm sure everybody in Añasco will know two brothers that go by the name, Los Batman, especially if they have a dubious reputation, don't you think?"

"As a matter of fact, why don't we head out there right now? We can take Flaco with us and if he hears anything on the way, fine. If he doesn't, we will find them."

"We can also call Sergeant Lopez in Rincón. If these brothers are notorious, he must know who they are," said Liz.

"I'll do that," said Bill. "I was the one who spoke to him about Peggy's situation aboard the Comfort, and got him to find a way to assign men to ensure her safety."

Bill spoke to Sergeant Lopez, who told him that he did know of Los Batman; that they were brothers in their late teens or early twenties who had not wasted time in amassing impressive rap sheets, and that they were suspects in more than one execution-type slaying.

'They are either evil or crazy, or perhaps both," the sergeant said. "People say that others use them to do their dirtiest work."

Bill asked him whether he knew where to find them and Sergeant Lopez asked why he wanted to know.

"We need to confirm whether they were involved in something," Bill told him.

"Mr. Heinrich, you should let us handle this, if you have information that these boys have committed a crime, they are dangerous."

"But that's just it, sergeant," said Bill, "we don't know whether they have done anything, that's what we're trying to find out. I assure you that we will be careful."

Sergeant Lopez gave Bill general directions to where they might find Los Batman. They followed Lopez's suggestions and wound up at a bar in the Caracol neighborhood of Añasco.

Flaco went in by himself and saw two boys of the right age. One of them was playing a video game, the other one was watching. Flaco walked up to them and identified himself as one of Santos's men. He told them that he was there to ask them to do a job, and could they walk outside to talk. Los Batman didn't seem very convinced, but they must have figured that they were two and he was one, so, worse come to worse, they could always roll him and make some easy money. They asked him to follow them to an alley behind the bar. Once there they confronted him.

"Pendejo, we know that you're not with Santos anymore," they punched him hard on the stomach, slammed against a wall and pulled out a knife.

They took his wallet and his watch, and beat him up some more, but as they concentrated on their easy prey, they failed to notice an unoccupied car parked nearby with its emergency flashers on. They didn't see, until it was too late, the two men who came up from behind and pushed them hard against the same wall that they had pushed Flaco.

"Get the fuck off," shouted one of them. "I'll kill you."

"I'm sure you would if you could, you little turd," said Bill, "but your luck just ran out. We're with the FBI and this gentleman who you just rolled is with us. You are both under arrest. We have reliable information that you were the ones who murdered an American military officer in Rincón, and a young man named Marcos in La Perla."

"That's a lie," said one of the brothers.

"No," said Bill. "And to show you how much trouble you're in, I'll tell you how we found out; Santos Otero, who also says that you were the ones who kidnapped his aunt, Peggy Ramos, the owner of La Ola in Rincón. He says that you called him asking for money, and threatened that if he didn't pay you would kill her."

"That's bullshit, we didn't kill or kidnap anyone," said the same brother.

"I would advise you not to say anything until you've consulted with an attorney," said Bill. "Killing an American military officer and kidnapping someone are crimes punishable by death in federal court, which is where you both are going to be in a few days, maybe even tomorrow. The killing of the young man in La Perla is not a federal crime. We don't look into that, but the police would be interested, I'm sure."

"Wait," said the brother. "I'm telling you. If Santos said that, he's lying. We didn't do any of that."

"As I said, keep quiet. We're taking you to San Juan," said Bill.

"Can we talk, please? Santos is lying."

"I don't think we can do that. What do you say, Agent Palou?"

"Let them talk," said Carlos.

"They can talk in San Juan," said Bill.

"No, please, listen."

"Let's hear them out," said Carlos.

"If you say so," said Bill. "Somewhere else, though. Not here."

"Flaco, where can we take them? Some out-of-the-way place nearby, out in the sticks, not near the beach," said Bill. "Guys, climb in the trunk."

"What?" they asked.

"Either that, or we go to San Juan. Your decision" said Bill.

"Okay, okay," they said, and climbed into the trunk.

"Get out of town and keep going east. I'll tell you when to turn," said Flaco.

Twenty minutes later, they were high in the mountains with not a soul around; it was almost midnight. They parked the car and told Los Batman, who didn't look very scary, only very scared, to climb out of the trunk.

"What do you have to say?" asked Carlos.

'We didn't take the owner of La Ola or kill any American officer. Santos is lying," said one of the brothers.

"What is your name?" asked Bill.

"I am Junior Velez, and this is my younger brother, Elvis Velez."

"What about Marcos in La Perla?" asked Carlos.

"Cholo came to hire us. Santos sent him. He told us that we had to do a job for an important American. He paid us to kill Marcos."

"Do you know the American's name?" asked Bill.

"No."

"Who paid you? How much?"

"Cholo paid us two hundred dollars. He said it was the American's money," said Junior.

"Two hundred for each of you?"

"No, total."

"So which of you killed him?" asked Bill.

"We didn't. We paid someone from La Perla fifty dollars to do it."

"Who did it?" asked Bill.

"A guy named Perico."

"Who talked to Perico?" asked Carlos.

"We both did. We went to San Juan, to La Perla."

"I'm going to show you some pictures. Both of you look at them, and tell me whether you see the guy who paid you to get rid of Marcos," said Bill.

"We don't need to see pictures; it was Cholo."

"I'm going to show you some pictures anyway. Look at them and tell me if you recognize anyone, either of you."

Elvis and Junior got into the back of the car, and Bill sat up front. He pulled out a flashlight from the glove compartment and showed the brothers the pictures, one by one. To Bill's surprise, Elvis pointed to the image of Sandra Martinez. He said that he had seen her once with Santos. Neither of them recognized anybody else.

"Hijo de puta, Santos," said Carlos. "I'm going to kill him. And that little bastard Perico. I had him in front of me with don Gilberto's nephew, Andrés. He was trying to lead us in the wrong direction."

"You're welcome to Santos after I'm finished with him," said Bill.

"Listen, guys, we're going to investigate what you told us regarding the killing of the military officer and the abduction," said Harry. "If you're telling the truth, you won't be charged with those crimes. As I said, what happened to Marcos is not a federal crime, so we don't have jurisdiction. We do need you to come with us to the Rincón police station to talk to Sergeant Lopez. You will sign a sworn statement about what happened to Marcos. You need to tell him everything, including who paid you, otherwise you're coming with us to San Juan and we will charge you with the other crimes."

Bill had Sergeant Lopez's private cell number. It was late, but he decided that the matter was important enough to wake him up. After he explained the situation, John Lopez agreed to meet them at the station as soon as they could get there. They drove there and handed Los Batman over to Lopez, who took their statements.

"The sergeant agrees that moving on Perico or anybody else at this time would be premature," Bill told Liz and Jack back in San Juan. "He says that because Cholo was the one who paid Los Batman, it would be useless, that the testimony of the brothers that Cholo, who is dead, told them that Santos had sent him to hire them, would be impermissible in court, something known in legal terms as hearsay."

"So what is our next step?" asked Liz.

"First of all, we're moving Peggy Ramos, at her request and with medical approval, to a private room at the Auxilio Mutuo Hospital. Harry is at the medical center at this moment making sure that all goes well. You never know what Santos may try to do," said Jack. "I don't think that she's ready physically or mentally to give a comprehensive statement. It will be up to her to decide when she wants to talk to law enforcement, and what she will tell them."

"Let's think about this. Why would Santos have two young hoodlums from Añasco come to La Perla, and kill Marcos?" asked Liz. "If we assume that Marcos was killed because someone wanted to scare us away from La Perla, where we know Santos was transacting business, they didn't want to use a local person that might be more easily found out than an outsider. I don't think that they're happy that the deed ended up being carried out by a local person".

"It may not mean anything, but I don't believe in coincidences. We know Perico, right?" she asked rhetorically, "how? We know Perico through don Gilberto."

"Are you suggesting that don Gilberto is mixed up in whatever happened?" asked Carlos.

"I'm suggesting that we may need to consider the possibility. Nobody is beyond suspicion, Carlos. We need to follow this through, see where it leads us."

"I understand, Liz, but I think that your suspicion is unfounded," said Carlos.

"I'm not suspecting anything yet, Carlos. I'm pointing out a fact which in the end may mean nothing. We know that Perico did what he did. That is the only place where we can start. You agree, right?"

"I do, wherever it may lead, but I'm sure that it won't take us to don Gilberto."

Chapter Fifty-One

Santos was on a tear: "Los Batman have been arrested, and Flaco had something to do with it. Jesse, this wouldn't have happened if you had done your job. How could you have let him get away?"

He had always kept Los Batman at arm's length, and not many people knew that they were connected to him in any way, including Flaco, so he knew that they couldn't directly implicate him, but they might point people in uncomfortable directions. The only person who could incriminate him was Cholo, who was always the go-between whenever he needed to use the services of the brothers, which wasn't often, and Cholo was dead. No, there were only two persons he needed to worry about, Peggy and Flaco. He had to find out where they were.

"Jesse, where could Peggy and Flaco be? We need to go to the medical center. They have to let me see her. I'm her nephew. As to Flaco, tell Jose Luis to take another of the guys with him and go to that guy Carlos's place in Llorens. Either Flaco is there, or Carlos will know where he is. If Flaco isn't there, they need to make Carlos tell them where to find him. Jose Luis is to do whatever it takes to make that happen. After you send them off, come back. We'll go find Aunt Peggy."

When they arrived at Peggy's room in the medical center, she was gone. Santos went to the nurse's station, where he was told that the patient had been transferred to another hospital at her request. When he asked which hospital, he was told that Peggy had left instructions that her new location not be disclosed. Santos walked away, stopped a male nurse, slipped a $100 bill into his pocket, and asked him to find out where his aunt had been sent. The nurse came back in a few minutes and whispered that she had transferred to the Auxilio Mutuo Hospital.

Santos and Jesse arrived at the Auxilio Mutuo Hospital and asked for Peggy's room number. Although Peggy had given specific instructions to hospital personnel not to give out that information, as often happens, things, including important instructions, often fall through the cracks. The person at the reception desk was a volunteer who didn't bother to look at the instructions on his computer screen. He gave Santos the room number, as well as visitor IDs for him and Jesse.

When they arrived at Peggy's room, Harry and Rita were there. Peggy looked at him and asked Rita to call security. Santos tried to get close to Peggy, but Harry got in his way.

"I think you should leave right now," said Harry.

"Why? I'm her nephew."

"No you're not, you're my ex-husband's nephew, not mine. Now, do what Harry says and get out."

"Peggy, you'd better keep quiet, or you will be very sorry."

"You know what I'm sorry about: that I took you in and brought you up. I should have left you with your father, Primo."

Jesse had closed and locked the door to the room, and now it was only Peggy, Harry, Santos and him inside.

"What are you going to do, Santos? People are waiting outside," said Harry.

"I want a minute to talk some sense into this old bitch. If I go down, you go down. You know that."

"So be it," said Peggy. "So be it."

"Let's go, Jesse," said Santos as he opened the door. "Sorry, folks. The door was jammed."

"I don't think he'll be back, Peggy," said Harry. "Although I think he is a very dangerous man right now, as he may feel that he is getting pushed into a corner."

Following Santos's instructions, Jose Luís and Sammy, another of Santos's acolytes, arrived at Llorens and asked around for Carlos Palou. Nobody seemed to know where he lived. After a while, four or five young men stopped them and asked why they were looking for Carlos. Jose Luis said that they had a message from a friend. The five asked them to follow them, that they would take them to Carlos. Jose Luis didn't like how things were going.

"No, thank you," he said. "If you can tell us where to find him, that's fine. If not, you can tell him that Jose Luís from Rincón was asking for him. He'll understand."

"C'mon," said one of the young men. "You're already here all the way from Rincón. Why would you waste your trip?"

"Deliver the message. We're leaving," said Jose Luis.

"No, you're not. You're in our house now, and you're coming with us."

By now, a larger group had gathered, and Jose Luis saw that he would have to follow instructions. They were surrounded and had no other choice. They walked to one of the buildings and up the stairs to the third floor. One of their hosts had called ahead, so when they arrived at the door of Carlos's apartment, he opened it without waiting for a knock. Jose Luís, Sammy, and the others, about eight additional persons, walked in. Flaco was sitting on a sofa. He waved, smiling, at Jose Luís.

"Sit down," said Carlos. "Why are you looking for me?"

"We're not looking for you, we're looking for him," said Jose Luís, pointing at Flaco.

"Santos wants to talk to him. I don't think that he should be smiling."

" Flaco," said Jose Luís, "you know Santos, so you know that you're in real trouble, don't you?"

"Look around you," said Carlos. "You two are the ones who are in trouble. Don't worry; nothing is going to happen to you. We're letting you go. Let your boss know that we're coming for him, that Llorens won't forget that he killed Marcos."

"Guys, take Jose Luís outside. No, Sammy, you stay," said Carlos.

"I'm not leaving without Sammy," said Jose Luís.

"Yes, you are. Now, get out," said Carlos, shoving Jose Luís out of the apartment. "Get out while you still can. We'll take good care of Sammy. He can leave after we talk to him if he still wants to."

"How old are you, Sammy?" asked Carlos.

Sammy remained silent, glowering at Carlos and Flaco.

"I asked you a question. I think you should answer it."

Still, no reaction.

"That's fine. Have it your way, but you look too young, so you haven't been hanging out with Santos very long. Flaco doesn't know you, and he used to be one of Santos's top men until a few days ago."

"Flaco is a traitor," said Sammy.

"Maybe so. Did you know, however, that Santos is a drug dealer and a killer? Did you know that? He is going to end up dead or in prison soon enough. Is that how you want to end up?"

Still silence.

"What do you think about his white supremacist bullshit?"

"I think we have to protect ourselves, our race."

"Ourselves, our race? Have you looked at yourself in the mirror lately? Have you looked at Santos, at Jose Luís, or at any other of those idiots that hang out in Mi Sitio? I have news for you: you're the outsiders that the white supremacists hate. So, how old are you?"

"Nineteen."

"Get out of here. Think about what I've said."

Chapter Fifty-Two

"Liz and Jack want us to meet in the office this afternoon, Harry. From what you've told me, I don't think that Santos will be returning to the hospital, so can you come over?" asked Bill. "I'll give Carlos a call, and I'll ask him to let David and Robert know."

"Jack, we need to get back to La Perla," said Liz. "When the others get here, they can wait for us. Perico is our only lead into what has happened, and we need to move fast before we lose him."

"I agree, Liz. How do we do it? It's difficult to know who to trust."

"I want to go see don Gilberto again. I know that there is a tie-in between him and Perico, the kid who is supposed to have killed Marcos. He is a friend of his nephew, Andrés. Not that he couldn't have been in on things, as well, but I don't see Gilberto mixed up with Santos and whatever happened."

"So, let's give don Gilberto a call and ask him to meet with us somewhere. Do you have his number?" asked Jack.

"I do."

"Don Gilberto, this is Liz, do you remember who I am?"

"Sí, claro que sí. Of course."

"Can my husband and I see you today?"

"Yes, of course. Same place on San Sebastián Street. Do you want to meet there in half an hour?"

"Yes, thank you."

Liz told Andy that she and Jack were going to meet don Gilberto and would be back soon, that if the others arrived at the office before they came back, Andy should ask them to please wait.

"Sure, see you soon."

The bar was not far from their office. It was not, however, a comfortable walk, so they drove. The issue was always finding a place to park. Today they were lucky and found a spot right on San Sebastián Street, a short walk away. When they arrived, Gilberto was waiting. He rose to greet them, kissed Liz on the cheek, shook Jack's hand after Liz introduced them, and invited them to sit.

"Don Gilberto, I don't know how else to say this. I trust and respect you, so I'll get right to the point."

"I appreciate that. What is it?"

"We have good information that the person who killed Marcos was Perico."

"No, that's impossible. That's a lie."

"Let me tell you what we know."

"It's a lie. Hija, why are you lying to me? You're making it up, why?"

"I wish it weren't true, I guess there's always a chance that it isn't, but let me tell you what we think happened, and you can check it out. Wouldn't you want to know the truth?"

"I'm sorry. I think that you have been told a lie. But tell me, I'll listen. I'll hear what you say, and I'll investigate."

"Thank you," said Liz. "This is it: We got in touch with two young men in Añasco who, despite their youth, already have extensive criminal records. It appears that they have done some evil things on behalf of Santos Otero. You already know that Santos is involved with drugs in La Perla, right?"

"Yes, I am aware of that."

"They told us that Santos sent his man Cholo to ask them to kill Marcos and that he paid them $200."

"So why are you saying that it was Perico?"

"Because those two young criminals told us that instead of doing it themselves they came to La Perla and paid Perico $50 to do it."

"$50? That's ridiculous."

"I agree. That's why we think that it's true."

"Why would Santos want to kill Marcos?" asked Gilberto.

"We think that it may not have been only him. He, and maybe others didn't appreciate that we were asking questions related to his business in La Perla."

"What others?"

"We're not sure. You have to know that there are many making money illegally selling supplies brought to help after Hurricane María, including controlled substances. We think that someone was selling drugs from the hospital ship USNS Comfort on the black market and that Santos was helping them do it. The navy lieutenant that was killed in Rincón was a nurse on the Comfort, and she was seen in La Perla."

"Very well. I'll look into it, and we will talk again."

"Be careful, alright? These are dangerous people," said Jack.

"Thank you. I have dealt with many dangerous persons in my life. What I want to find out now is whether it is true that Perico killed Marcos. I have my people, and we will find out. I promise you."

Chapter Fifty-Three

Gilberto returned to his house and called his nephew Andrés. He also called two friends who he had known for many years and trusted completely, Rafael and Hernán. They had faced many dangerous situations together and knew how to handle themselves.

Once they were all present, Gilberto asked Andrés how well he knew Perico.

"We have been friends for a long time, why?"

"Because I know that Perico killed that man from Llorens, Marcos, for $50, that's why. Did you know?"

"Why would I know it?" asked Andrés.

"I don't hear you denying anything, nephew. You're not denying that he did it and you do not deny that you knew."

"So what if he did, uncle? What was Marcos doing asking questions in La Perla? He wasn't one of us, and he should have kept his nose out of our business."

"You knew that he did it, then. And what do you mean, our business?"

"You're an old man, uncle, out of touch."

"You haven't answered my question. What do you mean by our business? Are you involved with Santos?"

"You don't matter anymore, old man. Goodbye."

Rafael and Hernan stood in his way, and Gilberto came up and gave him a solid punch, knocking him down on the floor.

"What do you say, nephew, not bad for an old man, right? You are a fool. You don't know who you're dealing with or what you've done. Hernan, find Perico and bring him here. And you, don't you move if you know what's good for you. Watch him, Rafa."

Hernan was back with Perico in half an hour. Perico didn't know what was happening. He suspected that something was wrong when he took a look at Andrés and don Gilberto.

"What's going on?" he asked.

"You killed Marcos, didn't you?" asked Gilberto.

"I don't know what you're talking about."

"Don't waste our time, Perico. I know you did it, and this is not a court. I don't need any more proof. I'll tell you how much I know. I know that you were paid by two guys from Añasco known as Los Batman and that they paid you $50 to get rid of Marcos for Santos, who was doing it for an American. Did you know that they were paid $200? So, they made a profit of $150, and you did their dirty work for pennies."

"Who says I did it?"

"I say you did it. I, Gilberto, say you did it, and that is enough. And here is what you're going to do. You're going to help me tie this to Santos. You're going to call Santos, and you're going to tell him that you need to talk to him because the police are asking questions. He may tell you that he doesn't know what you're talking about, and if he does, you tell him that you're not going to take the fall for this and you're going to give them your number, and he can then answer their questions."

"And if I don't agree to do as you say?"

"Well, I'm not going to call the police on you. I'm going to call friends in Llorens and tell them what you did, and then I'll send you to them gift-wrapped."

"What if Santos doesn't believe me?"

"I'll still send you to Llorens, so you had better sound convincing, you little hijo de puta."

"So you go ahead and call Santos, and you tell him to meet you tomorrow night at 9:00 pm on the same street corner here in La Perla where he meets his clients."

"You and Andrés are not leaving this house until then. Andrés, give Rafa your phone. Hernan, you stay with this other little shit until he makes his call and then you take his phone as well."

Perico made his phone call under Hernan's close supervision. As Gilberto had suspected, it wasn't an easy sell. Santos told Perico that he didn't know him or what he was talking about. He agreed to come when Perico made his threat as don Gilberto had instructed him. Hernan then took his phone and both he and Andrés were locked inside a room in Gilberto's house. Rafa and Hernan would stay in the house, along with Gilberto, guarding them until the following day.

Gilberto called Liz to fill her in on what he had found out and what he planned to do.

"Liz, you were right. Perico did it. I confronted him and my nephew Andrés today. They tried to deny it, but I told them that I already knew."

"I'm so sorry that it turned out this way."

"Perico is guilty, yes. Even so, we're after bigger fish, aren't we?" asked Gilberto.

"Yes, we are. Whoever ordered a hit on Marcos and whoever killed Pat Colberg."

"This is what I've arranged, Liz. I made Perico give Santos a call and set up a meeting with him for tomorrow night at 9:00 pm here in La Perla to talk about Marcos. I and some friends will be close by, and I hope that Perico can trick him into admitting his participation and that of any other person that may have been involved."

"Don Gilberto, please. These are dangerous people. If they feel threatened, you never know what they will do. It could get ugly. Aside from Santos, other players have much to lose, as they are involved in contraband and black-market operations."

"Santos and Perico are bad enough," said Gilberto, "I'll help you get them. If there are others, you will find out, and you will get them, Isabel."

As it turned out, Santos and Jesse had not returned yet to Rincón after their attempt to visit Aunt Peggy. Things were getting out of hand, and they decided to call their American partner.

Chapter Fifty-Four

"Why are you calling me? You know that you're not supposed to."

"Forget about whether I'm supposed to or not," said Santos. "We need to meet as soon as possible. This is an emergency."

"Very well, we can meet at the Cataño terminal of the San Juan Bay ferry tonight at 8:45, that should give me enough time to get there. How about you, can you be there by then?"

"Yes, I can make it. I'm already in San Juan," said Santos.

"Alone, Santos. Come alone, or you won't see me."

"That would be a serious mistake on your part. But that's fine, I'll come alone."

Santos arrived at 7:15 pm at the Old San Juan terminal of the ferry and boarded the next boat heading for Cataño. The fare is fifty cents each way, and the boats take approximately eight minutes to cross from one shore to the other, from San Juan to Cataño and back to San Juan. The last boat leaves Cataño for San Juan at 9:30 pm.

He came alone, as requested because anybody that he could bring would be spotted. When he got off the ferry on the Cataño side, he saw them waiting for him; his associates, Fred Rogers and Linda Perkins.

"What's going on?" asked Linda. "What is the problem?"

"The problem is that the person who did the hit on Marcos is afraid that the police are on to him and he wants to talk to me, I presume to ask for my help in getting away."

"Why you?" asked Fred. "I thought Cholo had set up the hit using some guys from Rincón."

"He did. He told them that he was acting on my behalf, mine and some American, and then those guys turned around and subcontracted the hit to this person from La Perla."

"Wait a minute," said Linda. "What hit? What are you talking about?"

"So now your name is being mentioned regarding the hit, yours and some un-named American. That's great," said Fred, disregarding Linda.

"They can't tie us to anything. Cholo is the only person who could, and he is dead," said Santos.

"Yeah, and if the idiot hadn't mentioned you, that would be it, end of story. He did use your name, however, and even if that isn't enough to pin anything on you, it still shines a spotlight, which is bad enough. What's his name?" asked Fred.

"Perico."

"Perico. That's the street name in Puerto Rico for powder cocaine, isn't it?"

"Yes," said Linda. "The name comes from the fact that when cocaine is inhaled, it bites like a parrot's beak. What hit, Fred?"

"Have you ever tried it?" Fred asked Linda, again ignoring the question.

"What hit?" she insisted.

"You need to take care of this," Fred said to Santos. "If this guy Perico mentions your name to the wrong persons, we're all in trouble. You do know, don't you, that some attorneys are going around asking questions because they represent the man picked up for the murder of Pat Colberg."

"I know, but I had nothing to do with that," said Santos.

"Whether you did or not doesn't matter. Whoever did it, the point is that they are asking questions," said Fred. "They've already talked to Linda, to me, and to several others, including Ann Miller and Sandra Martinez."

"We can't let this get out of hand," Fred warned. "We need to make sure that it won't go any further. Let me repeat it. It's up to you. You need to put a stop to this. Let us know when you do."

Santos took the ferry back to San Juan, while Linda and Fred went a long way around the bay by car. They didn't see Jesse, who had been watching from across the street. He waited ten minutes before leaving on his Harley.

"Fred, what hit?" asked Linda, again.

"The hit on Marcos," Fred said. "And there is only one solution. If Santos doesn't resolve the situation we will have to get rid of him. He's the only person who can bring us down. I'm not worried about our Red Cross operation," he continued. "I don't think anybody is looking into any improprieties there. I'm worried about the Comfort."

"It was stupid to get involved with that pharmacist," said Linda.

"Perhaps so," said Fred. "But at the time, we both agreed that it was a good idea to work with her."

"Sure, but it brought Pat Colberg and the NCIS into the picture," said Linda. "And myself, once Pat was killed. Now Liz Diaz knows that I am with the DEA."

"How did she find out?" asked Fred.

"Because they were asking questions and I felt I had to tell her."

"Well, we have other things to worry about. If Santos doesn't take care of things, we need to get rid of him. As I said, he would need to go."

"What do you mean by needs to go?" asked Linda.

"I mean that he needs to go, as Marcos had to go."

"Why did you ever have Marcos killed? Why didn't you tell me that you were going to do it? It was an idiotic thing to do," Linda said, alarmed.

Linda was thinking that when she agreed to join Fred in his contraband schemes, it seemed an easy way to make money. There were so many relief supplies coming into Puerto Rico after Hurricane Maria and so few controls, so many willing to turn a blind eye for the right incentive, that if a person was in the right place, as she and Fred were, it was like picking low-hanging fruit. It was so easy, and so many people were doing it, from relief workers to local politicians or others who had the right access, that it never occurred to her that people could get hurt. Now two people had died, Pat Colberg and Marcos, and there was the possibility of another death. She wasn't involved in those two deaths, Pat or Marcos, but she would be involved in this next one if it happened.

"Dammit, Fred," she said, "we were supposed to make money, not kill people."

Fred looked at her with disdain. "Do you want to get caught? Do you want to end up in federal prison? It's too late, Linda. You're involved, and you can't get out. You have as much to lose as anybody else, so stop pontificating."

Linda dropped Fred off at his hotel and continued to her own. It wasn't easy, navigating the darkened streets, the crater-like potholes that force a driver to be on guard and swerve her car from one side to another, the haphazard traffic lights, working in one intersection, out of order on the next, and other drivers trying to muscle their way through it all.

Keeping her mind on the road was hard. She wasn't so much worried about what could happen to Santos as about what could happen to her if he came to any harm, how she would be implicated. She was also worried about Fred. She knew that by letting him know of her misgivings, she had planted a seed of doubt in his mind about her reliability, and that was not good. She was in a very tight spot. She could go to the FBI and blow the lid off everything, she could try to talk to Liz Diaz, or she could let things play out. There was very little time left for her to make up her mind. She was sure that it wasn't wise to wait and see what happened tomorrow night at La Perla, how Santos handled his encounter with Perico. By then it could be too late. If someone was killed or hurt, she would be a part of it.

Chapter Fifty-Five

Back in the office, after they had heard from Gilberto and what he planned to do, Liz explained that she was worried that something could happen to him.

"I wouldn't worry about don Gilberto," said Carlos. "Do you know that he is a naturalized American citizen? He was born in Spain, his full name is Gilberto Alvarez. He was once a soldier in the Spanish Foreign Legion; served in the Spanish Sahara, today Western Sahara. He left the Legion after it was involved in an incident where units fired on demonstrators in the neighborhood of Zemla in 1970. Don Gilberto made his way to Puerto Rico soon after that and moved into La Perla with a woman he met in one of the waterfront bars of the day, before the area was cleaned up for the cruise ships."

"He doesn't talk about his time in the Legion or about his early days in Puerto Rico," continued Carlos. "It's a past that he prefers to forget. He will be furious if he ever finds out that I've shared this information with you, but I wanted to reassure you that Gilberto Alvarez can take care of himself. I count on your discretion."

"He can take care of himself, or he thinks he still can," said Liz. "But his Foreign Legion days are long gone, and he is no longer a young man. He may think that he still is, which means that he may try to do things the way he did fifty years ago, and will end up getting himself in trouble."

"Of course you're right," said Carlos.

"So I want us to watch out for him tomorrow. I don't want him to know that we're there, but we will be."

"Who do you mean by we?" asked Jack.

"I mean Harry, Carlos. and me."

"Also Robert and me," said David.

"No, you would be recognized. Besides, we're only going to watch."

Jack felt that the three who would be going wouldn't be able to get anywhere close to the action without being recognized by the dealer's lookouts, and might end up placing don Gilberto and his people in danger if the dealers were to think that he'd brought them.

"You could end up doing more harm than good," he said.

"We can't leave them on their own, Jack," said Liz.

"Why not?" he replied. "I think he knows what he's doing."

Liz agreed but was still concerned because she knew that Santos was capable of anything, and she didn't like the fact that they were trying to have Perico push him into a corner. They left it at that, for now. The following day would be an anxious one as they waited for the main event that night. Liz planned to speak with don Gilberto again to try to dissuade him from what she believed was a mistaken and dangerous course of action. Although she didn't expect to win him over, she would do her best.

As she and Jack were getting ready to go home, her cell buzzed. She looked at the screen, and it was an unknown and unfamiliar number, so she did not take the call. A few seconds later, she saw that the caller had left a voicemail. She was surprised to find a message from Linda saying that she needed to speak with her as soon as possible, and would she please return her call. Liz rang her back, and Linda told her that she needed to talk with her right away, could they meet somewhere? Liz told her that she was still in the office, and would wait for her if she wanted to come by.

"No, Liz, not in your office. You will understand why when we speak."

"Fine, do you know the Punto de Vista, the rooftop restaurant at the Hotel Milano on Fortaleza Street. Can we meet there?"

"Yes, I know the place, when?"

"We can have supper. Can you be there in half an hour?"

"Sounds good. I'll meet you there in half an hour."

"My husband will be with us, and I also want to bring Bill. Do you have a problem with that?"

"Not at all. I think it's a good idea."

The Hotel Milano was a short fifteen-minute walk from Liz's office. She and Jack had been there many times, and the views of the old city do justice to its name.

They arrived ahead of Linda, who arrived fifteen minutes late and blamed the heavy traffic. She looked worried, sat down, and without preamble got right to the point.

"I can't keep silent," she said. "I know that I may have to face severe consequences, but things are getting out of hand, and I won't be a part of it any longer."

"What is it that you can't be a part of, Linda? Why have you come to us?" asked Jack.

"I've come to you because you will know what I'm talking about and may be able to stop another murder," she said.

"Another murder, Linda?" asked Liz.

"Yes, another murder. Look, I'm sure you must have had your suspicions, and it's not easy for me to confirm them, but my hands aren't clean. I am involved with the contraband of hurricane relief supplies, together with Santos and others. Not with his operation of bringing in drugs, arms, and people, only with relief supplies."

"Did you have anything to do with the deaths of Pat Colberg or Marcos?" asked Bill.

"No, I did not, but Santos and others may have, and that's one reason why I'm here. Santos is desperate. He is meeting someone tomorrow in La Perla who is threatening to go to the police about his participation in one of those deaths, about his having paid for the murder of the young man that you mentioned."

"Are you saying that he ordered the hit on Marcos?" asked Bill.

"He did," she replied.

"Why?" asked Jack. "Why would Marcos be a threat to Santos? What would he, or we, learn about Santos that wasn't already common knowledge?"

"It wasn't about Santos, right?" asked Liz.

"Right, Liz. There's someone else who didn't want his identity revealed."

"Fred Rogers," said Liz immediately.

"How did you know?" asked Linda.

"Educated guess. I always thought that it might have been one of you, although I must say that I never expected it to be both."

"Are you sure you didn't have anything to do with the lieutenant's death?" asked Jack.

"I told you that I didn't. I don't know whether Fred did," she replied.

"Aren't you both with the DEA, Fred and yourself?" asked Bill.

"Yes, but he was looking into shipboard contraband operations out of the Comfort. I didn't come into the picture until Pat was killed."

"Are you sure you didn't have anything to do with Marcos's death?" asked Jack.

"Second time you ask me that too. I've already said that I did not. That's why I'm here because there may be another death and I want to stop it from happening."

"You mean Perico?" asked Bill.

"Perico, or Santos, if he doesn't take care of Perico."

"So Santos is supposed to take care of Perico?" asked Bill.

"And if he doesn't?" asked Jack.

"Then Fred will take care of Santos."

"But why?" asked Liz.

"Because Fred is afraid," said Linda.

"Santos is planning to take care of Perico when they meet," she said.

"Okay, so we have to figure out how to prevent that from happening," said Jack.

Liz asked Linda whether she felt comfortable returning to her hotel, and Linda replied that she was now afraid that Fred would harm her if he suspected that she would go to the police.

"Well, it might complicate things if he can't find you. But you don't have to place yourself in harm's way," said Bill.

"I know that it will it help my case if I help bring them down, Santos and Fred."

"Even though how things go for you is not up to us, I would say that it will if you didn't have anything to do with Pat or Marcos's deaths," said Jack.

"In that case, I'll return to my room in La Concha. I don't want him to suspect anything."

Chapter Fifty-Six

The next morning, Carlos went to La Perla with Liz to speak with don Gilberto. They told him that they had information that Santos would try to either kill or kidnap Perico and that he was acting on his behalf and also on behalf of another, un-named, individual.

"We can't be sure what's going to happen, don Gilberto, but it looks bad," said Carlos. "It's not about Santos now as much as about this other person, and Santos himself may be the target of this other person, who may feel that Santos can implicate him. We believe that Santos ordered the killing on behalf of this person."

"Who is he?" asked Gilberto.

"Fred Rogers, who is a DEA agent and has much to lose," said Liz.

"So why don't you go to the police, or the FBI, or the DEA?" asked Gilberto.

"Because we have no hard evidence of what we're saying and he would slip away. We need direct evidence of his involvement," said Liz.

"So, what do we do?"

Liz explained that they couldn't afford to let things happen that night because it could turn into a bloodbath with Rogers getting away. Or he could shoot Santos and Perico, claiming to have been afraid for his life when he was discovered watching them.

"We think that we need to find Santos so that we can try to convince him that his life is in danger," said Carlos.

"How are you going to do that?" asked Gilberto.

"I think we have the right person to scare some sense into him," said Liz. "We need to find and capture him before he finds Perico."

"I don't think that will be a problem," said Carlos. "But we need to identify anyone else who comes with him before we can grab him. I think he won't come with more than one person. He's been doing business in La Perla for a long time and will feel confident. We can use Flaco to tell us who's with him."

That night Rafa, Hernan, Harry, Carlos, and Flaco were standing close to where Santos was supposed to meet with Perico, far enough away so that he wouldn't see them. At the agreed-upon hour, Santos walked towards Perico and Flaco alerted Carlos to Jesse's presence, hiding close by. Rafa and Hernan then moved closer to Jesse at the same time that Carlos and Harry moved towards Santos. Rafa and Hernan grabbed Jesse while Carlos and Harry, aided now by Perico, pushed Santos into the back seat of a waiting car and whisked him away. As they did so, they saw Fred come out of hiding and start running after them together with Jesse, who had been released as soon as Santos was in the waiting car.

They left La Perla and drove to Carlos's apartment in Llorens where Liz, Don Gilberto, Rita, and Linda were waiting for them. Once inside, they asked him to sit on one of four chairs around the dining room table, with Liz, Don Gilberto and Linda occupying the other three.

Santos was surprised to see Linda. "What are you doing here? What am I doing here?" he asked.

"Mr. Otero, do you know who I am?" asked Gilberto.

"Of course I do. You and the rest of these people will be sorry for this."

"I think that once you hear what this lady is going to say, you may change your mind," said Carlos, who was standing behind Linda.

"This is Perico, Santos," said Liz. "You know me. I'm sure you remember me from that unpleasant business at Mi Sitio. I can't say that it's a pleasure to see you again. As far as you're concerned, this could be your lucky day. Now, please listen, and don't interrupt. None of what we're about to say is up for debate or revision."

"We know that Perico did a job for you and we're convinced that you planned to hurt him tonight," said Liz. "We know that you're going to deny knowing him or that you paid him to do what he did, but we know otherwise, and that's enough for us. We know that you sent your man Cholo to set up a hit on Marcos and that he paid $200 to a couple of boys from Añasco known as Los Batman to carry it out. We know that these boys came to La Perla and sub-contracted with Perico to do the job. We also know that Cholo is dead and that, since he can't finger you, you think that you're safe. We know more, and that is why Linda Perkins is here. If you listen to her, she may save your life. Go ahead, Linda."

"Do you know why I'm here, Santos? I have admitted to what I have done as one of your partners selling contraband, including controlled substances. Do you know why I confessed?" asked Linda, looking straight at him. "Because I didn't sign up for murder." Linda was getting worked up, and her hands were starting to shake. Gilberto told her to take a minute and asked Perico to bring her some water.

"Drink the water, Ms. Perkins, and calm down. You're doing the right thing," said Gilberto.

Linda continued. "Santos, believe me, Fred is ready to kill you and planned to do it tonight. He knows that you're the only one who can connect him to Marcos, and perhaps to Lieutenant Colberg."

"I don't know anything about Lieutenant Colberg. We never discussed her. He makes money from me, why would he want to come after me?"

"Because you know too much, Santos. Look what happened to Marcos, and you're far more dangerous. Why would I be here if I'm not telling the truth?"

"So let's say I believe you. What do we do next?

"Well, you would have to start by admitting your participation in everything that has happened," said Liz.

"I'm not willing to admit to anything. The only reason why I was in La Perla was that this guy, Perico, wanted to talk to me. He accused me of having been involved in some murder conspiracy. I wanted to hear him out because I prefer to avoid any interaction with the police. Even when I didn't have any idea of what he was talking about, I thought that by talking to him I might be able to talk him out of taking some rash action."

"So, what, you were going to pay him off?" asked Liz.

"To tell you the truth, yes, that did cross my mind, I was willing to buy him off to prevent him from making false claims against me."

"But if you're innocent, why would you pay?" asked Rita.

"You know what people say: where there's smoke, there's fire. That is what most people do think. Innocence is not an effective defense once people start talking," said Santos. "So, can I leave now? I assume that one of you will take me back to where you got me."

"Santos, you're making a big mistake. Fred will come after you," said Linda.

"He will come after you, Linda, for betraying his trust and spreading false rumors."

Everybody looked dejected. They had been sure that this man would listen to reason, but forgot that some people are willing to do anything to get and defend, their pot of gold. Not even fear of death will stop them.

"Many people will do anything, anything, for money," said Gilberto. "I've seen people do unimaginable things: kill their children and their spouses to collect insurance benefits, or risk their own lives, sacrifice their bodies, amputate limbs, and do horrible things to get their treasure. Not to feed their families, mind you. No, they want to buy a boat, or a bigger house, to buy, to have. It is greed, and what is greed if not that: to lust after money and after things that you don't need, only to have them, and then to have even more."

"Sure," said Liz. "It is ambition out of control. Like a fire that can warm your house, but will burn it down if left unattended."

"Yes, I guess you're one of those people," Liz said to Santos. "Harry, take him back."

Harry and Carlos left to take Santos back to La Perla with instructions to keep a discreet eye on him.

Chapter Fifty-Seven

They drove Santos back to La Perla. He called Jesse on the way to let him know that he would meet him by their bikes on Norzagaray Street. By the time they got there, it was past midnight, and Jesse was waiting for him. Santos, who hadn't said one word on the trip over, got out and slammed the door shut, making an obscene gesture on the way out. He and Jesse mounted their bikes and roared away. There was little traffic at that hour, which meant that it would be impossible to follow them undetected, especially as Santos would be expecting them to do so.

Harry guessed that Santos and Jesse would be heading back to Rincón. They called Bill to let him know. He had already heard what had happened in Llorens and said that despite the late hour, he wanted them to go to Rincón. They agreed to do so and got underway.

They went straight to Mi Sitio. The bar closed at that two in the morning but Santos had a key. Harry and Carlos arrived within minutes and parked nearby. By then it had started to rain. They had shut their motor off, and now, with the windows closed against the rain, the interior of the car was stifling hot and humid. The windows were steamed up, which made it impossible to see what was happening outside.

After a while, they saw the lights of an approaching vehicle. It stopped in front of the bar. In a couple of minutes, the driver doused his lights and shut off the engine. It was raining hard, and they were far, but they heard the door of the car open and then slam shut, and saw a person get out without an umbrella and move quickly to avoid getting soaked. Despite the heavy rain, they too left the car and approached the bar, also getting drenched in the downpour.

The person ahead of them had entered the bar, and Harry concluded that he had been expected. Harry and Carlos were not, or so they hoped. They stayed outside and were able to peer through a window. The visitor was Fred Rogers. They were too far to hear the conversation, so they looked around until they found a window that was half open. They moved closer to it and were able to listen in.

"Did you take care of Perico?" asked Fred.

"No, things got a little complicated. You were there and saw what happened," said Santos. "Some people were waiting for me. I was captured and taken to an apartment where others questioned me."

"Who? What did they want?" asked Fred.

"You'll be surprised when I tell you the name of one of those who were waiting. Your associate, Linda Perkins. The others were trying to use her to scare me into talking to them. Do you know how? By telling me that you were planning to get rid of me."

"Linda? How did they get to her?"

"That's not the point. Were you planning to kill me?"

"That's Linda making things up to try to save herself. She has sold both of us to get a deal for herself."

"Sold us to whom? The people that she was with were not law enforcement. They couldn't offer any deals, could they? They are representing a suspect in the death of the Navy lieutenant and are trying to find out what happened to her and to the other person, Marcos, that Perico killed."

"I had nothing to do with the lieutenant's death. Did you?"

"No, I didn't."

"Look," said Fred. "Perico killed Marcos, not us. Anyone who says that we were involved has no proof. Neither of us ever interacted with Perico, and he cannot tie us to that crime. Sure, it would have been better to eliminate the threat. That is impossible now. Let's not panic and end up hurting ourselves."

"Aside from that," he continued, "I've decided that we need to take a break from the black-market distribution of hurricane assistance supplies. The feds are investigating, and it's too dangerous for us to continue. Maybe we can resume those activities in the future."

"As to the lieutenant's death, I know that these people are trying to exonerate their client, and that has been a problem for us because in the process they have stumbled on our business. We were not the killers," said Fred. "You saw her that night after I did, didn't you?"

"Sure," said Santos. "I spoke to her at The Islander. We argued, and I left. Then she went to the beach party, and I know that you saw her there."

"How do you know that? Anyway, it was before she left the party with Robert."

"You forget that we had a delivery that night. I went to Mi Sitio and returned to set things up. I saw her with Robert Montes. They were relaxing on their beach blanket for around forty-five minutes until they started to argue and he got up and left."

"You had a personal relationship with her. I didn't," said Fred.

"How would you know that I had a personal relationship with her?"

"You forget that I am a DEA agent and that I have you under surveillance," said Fred. "Anyway, this is getting us nowhere. Let's leave things as they are and stop communicating with each other for the time being, agreed?"

As Fred was getting ready to leave, Harry and Carlos hurried to their car under rain that was still coming down hard. They watched Fred get into his vehicle and drive away. Minutes later, Santos and Jesse also left.

Chapter Fifty-Eight

"Santos didn't break. What do we do next?" asked Jack.

"Why don't we lean on Fred?" asked Liz. "I think we can get to him using Linda, if he knows that she has turned on him. I can call him and ask him to meet with me at La Bombonera. I'm sure he would come. He would want to continue playing his part and would also be curious to hear what I have to say. He wouldn't anticipate any problems."

"And meanwhile," she continued. "I'll be waiting for him with Linda, if she agrees."

"I don't see how she could refuse," said Rita. "She's already committed herself."

"Let's give her a call first and then set up the meeting with him," said Liz.

Linda did not sound thrilled with the idea of confronting Fred.

"I'm sure she is apprehensive because she doesn't know how Fred will react, and he may have something to say about her," said Jack.

But Rita was correct. Linda had already committed herself, and there was no plausible reason for her to refuse.

Fred, too, had no reason for refusing to meet with Liz, and he was not told that Linda would be present, so the meeting was arranged for three o'clock that same afternoon.

When Fred arrived at the restaurant, he was met at the door by Jack. He was taken aback, but they shook hands, and Jack led him to the table where Liz and Linda were waiting. Had he been alone, he would have turned around and left, but with Jack at his side, he couldn't do that without raising suspicions. Why would he not want to meet with his friend, Linda? They had sprung their well-laid trap.

"Hello, Liz," said Fred. He then turned to Linda. "I'm surprised to see you here. Liz didn't tell me that you were joining us."

"Would you have come?" asked Linda.

"No, I wouldn't have," he replied. "But that's beside the point now that I'm here."

"Linda has admitted her participation in the black-market sale of federal disaster relief supplies in Puerto Rico. She says that you were also involved," said Liz.

"So why are we sitting here with you instead of with federal law enforcement agents or local police?"

"I can't answer that. They don't tell me what they are going to do, and besides, you're a federal agent, so they may not even be looking at you," said Liz.

"Does that mean that you haven't reported anything to the FBI, Linda?"

"No, she hasn't, not yet," said Liz.

"Look, Fred, we know who killed Marcos, and we think we know who hired the house painter," said Liz, using a term sometimes used to describe a hired killer. "We think that the same person killed the lieutenant, but we can't prove it. Now, if you help us do that, you will be in a much better position with the feds."

Liz didn't tell him that they suspected that he was involved in ordering Marcos's death.

"And how are we going to do that?" asked Fred.

"Well, I think we should all pay a surprise visit to his favorite hangout," said Liz.

"Why would I go?" asked Fred.

"Because if you don't, we will go straight to the FBI to report you, and you will not have the benefit of telling them that you helped solve the Pat Colberg case."

Fred decided that it was better if he went. It was preferable to declining and not knowing what would happen.

"Very well," he said. "I suppose I'll go with you."

"What are you talking about, Liz?" asked Jack. "We haven't discussed this. It's a crazy idea. Visiting Santos in his lair? No, Liz, that's not going to happen. It's too risky."

"Jack, it's the only way. We have to do it. Trust me."

"When would we go?" Jack asked.

"Right now. Bill and Robert are waiting for us at the office, ready to head out."

Jack called Bill, still somewhat upset because it seemed that he was the only one that wasn't in on the plan, even after Liz had explained to him that the reason was that he would have argued against it.

Liz, Linda, Jack, Bill, Robert, and Fred left for Rincón. By seven thirty in the evening, they were in front of Mi Sitio. Several motorcycles were in the parking lot, including Santos's Harley.

When Santos saw them come in, he didn't know how to react because Fred was with them, and as far as he was concerned, he and Fred were on the same page. He knew where Linda stood, which increased his confusion. After all, she had tried to throw him and Fred under the bus regarding Marcos's killing.

"What do you people want?" Santos asked.

"We want to talk about Pat Colberg," said Liz.

"At least four of the people here tonight were at María's Beach on the night when she died. Four of you who knew her: You, Santos, Fred, Linda, and Robert.

Oh, and I assume that you were there as well, Jesse," said Liz.

"There was still another person who was at the beach, Tony. Here he is now with our friend Carlos," continued Liz.

"That's Flaco," said Santos.

"Yes, Flaco, or Tony," said Harry.

"What does he have to do with anything?" asked Robert.

"As Liz said, Tony was at the beach," said Bill.

"Anyway, the point is that all of you saw the lieutenant that night, some of you more than once," said Liz.

"Santos," she said, "as far as we know, you were the last one to see her alive, after Robert. Fred, we think that you were at the beach late that night, and of course, you knew Pat Colberg, as did you, Santos."

"So, Tony, do you recognize anyone here as the man who met with Santos late that night?" asked Bill.

"Sure, it was that guy," he said, pointing at Fred. "I'm sure it was an American, and it was him."

"What do you say, Fred?" asked Jack.

"I say nothing, other than that I did not kill Pat Colberg."

Jack told them that he had another piece of critical information, the estimated time of death. He said that, as some of them knew, establishing the time of death is an essential but inexact process. Essential because, inexact as it is, the estimate is accurate in determining a timeframe: for example, that death occurred between one and three o'clock in the afternoon.

"It is an inexact process," he continued, "because unless death occurs in a hospital, where medical personnel observes it, or is otherwise witnessed through competent means, the technology has not been perfected to where a time of death can be precisely determined. But through other observations, rigor mortis, for example, or discoloration, an exact time frame can be determined, a range of time during which the person died, if not the precise moment."

"That means that if a person has an alibi that covers the period when the death could have occurred, she can be ruled out as a suspect," said Liz.

"In the case of Pat Colberg," said Liz, "the medical examiner determined that she died between the hours of two and four in the morning."

"I suppose your alibi could be that during those two hours when the murder took place, you have otherwise occupied smuggling drugs and weapons into the country," Jack said to Santos. "Of course, those are serious crimes which will land you in federal prison for a very long time."

"Fred, you were on the beach at the right time. It could have been you," said Jack.

"Or it could have been the original suspect, you, Robert," said Fred. "I saw you were lurking around after I finished speaking to Santos, so you were there at the right time."

"What possible reason could I have to kill Pat?" asked Robert.

"One of the oldest motives in the history of the world, jealousy," replied Linda. "It was you, wasn't it? You couldn't stand the thought that Pat was seeing Santos. You came back to the beach to apologize for the argument that you had just had and you saw her with him. You waited until Santos left and followed her when she left the beach. You then confronted her with her betrayal and killed her."

"No, that's all wrong," said Robert. "That's not what happened. Yes, I saw her with Santos. Yes, I was angry and confronted her when he left. She told me that she could see who she wanted and that it was none of my business. I grabbed her by the arm and shook her. She pulled away, stumbled, and fell to the ground hitting her head against a rock. She wasn't moving! I tried to revive her but nothing happened."

"Is that why you said you were afraid of other people when we first interviewed you, because you killed Santos's girlfriend?" asked Liz. "And you've lied to all of us, including to your father and your friends. Marcos lost his life trying to help you. We all believed in you."

"You coward," said Carlos as he lunged at Robert.

Bill stepped in front of him and held him back. "Easy, Carlos, he will have to answer for what he did."

"Why did you put us through this? What did you expect would happen? asked Jack. "How were we supposed to prove your innocence?"

"I don't know. It was an accident. I didn't mean to kill her, but I knew that nobody would believe me. Everybody was after me, the Police, the FBI, and all those federal agents. They were saying I killed her. It all got out of hand. I wanted to run. It was my father who decided to call you. If he hadn't done so I would be gone, but once he did, I didn't know how to stop everything."

"You could have told the truth, we would have still defended you if, as you now say, it was an accident," said Liz.

"Nobody was going to believe it. Nobody saw what happened. They had made up their minds, and I knew that they wouldn't change it."

"If it happened where you said it did, how did she end up on the beach?" asked Jack.

"Robert, answer me, how did she end up on the beach?" asked Jack.

"I don't know; I don't know! I left her where she fell."

"I'm afraid that was me," said Santos. "I didn't want the police to be looking in the area where I was operating—who knew what they could find? I carried her body to the place where it was found in the morning. I don't care who killed Pat Colberg, or who killed Marcos. What I care about is staying out of prison for any reason, be it murder or trafficking drugs, weapons, or people."

"She wasn't dead," said Flaco.

"What?" asked Liz.

"After Robert left, she got up. I saw her get up, bleeding and dazed, and walk away."

"Are you sure?"

"Yes, Ms. Diaz, I'm sure. I saw her."

"Santos, if the lieutenant was alive you couldn't have picked up her dead body. You must have killed her. You are playing it safe. Now that Robert has said that it was he, you decided to use him for cover, in case somebody saw you carrying her to the beach afterward. If Flaco hadn't seen her walking it would have worked," said Liz. "But it turns out that you have been too clever for your good. If you hadn't made up this last-minute story, nobody would have been the wiser."

"What is your explanation now?" asked Jack. "That a third person was hiding in the sea grapes and killed the lieutenant after her argument with Robert," said Jack.

Santos pulled out his gun. Jesse and the rest of his men did the same.

"What are you doing?" asked Fred.

"What does it look like I'm doing? I'm taking charge. We need to figure out what to do. I need time to think. I'm not going to prison. That's why I killed her in the first place. She was going to turn me in. All the time that she was with me she was gathering information, and that night she saw us preparing for our operation. I hadn't expected to see her at The Islander, nor did you Fred. We argued there because I tried to talk her out of going to the beach party. Of course, she went anyway and figured out what was going on. She confronted me later, on the beach. How stupid of her. Later, I saw her arguing with Robert, saw her fall and Robert leave. I went to where she was, expecting to find her dead. She wasn't, and I did what I had to do and finished the job, smashing her head against the same rock on which she had previously fallen."

"I'm going to hold on to these people until we think this through, Fred. I assume you don't want to go to jail either."

Chapter Fifty-Nine

"Jose Luis, bring the van to the back door," said Santos. "Luis, get a rope and tie these people up," he said, pointing at his seven prisoners, Liz, Jack, Bill, Linda, Carlos, Flaco, and Robert.

"What do you plan to do, kill seven people?" asked Fred. "That would be a massacre and would kick up quite a shit-storm."

"I don't know what I'm going to do, but we can't let them go. I need to think. Do you have any ideas? If we let them go, all of us—me, you, and all my men—will go to prison, as this gentleman said, for a long time."

"Look, I don't know," said Fred. "We should think this through before we do anything drastic. Do you have a place where we could hold them while we decide how to resolve this?"

"There's only one way to resolve this," said Santos. "Yes, I have a place. My stash house in Moca."

"Have your men take them there."

"Jesse put them in the van and take them to Moca. Take Jose Luis and two other guys with you. Stay there until I call and tell you what to do."

Jesse rounded up their seven prisoners and packed them into the van. He told Jose Luis to drive and got into the front passenger seat with his AR-15 at the ready. Two other men, Pancho and Juan, followed on their motorcycles. Santos, Fred, and another man, Frankie, remained in Mi Sitio.

"Frankie, get us a bottle of rum, ice, and two glasses. Make sure they are clean," said Santos.

Frankie did as he was told, and Santos served himself and Fred a drink.

"No, thank you," said Fred. "I can't believe that you would be drinking at a time like this."

"Fine," said Santos. "I'll drink alone."

"What are we going to do to resolve this mess?" asked Fred.

"Fred, there's only one solution, and you know it. We couldn't do it here. We can do it in Moca. There are no neighbors for miles around, and we can take their identifications, even remove their teeth and their fingers, if need be, and then burn the house with the bodies inside. By the time firemen get there, they will be charcoal."

Fred stared at Santos as he finished his drink and prepared himself another one. He was horrified by what this man intended to do. Fred could be charged as a co-author if—no, when, they were caught. He knew that he would be charged with a crime for his contraband of federal government materials and supplies, but if Santos killed seven people, which seemed to be his plan, everything would be elevated to another level altogether. He didn't want to be associated with this lunatic and saw no way of dissuading him from what he was going to do. There was only one thing that he could do.

Fred pulled out his gun and shot Santos between the eyes, then turned around and shot the surprised Frankie before he had time to react.

He knew where the Moca house was. Jesse, Jose Luís, and two other armed men were there, and it would be foolhardy to go alone. Plus, he didn't want to leave two bodies in Mi Sitio, killed with bullets that could be traced to his official firearm. Fred knew that he had done the right thing, what he had to do to save the lives of seven people, whether he did it altruistically or for self-preservation. He called the police at the Rincón station and asked to speak with the person in charge. Sergeant Lopez happened to be there and took his call. Fred explained who he was, that he had shot a man named Santos and one of his men, that other lives were in imminent danger, and that he needed assistance. Lopez said that he would come at once. He was there within fifteen minutes with two of his men.

"Sergeant there are seven persons at risk of losing their lives right now. I shot Santos and the other man; I think his name was Frankie because Santos planned to kill them. At his direction, four of his men are holding them in a house near Moca. I know it sounds crazy and unbelievable, but he intended to kill them and burn down the house with the bodies inside to impede identification. I tried to talk him out of it, to no avail. I saw no other way to stop him other than to shoot him and Frankie. The people that they are holding are the ones investigating the death of Lieutenant Pat Colberg, plus Robert Montes and a man nicknamed Flaco. I think we need to hurry there now if we want to save their lives."

At the Moca house, the seven prisoners were sitting on the floor with their backs against the wall. Sergeant Lopez arrived with two other agents and Harry who had followed Liz and the others from San Juan. The sergeant shouted to the men inside that Santos was in custody, and they should surrender. Jesse shouted back that they wouldn't surrender and would kill all the hostages if the police tried to enter the house by force.

"We'll have to wait them out," said Lopez.

"Are the hostages hurt?" shouted the sergeant.

"No, they are fine," said Jesse. "But they won't be if you try anything funny."

"I understand. Could we send one man in, unarmed, to take a look at them?" asked Lopez.

"It would have to be the American," said Jesse.

"Sure, I'll go," said Fred.

"You don't have to," said Lopez.

"Yes, I do," replied Fred.

"The American is coming in, unarmed," shouted the sergeant.

Fred climbed the precarious front steps and came to the front door. Jesse was waiting and pulled him inside. He had him searched for weapons and, once the guards were satisfied that he was clean, asked him what had happened.

"Where is Santos?" asked Jesse.

"He and Frankie are in custody," Fred lied.

"And you, why aren't you in custody?"

"Because I'm a DEA agent."

"You're an hijo de puta. Turn around."

"Jesse, if you don't let me leave, they will come in."

Jesse tied Fred's hands behind his back and made him sit with the rest of the hostages, then shouted out to Sergeant Lopez that nobody was getting out until he was able to talk with Santos.

"That is not going to happen, Santos is in custody. The FBI has him, and he is on his way to San Juan. They are not bringing him here. They know he killed the lieutenant and that is all they need. The only question now is how to end this without anybody getting hurt, the hostages or you and your men," said the sergeant.

"Jesse," he shouted. "Things are only going to get worse, and soon. More police are on their way here, including local and federal SWAT teams. They don't mess around, they don't negotiate, and you and your friends may well end up dead. Let's stop this while we can."

"If you don't let us leave, I'm going to start shooting the hostages, starting with this piece of shit traitor, Fred."

"Jesse, you've done stupid things in your life, but as far as I know, you've never killed anybody, much less a federal agent."

"I don't think that you believe what I'm saying. Watch this."

Jesse pulled Fred up from the floor and began to push him toward the door. He opened it and made Fred stand there while pointing the gun at his head.

"You have one minute to get out of here. If you don't do so, I will shoot this man."

Sergeant Lopez ordered his men to step back.

"Not enough. I want to see you get in your cars and drive away," said Jesse.

The police got in their cars and drove far enough away to where they would not be able to see them. Harry stayed hidden near the house, and when Jesse pulled Fred back inside, got closer.

Inside the house, Liz's cell phone rang. Jesse told Jose Luis to get it for him. Jesse took the call, and it was sergeant Lopez.

"Jesse, this is sergeant Lopez. We need to find a way out of this."

"Lopez, I need you to send food and water, then we'll talk," said Jesse.

"I will do that, Jesse, but we are running out of time."

"Just do it, sergeant."

Lopez sent a car with a few sandwiches and water. The driver took the supplies to the door, left them there, got back in his car, and left. Jesse opened the door and brought the food inside. In the meantime, Harry had positioned himself by the front door. He waited patiently for one hour knowing that the men inside, who despite being criminals had probably never been involved in a drawn-out hostage situation, would start to let their guard down when time passed, and nothing seemed to be happening. He knew that they would also be thinking about how to get out of the mess that Santos had gotten them into, and in effect, he could hear them saying so to Jesse.

He heard Jose Luis saying that he was leaving. Jesse warned him not to, but Jose Luis insisted. He opened the door and started to step out, but as he did so, Jesse shot him in the back. The other men began arguing with Jesse and Harry took advantage of the distraction and ran into the house through the open door. He fell on Jesse before he could react and wrestled him to the ground.

Pancho and Juan, startled, turned towards them, taking their attention away from the hostages. Liz, Bill, and Carlos, who had surreptitiously untied themselves, jumped on them.

Liz made use of her Krav Maga skills and took down Pancho. Jesse got off two shots before Harry and Bill were able to take away his firearm. One bullet hit Fred and the other Primo. Bill pulled Jesse from the floor, punched him hard and pushed him on the sofa next to Primo who was bleeding profusely. By now, Lopez and his men had returned. Between them and Carlos, they disarmed and captured Juan and helped Liz with Pancho, who she had face-down on the floor.

Primo had been shot below the groin, on the inside of his right thigh. He was hemorrhaging copious amounts of blood, and by the time Bill applied a tourniquet around his leg to stop the bleeding, too much time had elapsed, as exsanguination would have taken no more than four minutes. Primo was beyond help. In those last moments of life, the old drunk seemed at peace. Sergeant Lopez called for an ambulance ASAP, for both Fred and Primo. By the time it arrived Primo was gone.

Fred had been shot in the head and was unresponsive, but alive. He was transferred to the hospital, where he was stabilized, but the damage had been extensive. The swelling caused by the bleeding, and by the pressure wave created by the bullet traveling through brain tissue, was too severe, and Fred did not survive.

Epilogue

The investigation into Lieutenant Pat Colberg's death was closed after it was determined that Santos Otero was the murderer.

Perico was placed on trial and convicted of Marcos's murder, as were Junior and Elvis Velez, the Batman brothers.

Peggy Ramos remains hospitalized and has not been charged.

The pharmacist at the USNS Comfort was court-martialed and sent to the Navy Brig. She also received a Dishonorable Discharge. Other personnel aboard the Comfort were also court-martialed and similarly punished.

Cris went to Europe with her boyfriend. They broke up in Amsterdam, and she continued her travels by herself.

Liz frets.

La Perla remains a devastated community.

www.ingramcontent.com/pod-product-compliance
Lightning Source LLC
Chambersburg PA
CBHW021500240626
47154CB00002B/456